Dessert Flirt Repeat

Grant Siblings Series book 1

Sarah Smith

Cover design © 2023 Elle Maxwell

ISBN 9798397795586

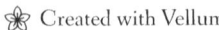 Created with Vellum

For Kare Bare. LYLAS <3

Chapter 1

Becca

"**B**ecca baby, what in the world are you doing?"

I take in the expression on my boyfriend's face, how his gaze is fixated on my whipped cream–covered breasts. Except instead of the hungry look I expected, he looks...confused? Wow, yeah. Confused.

I push aside the doubt and flash what I hope is a sexy grin. I can understand the momentary confusion. Ben isn't used to seeing me like this, all sexed up. I'm standing in our living room, buck naked save for the dollops of whipped cream on my boobs and my hoo-ha.

"What does it look like I'm doing?" I take a step toward him, shimmying my hips a little. A tiny teardrop of whipped cream falls to the dingy hardwood floor of our apartment.

His eyebrows crash together as he gazes between my legs. A hard swallow moves down his throat. He blinks furiously, like he's still trying to make sense of why I'm standing there covered in Reddi-wip.

I'm not normally a doll-myself-up-in-whipped-cream kind of girl. That's something a sexy, super confident vixen would do. Me? I'm pretty much the exact opposite of that.

I'm as "girl next door" as they come. Yoga pants, hoodies, sneakers, and other comfort wear are my uniform. And as much as I wish I could prowl around with the unflappable confidence of a sex goddess, that's not me. Save for tonight, the sexiest thing I've ever done is surprise Ben with a few matching lace bra and thong sets for his birthday, Valentine's Day, and our anniversary. If vanilla were a person, it would be me. Even my blonde hair and light skin denote simplicity. One-note. Bland.

But I've had enough of being vanilla. Vanilla is exactly what our life has been the past few months, and I'm tired of it. It's summertime, which means I've been slammed at Sweet Cheeks, the ice cream shop I own in the LoHi neighborhood of Denver. For the past nearly three months I've been working fourteen-hour days making ice cream, serving customers, marketing my business, and doing all the behind-the-scenes stuff, like paying bills and fixing whatever equipment craps out in the shop. My life has been a nonstop stream of cream, sugar, and waffle cones, and as a result, I haven't been the most attentive girlfriend. Our romantic life has been hurried I love you's and quick kisses in passing while Ben is on a work call or before I run to the shop, which is located on the first floor of our apartment building.

That's why, tonight, I wanted to surprise Ben, to be the exact opposite of the sweet and sensible woman he's been with for the past almost three years. He's mentioned to me before that nothing is sexier than when I'm naked, so that's what I want to deliver: nudity with a bit of whipped cream as a fun little cherry on top. That's the ice cream part of me coming out. I can't help it.

When I think about how we've gone from getting kicked out of movie theaters for making out in the early days of our relationship to two workaholic thirty-year-olds who barely peck on the mouth before passing out due to exhaustion in bed, there's a stinging in my chest.

This isn't the life I want. This isn't the kind of girlfriend I want to be.

I'm on a mission to change that. I'm determined to go all out, to show Ben that I can be a sex kitten who can't get enough of him, that I'm still thoughtful and romantic and wild for him.

I step up to him and slide my palms against his chest. I'm careful to keep a couple inches of space between us. He's wearing a suit, and I know that even the tiniest smidge of whipped cream on the fabric will result in a trip to the dry cleaners.

"Do you know what today is?" I tiptoe up and gaze into Ben's gold-green eyes.

The furrow in his brow eases. He swallows again. "Um, no..."

"It's Naked Saturday," I say, my voice raspy and low. I start to unbutton his dress shirt.

"Oh. Is that, like, an official holiday?"

I smile up at him. "I know I haven't been the most attentive girlfriend lately, so I want to make it up to you with something spontaneous. And sexy."

His shirt falls open, revealing an expanse of peaches and cream skin. I lean down and press a soft kiss to his chest. I take my time, trailing slow, soft kisses down his stomach.

"Happy Naked Saturday," I whisper between kisses.

Ben hisses out a breath. "God, Becca..."

His ab muscles flex under my kiss. I smile to myself as I plant another kiss right above the waistband of his pants and reposition so I'm on my knees. That ragged breath means he's turned on.

When I start to undo his belt, he grips my shoulder. "Wait."

I take in the worried look on his face, how he's gone pale. "What's wrong?"

He opens his mouth, but no words come out. Then he shakes his head. His expression turns pained. I hop to my feet and grab his hand in both of mine.

"Honey, what's going on? Are you okay?"

Eyes pressed shut, he shakes his head. A beat later he opens his eyes. "I can't do this."

"Do what?"

He pulls his hand out of my grip and gestures between us. "This. Us. I can't do this anymore."

"Wh-what do you mean?"

His mouth turns into a straight line at the exact same moment the look in his hazel eyes shifts. He no longer looks confused; he looks guilty.

"There's someone else."

My ears ring. No way. This...this can't be happening.

"There's someone else?" I finally squeak out after a long stretch of silence.

His shoulders hunch, and his head hangs. He nods. He doesn't even look at me. The dread inside of me flips. It turns into something hot, something angry.

"Becca baby, I'm sorry. I—"

"No," I croak out. "You don't get to call me baby."

I stand there, practically naked, and glare at my boyfriend as I struggle to process what's happening right now. My boyfriend of three years is cheating on me.

I swallow past the lump in my throat. "How could you do this?"

He tugs a hand through his sandy blond hair. He

exhales, his jaw hard set like he's irritated. "Come on, Becca. Don't act like this is shocking news."

"What the—are you saying that I should have expected you to cheat on me?"

He presses his eyes shut once more and shakes his head. "No, that's not…Look, things between us haven't been all that great lately. You've been working such long hours. I have too. We've been growing apart. You can't say that you haven't felt things between us changing."

I stand there, mouth agape. "Ben, are you serious right now? Of course I've felt the disconnect between us due to how crazy work has been. But it's been, like, three months. You cheated on me because we've both been busy with work for three months?"

He winces when my voice turns pitchy at the end, but I can't help it. Is he seriously saying this justifies him cheating on me?

There's another shift in his expression. That guilty look again. "I'm sorry, Becca. Someone else came along, and it just feels different this time. It feels…right."

I stumble back a step.

He starts to reach for me, but I hold up my hand. "Don't you fucking touch me."

I don't miss the way his eyes go wide. I hardly ever swear, so when I do, it's a bad, bad sign.

"Becca, I'm sorry. I didn't plan for this to happen. It just did."

His tired gaze turns pitying as he glances up and down my body. A hot flash of embarrassment travels across my skin. God, I'm pathetic. And clueless. I'm a pathetic, clueless loser covered in whipped cream who just got dumped by her cheating boyfriend.

Tears prick my eyes. I try to blink them away, but they tumble down my cheeks anyway in hot streams.

Through my blurry vision, I can still make out Ben's pitying stare. "Becca. Oh, baby, I'm so sorry."

I press my eyes shut. "Stop. I don't want to hear your apology."

He starts to speak again, but I stop him.

"Get out."

He hesitates for a second. "Can I at least pack a bag?"

"No," I blurt.

He babbles something about not having enough clothes for tomorrow.

"Have your new girlfriend get you some clothes." I sniffle.

"Come on, Becca. I know this situation isn't ideal, but there's no need to be cruel."

I almost laugh, I'm so blown away by the entitlement in his words. "You cheated on me, and *I'm* the one being cruel?"

He throws his arms up, clearly frustrated. "God. At least be reasonable. I'll come by some other day and get the rest of my stuff. Right now all I'm asking for are my clothes."

I don't know if it's the impatience in his tone or the annoyed look on his face or the fact that I'm still processing being cheated on *and* broken up with, but something inside of me snaps. I dart to the bedroom, yank open the closet door, and randomly grab at his suits. I march back to the living room and chuck them out the open window, leaving a trail of whipped cream behind me.

"Becca, what the hell!" Ben runs over and hangs his head out the open window of our fourth-floor apartment.

He pivots back to me, his eyes wide and unblinking. "You threw my clothes onto the street!"

My heart is pounding so hard, I can feel it in my throat. "I did," I manage to say in a weirdly calm voice. "Wow...I... really did that."

This is so un-vanilla of me. Vanilla girls are sweet and calm and accommodating and predictable...until you cheat on us, I guess.

I stare at Ben's clothes scattered across the sidewalk, a strange mix of shocked, confused, and heartbroken.

He leaves in a huff of muttered curse words, slamming the door behind him. The clap of sound snaps me out of my haze. I rush over, lock the deadbolt, spin around, and fall back against the door. My brain feels like it's on an out-of-control Tilt-A-Whirl. My thoughts are fuzzy and muddled.

How could this have happened? Ben is my dream guy —*was* my dream guy. I think back to how he'd surprise me with breakfast in bed on weekend mornings, how he'd gas up my car whenever he noticed it was nearing empty, how he'd surprise me by stocking up on my favorite coffee when he saw I was about to run out. How he cheered me on as I opened my ice cream shop just over a year ago. How, in the first six months that Sweet Cheeks was open, he spent his weekends and evenings working alongside me, refusing whenever I tried to pay him so I could save money instead of hiring help.

How is this guy the same guy who cheated on me?

Soon I'm crying so hard that I slide down to the floor. The dingy hardwood is cold on my bare butt, but I don't bother to get dressed. I don't have the energy to walk or even crawl to my bedroom closet to dress myself.

I stay slumped on the floor of my apartment, a pathetic naked pile of snot and whipped cream, and cry until I pass out.

Chapter 2

Becca

I stare at my computer screen, too shocked to formulate words.

"Ms. Briarwood? Ms. Briarwood, are you still there?"

The customer service rep's insistent tone jerks me out of my stupor. "Um, yes. Sorry."

I press my eyes shut in an attempt to refocus, but as soon as I open my eyes and see my bank account balance, I'm rattled all over again.

"As I said before, there was a withdrawal made last night from the other name on this account. A Mr. Ben Holt."

Just hearing him say those words out loud sends a wave of panic and fury through me. I had twenty thousand dollars in this account yesterday. But when I went to pay my bills this morning, I nearly vomited when I saw that my account had just $111 left in it.

Which meant only one thing: Ben emptied the account.

He and I opened this bank account together two years ago when we moved into this apartment to pay bills together. But when I started my business last year, I began using the account to save money to pay my ice cream shop bills too. Because of that, I was contributing the bulk of my earnings to that account. Ben hardly ever deposited money into it anymore. We even talked about taking his name off the account, but we were always too busy and never got around to it.

"I understand that, but I didn't authorize him to make withdrawals from my account," I say. "It wasn't even his money in the account. It was all my money."

A heavy sigh echoes from the other line.

"As I explained before, Ms. Briarwood, this is a joint account. Both of your names are on it, so that means you're both authorized to make withdrawals and deposits. Neither of you needs permission from the other to access this account to withdraw or deposit money."

My throat tightens with the urge to sob. "Of course, I know that, but this is an extenuating circumstance. We've just recently ended our relationship—the other night, actually."

I think back to yesterday when I came home from work and saw that Ben had been by to get the rest of his stuff. He had taken the zebra plant next to the fireplace and the vacuum cleaner—both items I'd paid for. I was too exhausted and sad to do anything about it though. I figured if he wanted them that bad, he could have them. But for him to steal my money? How could he be so selfish and greedy?

"I hadn't gotten around to dividing our assets, so I'm just really shocked and frustrated to find out that all of the money—all of *my* money is gone." I speak so quickly and frantically that I wonder if the bank customer service rep can even understand me. But if I slow down, the urge to cry hits, and the last thing I want is to break down sobbing to a complete stranger.

"I understand, Ms. Briarwood. And I'm very sorry to hear about your breakup. But there's nothing I can do. Mr. Holt has the right to access this account."

I'm sputtering until my throat aches. And then a sob hits. "Okay," I manage to mumble before I start to cry.

My screen goes blurry as tears flood my waterlines. I'm screwed. Actually, I'm beyond screwed. That was rent money for the ice cream shop for the next six months. And just like that, it's gone.

My head aches at the thought of how cruel Ben was to do such a thing—to outright steal from me days after he confessed to cheating on me.

"I'm sorry I can't help you, Ms. Briarwood," the customer service rep says in a gentle voice. "Your best bet at this point would be to reach out to Mr. Holt and ask him to return the money."

I'd laugh if I weren't currently using all the energy in my body to keep from ugly sobbing. If Ben was bold enough to take my money without asking me, no way he's going to give it back, even if I ask.

But as I rack my brain to figure out what my other options are, I come up empty.

"Okay, maybe I'll do that. Thank you." I sniffle and hang up, take a breath, then call Ben. It goes straight to voicemail.

"Ben, how dare you," I say. "You stole my money. How could you? How could you think that was an okay thing to do? You knew that was my money in that account." I force myself to take another breath. "You know how hard I've worked to build my savings. That money was for my business—to pay the rent, to pay for repairs, to pay my suppliers—and you just steal it right out from under me?"

I'm shaking as I speak.

"I can't believe I ever loved you. I can't believe I ever thought you were a good, decent—"

The voicemail cuts me off. I throw my head back and growl. I squeeze my phone in my hand so hard, it's a wonder it doesn't shatter. Anger and frustration collide in the center of my chest. I want to scream and punch a hole in the wall and chuck a rock through a window and—

My phone buzzes with a text.

Ben: *You know I had just as much claim to that money as you. Remember all those hours I worked at the ice cream shop? You never paid me.*

Me: *I offered to pay you and you refused!*

Ben: *Well, I changed my mind.*

Me: *God, you're the lowest of the low.*

Ben: *What I've done is perfectly legal.*

Me: *Legal but unethical. Gross. Immoral. Disgusting. You know it's not right, Ben.*

I wait for a response, but a minute passes and nothing.

I toss my phone onto the kitchen counter and slump on the floor. That's it. There's nothing I can do. Legally, I have no recourse. I just lost twenty grand of my life savings. And now my business is in jeopardy.

For the second time in three days, I end up a sobbing pile on the floor, except this time I'm clothed.

* * *

"I know a guy who can break Ben's kneecaps," my best friend Tori says as she hands me a takeout container of shrimp fried rice. "He owes me a favor."

I shake my head. "Very funny."

"I'm dead serious, Bec." She plops down next to me on the couch. "What Ben did was goddamn unforgivable. He stole your money *and* he cheated on you. That fucking asshole deserves to rot in hell."

I nod along and eat a forkful of fried rice, but even my favorite food tastes bitter on my tongue. I swallow it down but hand the container back to her. I hug a fuzzy pillow to my chest and tuck my feet under my legs. "As satisfying as that would be, I can't give Ben any more of my brain space or energy. I need to focus on figuring out what I'm going to do."

Tori pulls me into a side hug. Her wild auburn curls tickle my cheek.

"I can dig into my other savings account, but that'll only float me a couple of months," I say. "And then that's it. I won't be able to pay the rent for my ice cream shop. I'll get evicted. I'll lose my business. All because of Ben."

Tori's jaw bulges with how hard she's gritting her teeth. "This is so fucking unfair."

I nod, my eyes burning with tears yet again.

Tori sets the takeout on the coffee table and pulls me into another hug. "We'll figure this out. I promise."

I sniffle and manage a meek "thanks." Even though I don't believe her, I'm still heartened by Tori's support, how angry she is on my behalf, and how she's just as heartbroken as I am over this mess.

She pulls her phone out of her pocket and pulls up TikTok. "I was so excited to show you this, but then Ben decided to be a monstrous dickhead, and now this doesn't seem all that fun anymore."

She shows me that Sweet Cheeks has been tagged on TikTok in a bunch of videos.

"People are loving your new unicorn swirl flavor." She tilts her phone screen so I can see it. A sad smile tugs at her lips. "Kinda cool."

I feel myself brighten the slightest bit watching people's faces light up as they try my signature summer flavor: strawberry and blueberry sherbert swirled with vanilla ice cream and pop rocks sprinkled throughout.

I turn to Tori. "That's really awesome. Thank you."

"Now if one of these videos could go viral, that would send you a wave of new customers, which would result in tons of business. Then you wouldn't have to worry about money anymore."

I let out a sad laugh. "That would be a dream come true."

Tori points to the container of food. "More?"

I shake my head. "I'm too stressed to eat."

She hops up, darts to the kitchen, and returns with a bottle of wine. "Alcohol?"

"God, yes."

* * *

Two bottles of wine later I'm comfortably drunk and lying on my couch. Tori left to go home so now I'm scrolling TikTok to distract myself from my dumpster fire life. God, I love the randomness of this app. On my FYP, I watch some dude pull off what seems like a complicated dance routine effortlessly. Then I watch a group of drunk partygoers group-hug, then fall into a nearby pool, then laugh hysterically. Then I watch a woman lip-sync a scene from a Disney movie while cuddling her cat.

And then I see my favorite TikTok account has just posted a new video. His name is Gage Grant, and he posts videos of himself cooking and plating elaborate dishes with a sexy twist: he's usually shirtless and performs suggestive movements with the ingredients. I think back to the video he filmed of himself leaning over a metal bowl, whisking heavy cream into stiff peaks, all the while flicking his impressively long tongue. He never speaks. And he always kicks off his videos with a sultry scowl or cheeky smirk, then gets right into the cooking and plating.

He's pretty much everyone's fantasy come to life: a hot, ripped guy who lives to pleasure you...with food.

I tap on his video and watch with wide eyes as he plates what looks like a fancy deconstructed ice cream sundae. Two oval scoops of vanilla ice cream rest on one side of the plate. On the other is a pool of hot fudge, poured into a perfect circle. In the middle is a delicate cloud of whipped cream. Around it is a thin ring of finely ground peanuts. As Gage works his expert hands around the dish, he displays that insanely sexy scowl. He's shirtless, as usual. God, even in the dim lighting of his kitchen, he looks incredible. His tan skin practically glows. There's lean muscle everywhere —neck, shoulders, arms, forearms, chest, stomach...

I shake my head, mesmerized and mystified. How is this guy ripped when all he does is whip up rich, calorie-laden dishes day after day?

He sprinkles edible gold flakes on the plate. The video ends with him running a hand through his short-cropped jet-black hair. Then he looks at the camera and winks.

I swallow back the saliva that's pooled in my mouth. I skim the caption.

I scream, you scream, we all scream for ice cream...and then we head to bed and I make you scream even louder #wet #dripping #yum #melt #sosweet #sweetcheeks

I can feel my cheeks heating. I wonder if he's as good in

bed as his food and his captions make him out to be...

Judging by the thousands of comments his video already has, everyone is convinced he is. I skim the comments. There are endless flame and mind-blown emojis, proclamations of love, and even a few "will you marry me?" requests.

I laugh to myself. This guy probably doesn't even read the comments. I've noticed he hardly ever replies.

My phone buzzes with a text from Tori.

Tori: *Tell me you've seen Gage Grant's latest TikTok??*

Me: *Obviously lol*

Tori: *Ice cream this time! And the hashtag #sweetcheeks! Can you believe it? It's like he's channeling you lol*

Me: *Haha I wish*

Tori: *You should slide into his DMs. He lives here in Denver. Bet he'd make a hell of a rebound ;)*

I zero in on Tori's text.

You should slide into his DMs.

Maybe it's the alcohol infiltrating my brain, but this actually seems like a good idea.

Not the rebound part. God, I could never in a million years proposition a guy for sex via DM, let alone a total stranger.

But I could ask Gage for help. Actually, guidance is a better word.

Before I know it, I'm tapping out a message to Gage. My drunken, fuzzy brain can manage a pretty quick typing speed. Wow. When I finish, I do a quick skim of my message.

Whoa. I sound so ballsy. And confident.

I send it, then hop off the couch and head to the refrigerator for more wine. I don't bother with a glass. I just down the last half-bottle of pinot noir Tori left me in a few long gulps. And then I pass out.

Chapter 3

Gage

I squint at the message in my DMs. Is this serious?

I read it again.

Gage Grant! Hello! Okay so you probably don't know me, actually what am I saying, you definitely don't know me hahahahj, you're a TikTok celebrity and I'm a regular person, but I have a question for you! You're a social media/TikTok genius with your millions of followers and I need your help to go viral! See, I own an ice cream shop in Denver (it's called Sweet Cheeks—isn't that so cool? Like the hashtag you posted on your latest video! OMG it's like fate hahahahhh), I'm screwed financially because my cheating ex-boyfriend stole money from me and the quickest way I can think to earn more money is to go viral on TikTok by making sexy TikToks. Like you!! I have a TikTok for my ice cream shop, it's @sweetcheekscreamery and it does okay, I mean, the content is pretty tame, just cute shots of ice cream scoops and sundaes and malts and shakes and sometimes I'll be in a video. But I need to be sexy to go viral and be successful! Like you! And someday I want to see my ice cream in restaurants and stores yaaay wouldn't that be so cool? So can you please help me? Like, teach me how to make sexy TikTok videos that go viral? Pretty please?? I'll love you forever! And I'll give you a lifetime of free ice cream too! But hey, do you even eat ice cream? I've always been curious if you eat the food you cook because it's so rich and high calorie, but you're absolutely ripped, like you've got the body of a freaking Roman god who goes to the gym all the time. Do you go to the gym all the time? Okay so let me know thank youuuu

This time I laugh after reading it. I get a lot of random DMs mostly from companies who want to pay me to use their products in my videos since I've got a large following. I'm used to it by now; it's how I make a living, after all. Given the overt sexual vibes of my videos, though, some of those random DMs are wild. I get everything from marriage proposals to nude pics to messages that say, "DTF. You?" But this is the first time I've ever gotten...this. A rambling, semi-coherent paragraph of borderline nonsense.

Someone's gotta be fucking with me. I try and think of which one of my friends would have made a fake account to DM me. Henry or Manny? Probably not. Maybe Micah, if he was high. Definitely not Tyler. He's not clever enough to create an entire fake account just to DM me. My older brother is more of the "I'll make fun of you to your face" type.

I tap the name of the account. Sure enough, it's an actual account. Okay, so maybe someone associated with Sweet Cheeks Creamery's TikTok account messaged me as a joke? Or when they were drunk? I read it again. Okay, yeah, the more I look this over, the more this feels like a drunk DM.

I see that Sweet Cheeks is here in Denver, near downtown where I live. I do a quick skim of the few dozen videos on their account, most of which are videos of ice cream being scooped and prepared, overlaid to pop music. This all looks legit.

I Google Map it. This place is just a few miles from my apartment. Huh.

I go back to their TikTok account and scroll through the videos again. It's really wholesome stuff. There are videos advertising free scoops for kids on their birthdays and offering senior citizen discounts. I smile to myself as I watch a video of the ice cream shop hosting a fundraiser for the local humane society. Even the aesthetic of this ice cream shop screams cute and sweet: pastel pink walls, a neon pink sign that says "ice ice baby" in cursive writing behind the counter, and a greenery backdrop that makes up the entire wall on the far side of the shop.

I stop scrolling when I see a cute blonde beaming in the preview of one video. I tap on it and watch a quick video of a woman in wire-rimmed glasses, her long golden hair in a braid. She grins, flashes a thumbs-up, and scoops three scoops of ice cream into a waffle cone before handing it to a customer. I read the caption.

It's Triple Scoop Tuesday! Yay! How many scoops can you handle?

I watch the video a couple more times. That can't be the woman who messaged me...can it? She seems so wholesome, from her giddy smile to her ski-slope nose to her bright blue eyes. Christ, even the messy braid she's sporting. She looks like the girl next door who spends her time giving out free ice cream to kids or reading to elderly people or rescuing stray animals, not getting shit-faced and sending rambling DMs. *She* wants to learn how to be sexy in her TikTok videos?

I mean, if she wanted to come off as sexy, she totally could. She's got that cute-beautiful vibe down pat. All she'd need to do is give a sultry expression or show some cleavage. Bam, sexy as fuck.

The reminder on my phone goes off.

Meet Tyler at the gym

Crap. Is it three o'clock already? That's when I realize I've spent an hour trying to solve this mystery.

I lean back against my couch and tug a hand through my hair. Damn, I really lost myself in this. Normally I do a quick skim of DMs to make sure I don't miss any messages from companies, then delete the sexy ones. But something about this message got to me.

I watch the video with the blonde scooping ice cream one more time.

Something about *her* is getting to me.

Yeah, it's ridiculous, but I'm curious. I gotta know—is this cute and wholesome-looking woman the one who sent me that drunk DM?

I type a quick reply, send it, grab my gym bag, and jog out of my apartment to my car parked down the street. I text Tyler to let him know that I'll be a few minutes late. He's gonna run my ass off as payback, but whatever. After that ice cream sundae I ate yesterday, I could use the conditioning.

As I speed to the gym, I laugh to myself. I'm amused as hell by this. I can't stop thinking about that message—about that cute blonde.

And as I head to the gym, I find myself hoping that she'll message me back.

Chapter 4

Becca

I try to open my eyes, but it's a no-go when my eyelids feel like they're filled with cement. My head does too.

I groan into the arm of the couch, where I must have passed out last night. God, what was I thinking, drinking all that wine?

You weren't thinking. You were wallowing because your life is in complete shambles.

Oh, right.

A full minute later I manage to sit up, but not for long with how dizzy I am. It feels like a tiny, invisible person is banging on bongos inside my skull. Okay, no more wine ever.

My stomach curdles. Hot acid claws its way up my chest to my throat. Crap.

I dart to my bathroom and hurl all the wine I downed last night into my toilet bowl. When I finish retching, I land on my butt and fall against the nearby wall for support. I'm a mess. Thank god Sweet Cheeks is closed today. There's no way I'd be able to work in my current state.

My phone buzzing pulls my focus back to the living

room. I crawl on my hands and knees to the coffee table and see a notification from TikTok. I also see that it's three in the afternoon.

My shoulders slump with shame. I'm thirty years old and have adopted the drinking and sleeping habits of a college student. Real classy.

I tap the TikTok icon and see that I've got a message.

When I open it, I squint in confusion. Who's Gage? Have I ever met someone named...

Oh my god...No way...It can't be...

I stare at the username for a solid ten seconds. Gage Grant, the TikTok star, DMed me. But why?

It doesn't take long to read his message, considering it's one line.

Hey. Is this a joke? Are you serious?

What in the world...?

I see the message above his—the message I apparently sent last night.

Dread pools in my stomach as I quickly skim. No way. Oh my good lord, no, no, no, no...

My memory claws its way out of the hangover haze, and I piece together what happened last night. I remember scrolling through TikTok. I remember watching a bunch of random videos. A visual of a shirtless Gage delicately plating ice cream flashes in my mind. It triggers a wave of other memories, of me thinking of Sweet Cheeks, of the hashtag #sweetcheeks, of thinking that it would be a good idea to message Gage to see if he could help me go viral to save my business...

My stomach churns yet again, but this time it's embarrassment fueling the nausea. Did I seriously send Gage Grant this barely coherent message?

I blink at the block of text that I drunkenly typed. Yup. I definitely did.

I toss the phone to the far side of my couch like it's on fire and cover my face with both hands. It doesn't do me any good though. It's not like I can shield myself from the humiliation. It already happened—I'm already experiencing it.

My phone buzzes again, and I pray to the universe that it's not Gage. When I see it's Tori, I huff out a breath.

Tori: *You alive? You were pretty wasted when I left you last night.*

Me: *Yeah...but I kinda wanna die at the moment.*

Tori: *Bad hangover?*

Me: *Well, yeah, but something else happened...*

Tori calls me less than a minute later.

"Hey, what's wrong? Are you alright?"

I just now realize how cryptic I sounded in my text.

"Sorry, yeah, I'm fine," I say. "It's just that, I did something really, really humiliating last night."

There's a long silence.

"Well, are you gonna tell me?" Tori asks.

I wince just thinking about what I've done. "Oh my god, Tori, I can't even say it. It's too mortifying." I grab a nearby pillow and smother my face.

"Come on, it can't be that bad." She gasps. "Wait, please don't tell me you drunk sexted Ben."

I toss the pillow aside and scoff. "No way."

She exhales like she's relieved. "Good. Honestly, nothing you could have done would be worse than that."

I groan. "I don't know about that."

"Becca, you can tell me anything. We've been best friends since middle school. We work together. We've lived

22

together. We hold each other's hair back when we vomit. Nothing is too embarrassing. No matter what it is, I won't judge you."

I huff out a breath. "I sent Gage Grant, the TikTok star, a drunk DM last night. And, um, he messaged me back."

She chuckles. "Very funny."

"I'm serious, Tori. I was absolutely wasted last night after you left, started scrolling TikTok, and watched his video. Then your text popped in my mind, the one where you joked that I should slide into his DMs."

"Holy shit. You asked him to hook up with you?"

"What? No way! No, I asked him to teach me how to make sexy TikToks for Sweet Cheeks because he's so good at sexy TikToks and I thought that could help my business." I give her a summary of what I wrote in my message to him and what he wrote in his reply.

She sounds like she's choking on her own laughter. "I can't believe you did that. And I can't believe he replied to you."

"I know. God, this is beyond humiliating."

Tori makes a huffy sound. "No way. Don't you see what a golden opportunity this is?"

"Um, what?"

"He messaged you back! Gage Grant messaged you back! Dude's got, like, three million TikTok followers, and he actually replied to you. Becca, you have to message him."

I'm sputtering. "No way. I've humiliated myself too much to ever reply to him."

"You have no reason to be humiliated. Clearly he's intrigued by you. You have to look at this as an opportunity to save your ice cream shop."

Tori's tone is firm, which means she's dead serious.

"Yeah, maybe this all started as an embarrassing drunken moment, but this could be what ends up saving Sweet Cheeks. If Gage Grant can coach you on how to go viral on TikTok, this could mean serious money for Sweet Cheeks, just like you said in your DM to him."

I think for a second. She has a point.

"Okay. Okay, maybe you're right..."

"*You're* the one who's right, Becca. This was your idea in the first place." I can tell Tori is smiling. "Message him back, now. Tell him that you're dead serious and that you'd love his help."

My head spins, but not because I'm hungover. It's because my adrenaline is pumping at the thought of messaging Gage. I can't believe I'm actually considering this.

"Okay. I will." It's a second before I realize what I've said.

Tori squeals. "Keep me posted on what he says!"

"I will." A cold sweat breaks across the back of my neck at the thought of having an actual conversation with my TikTok crush.

We hang up, and I stare at the message exchange between Gage and me. My fingers hover over my phone screen. Holy crap. I'm really doing this.

Hello! Yes, I'm totally serious. Would you be willing to chat with me about helping me go viral on TikTok? Also, my sincerest apologies for how long and rambling my prior message was! It was kind of a rough night lol

I read the message over once, then another time. Is that "lol" at the end too much? Too cutesy? Too unprofessional? I roll my eyes. I pretty much annihilated any semblance of professionalism the moment I sent that drunken ramble of a DM to Gage.

Each time I read it over, I feel my nerves dissolving more and more. Before I lose it completely, I send it. And then I toss my phone aside and run back to the bathroom to puke again.

Chapter 5

Gage

Sweat drips down my forehead, landing in my eyes. I growl as I drop the barbell on the ground.

"Damn, dude. That's a new deadlift PR for you, right?" Tyler pats me on the back as I hunch over, hands on my thighs, bracing myself as I catch my breath.

"I guess so," I huff out.

"I thought those incline sprints on the treadmill at the beginning of the workout would smoke you, but I was wrong."

I stand up, wipe the sweat from my brow, and shrug at him. "It must have been the ice cream."

"Nice work on your latest video, by the way. Crap tons of thirsty comments. How many marriage proposal DMs did you get with that one?"

I roll my eyes.

He nudges me with his elbow. "Just giving you shit."

My older brother loves to give me a hard time about my TikTok, specifically how I make a living as a social media thirst trap. I'd normally tell anyone making fun of me about my TikTok to fuck off, but I let it slide when it's my brother and close friends. I give them all a hefty amount of shit for the random stuff they do. It's only fair they dish it back.

Still catching my breath, I wring out my hands and wait as he kicks out his legs in preparation for his deadlift set.

"Speaking of ice cream, Mom told me that's been Millie's biggest craving so far in her pregnancy," Tyler says. "You and I are supposed to bring a bunch when we all get together next weekend."

"I thought it was *lumpia* dipped in ranch dressing?"

"Nah, that's making her nauseous now."

"Damn. Poor girl."

Millie's our cousin and a year younger than me. All of us grew up together and feel more like siblings than cousins.

"I'll text Millie tonight and ask what flavors she wants us to bring," I say.

"You still in charge of planning her baby shower?"

I groan. "Yeah. Don't remind me."

Tyler laughs. "You'd better get to it, man. You know our cousin. She'll rip you a new asshole if you blow it off."

"You're not gonna believe what she wants to do."

"What? Cirque du Soleil? Princess tea party?" He guzzles from his water bottle.

"Worse. Thunder From Down Under."

Tyler spits out his drink. A half-dozen people in the weight room spin around to gawk at him as he coughs. I thump him on the back and hand him a clean towel. He quickly wipes up the water, then looks at me. "You're kidding."

"Nope. Leave it to our cousin to want male strippers at her baby shower." I chuckle and shake my head. "She said that's why she requested I plan it—because she knew I'd do exactly what she wants. She doesn't want her mom or our mom or any of our aunties or cousins to do it because then

27

it'll be a standard frilly baby shower with annoying games and finger food—exactly what she doesn't want. She told me wants to have a blowout party before the baby comes."

Tyler shakes his head, laughing. "That's wild, man."

"She's practically our second little sister. Of course I'll plan it for her, no matter how awkward it's gonna be."

Tyler moves to load up the barbell.

"Hey, have you heard from Maya lately? Is she coming home anytime soon?" I ask.

Tyler shrugs. "No clue. I texted her this weekend to see how she was doing and radio silence. The only way I know she's alive is from her daily posts on Instagram."

"Sounds about right."

Ever since our little sister Maya has been old enough to drive, she's been on the move, always wanting to road trip and travel with family and friends. When she turned eighteen, she kicked off her moving spree, never staying in one place for more than a handful of months. She's since lived in a dozen different cities.

"I'll try to get her on the phone this week and check up on her," I say.

"What's she doing in LA now? Staging homes?"

I shake my head. "That was when she first moved there. Now she's a personal assistant for some celebrity astrologist."

Tyler frowns. "What the hell is that?"

"Dude, I don't even know. I'm just glad she's somehow managed to find a job and hasn't hit me up for money."

"Yeah, good point."

Tyler pauses, and I think he's going to set up so he can do his set of deadlifts. But he doesn't. He looks over at me, the expression on his face hesitant.

"Hey, um, so you know that Dad has that pop-up for his restaurant in a couple of months, right?"

Just the mention of him has me gritting my teeth. I rip the plates from one end of the barbell.

"Nope," I mutter.

Tyler tugs a hand through his ink-black hair, which is shaggier and wavier than mine. He's working up the nerve to say all this. I wish he wouldn't.

"It's just that, he asked me to let you know—"

The plates clank so loud when I slam them on the floor, everyone around us spins around to look.

I straighten up and glare at Tyler. "I thought I made it clear that I don't give a fuck about Dad anymore."

Tyler's brows crash together. "Dude, why do you have to be so stubborn about this? Can you just set aside your feelings for one day? It's been over a year."

Anger simmers in the center of my chest, like someone's boiling a vat of hot acid in my ribcage. I fucking hate when my older brother does this, trying to play mediator. It doesn't seem to matter how many times I tell him no, I'll never, ever want to be in the same room as our dad after what he did. He always says he understands, but clearly he doesn't. I guess you can't really know how it feels to be betrayed by the one person who's always supposed to have your back until it happens to you.

"Tyler. Don't fucking start this again, okay?"

He clenches his jaw, and I know he wants to say more, wants to fight me on this. But he just looks off to the side and shakes his head.

"Fine, Gage. Have it your way."

Instead of finishing our workout together like we normally do, I walk off to the mats and stretch. Yeah, it's shitty for me to leave without saying bye, but I'm too pissed. He knows my one rule: never, ever bring up our dad.

I finish stretching and head into the men's locker room to clean up. When I check my phone, I tap the TikTok icon and see a slew of unread messages. I start to delete them, but then I stop when I spot a message from @sweetcheekscreamery.

Hello! Yes, I'm totally serious. Would you be willing to chat with me about helping me go viral on TikTok? Also, my sincerest apologies for how long and rambling my prior message was! It was kind of a rough night lol

I smile at the reply. It's so damn adorable. I still have no idea who this person is that's messaging me. But part of me hopes it's that cute blonde in the video I saw earlier.

Before I hit the shower, I reply.

It's all good, no worries. Hope things are better for you today. Before we start talking about this, can I get your name? Also, is this you?

I link the video of the blonde woman scooping the triple waffle cone. I get a response almost immediately.

My name is Becca Briarwood and yes, that's me in the video.

I grin to myself. I knew it. And god, even her name is adorable and sweet.

Nice to meet you, Becca. Look, instead of DMing back and forth, you wanna meet and talk in person? I feel like that would be easier. You could tell me exactly what you're looking for and I can figure out if I can help you.

Before I send it off, I stop myself. I have no idea if I'll be able to help her. I've never had this kind of request before. But something about this woman intrigues me.

Because you think she's pretty.

Yeah, that's part of it. And yeah, I know that's shallow as fuck. But that's not the only reason.

I think back to her initial message, how honest and open she was. How she mentioned an ex who stole money from her and why that's the reason she was reaching out to me. Maybe that's the reason she got drunk, to drown her sorrows a bit.

I clench my jaw. I've never had an ex do that to me, but I know what it's like to feel betrayed by someone who you thought had your back.

Yeah, I don't know this girl from Eve. But there's something about her. As I peel off my sweaty clothes and shove them in my gym bag, I think back to all those videos of hers that I watched. How she offers free ice cream to kids, how she gives senior citizen discounts, how she donates her time to the community. She seems really kind-hearted. She also seems to be in a rough patch. I want to at least hear her out.

I send the message, then hit the shower. By the time I'm dried off and dressed, she's replied.

You want to meet? Like in person?

I chuckle.

Me: *Yes, in person. I saw that your shop is in Denver, so I'm guessing you are too? So am I. You're not far from my neighborhood. I could stop by tomorrow if you want and we can talk this out.*

Becca: *Okay, great! Can you come by before I open? Like around 9 in the morning?*

Me: *I'll be there.*

Becca: *Perfect! Thank you! I'll have a scoop of whatever flavor you want waiting for you*

Me: *Mint chocolate chip?*

Becca: *You got it! It won't be as fancy as what you prepare in your videos, but I promise it'll be just as yummy!*

Me: *That's a big promise.*

Becca: *Ice cream is my specialty. Just wait till you taste it ;)*

I'm taken aback by the winky face she sends me. I wasn't expecting that. For the rest of the night as I make dinner, do laundry, and clean up my place, my mind periodically drifts back to Becca and that winky face.

Chapter 6

Becca

"Will you calm down? You're going to bore a hole in the glass the way you're staring at it."

I pivot my gaze to Tori, who's unloading a new batch of browned butter brickle ice cream into the front. "I'm calm."

She sets the massive container of ice cream into the display freezer, takes a breath, then rolls her eyes at me. "Becca, you're about as calm as a rabid prairie dog."

I choke out a laugh. "Rabid prairie dog?"

She lightly tugs on my ponytail. "You have the same hair color."

"Ha." The momentary lightness is replaced by the nerves that have been churning inside of me all morning. I finish opening the register, then start refilling the napkin dispensers.

"Becca, I swear it's not that big a deal," Tori says as she frosts an ice cream cake. "So you sent that Gage guy a winking emoji. So what?"

My jaw unhinges. "So what? Tori, he probably thinks I'm a creep. First, I send him an unhinged drunken DM, and then I send him a winking emoji. What kind of a maniac sends a winking emoji to a total stranger?"

"Lots of people do." Tori laughs. "Come on, you're acting like you sent him a pic of your boobs."

Just the thought of that has me dizzy with humiliation. I press my eyes shut and shake my head. "Oh my god, I can't even imagine doing that."

Tori's laugh bounces around me. I still can't believe I sent Gage Grant a freaking winking emoji. I meant to send a smiley face when I sent my last DM to him, but I hit the winking face by mistake and didn't realize it until the message had already sent. Just thinking about that moment sends the same wave of shame and panic crashing through me. I froze. I had no idea what to do—send a message apologizing and sound like an overthinking maniac? Or ignore it and come off like a creep?

Tori pats my shoulder. "I promise you're freaking out for nothing. This dude probably receives way more risqué things in his DMs. Like, just think of all the sexy messages and nude pics he gets. I mean, the comments on his videos are pretty X-rated. His DMs have gotta be worse."

I take a breath, feeling the tension in my muscles ease the slightest bit. That's a valid point.

"A winky face emoji was white noise for him, guaranteed." Tori says it with such confidence, I almost believe her.

Just then the door swings open. I look up, and my eyes go wide. I pull my lips into my mouth to keep from gasping. Holy crap. There's Gage Grant in the flesh, standing in my ice cream shop, three feet from me.

The right corner of his mouth hooks up when he looks at me. "Hey. Becca?"

I don't say anything in return. I want to. I know it's the polite thing to do, but I'm physically unable to move my mouth or blink or speak a single word. It's impossible when I'm standing three feet from unquestionable nuclear hotness.

It's not surprising that Gage is hot. That's the most obvious thing you could say about him. It's just that in person, he's insanely hot—especially when he smiles—and it's doing something strange to my brain.

God, have I always been this...shallow? I've been in the presence of attractive men plenty of times. And yeah, I've felt nervous. But this? This frozen state I'm in? I've never experienced that before.

I zero in on his mouth, those pouty lips, how they're hooked up in the most perfect crooked smile.

Tori clears her throat behind me, breaking my trance. "Yes, that's Becca."

"I'm sorry about the winking face," I blurt.

Tori's disappointed sigh sounds behind me. Shame heats across my skin. I can't see myself, but I'm willing to bet I've got one hell of a flush igniting my pale skin. God, he must think I'm such a freak.

But to my utter shock, his half-smile turns full. "No apologies necessary." He sticks out his hand. "I'm Gage. It's nice to meet you."

Tori was right. It wasn't a big deal.

Just act normal.

"So nice to meet you too," I manage with a smile of my own and shake his hand in return. "Thank you so much for meeting me."

I fight the urge to shrink into myself and summon all the normal person energy I have. I gesture to a two-person table off to the side. We both take a seat. I'm about to dive into the pitch I've been rehearsing ever since we decided to meet when I hear Tori clear her throat.

"Oh!" I look behind me and gesture for her to come forward. She practically sprints over, a wide grin splitting her face in half. "This is my best friend, Tori. She works here at Sweet Cheeks. She's amazing, keeps this place running."

Gage reaches up, and they shake hands.

"No way. That's Becca all the way," Tori says. She grins as she stares at him. "I just help where I can. I'm a huge fan, by the way."

A roguish smile pulls at Gage's lips, and I feel my body going hot once more. "You're very kind. Thank you."

He glances down, and that's when I notice Tori's still gripping his hand. I rest my hand on her forearm. "Can you get started on mixing a new batch of unicorn swirl in the back?"

Tori's starry-eyed gaze dissipates. "Oh, sure! Have fun, you two."

She disappears into the back, and I focus back on Gage.

"Oh wait! I promised you mint chip, didn't I?" I hop up, scurry to the counter, and quickly dish up a scoop for Gage.

When I set it down in front of him, he chuckles. "You didn't have to actually give me ice cream."

"Oh..." I look between the ice cream and the counter. "Sorry. I, uh—you don't have to eat that then."

I reach for it, but he shakes his head and grabs the spoon. "Let's see if it's as good as you claim."

His teasing tone sends a flock of butterflies to my stomach. I try to ignore it as I sit back down.

When he moans after that first spoonful, I can't help but smile.

"Holy..."

"Good?" I ask.

"Incredible." He inhales the rest of the ice cream in the

small dish. "You weren't kidding. That was the best mint chip I've ever had."

I grin so wide, my cheeks hurt. "I love seeing people try my ice cream for the first time. It makes me happier than anything."

There's a quiet moment where Gage's smile turns soft as he looks at me. "So," he says with a glimmer in his mahogany brown eyes, "you need help with some sexy TikToks?"

I nearly jolt at the change in topic. I shouldn't be so shocked. That's the reason he's here.

"Um, yes," I say.

He leans forward in his chair, and that's when I take in his size. He's not huge. He looks just shy of six feet. Definitely not short, but not necessarily tall, though he's plenty tall to me given I'm barely five-five.

But it's his broad build that's most striking to me. I've watched all of his TikTok videos, so I'm well aware that he's jacked. But now that I'm sitting just inches from him, his physique is mesmerizing.

He shifts, lightly bumping the table with his knee.

"Sorry, the tables and chairs in here are a bit on the small side," I say quickly. "It's just that a lot of my customers are kids, so I thought it would be good to have some smaller furniture and..."

He leans forward, closing the space between us to just a handful of inches. "You're not allowed to say sorry anymore."

I laugh nervously. "What do you mean?"

"You apologize a lot. You don't need to."

"Oh. Okay."

His tone is so definitive but gentle, so firm and commanding yet kind.

I think of his videos, how he embodies this very same self-assuredness in the way he moves, the way he looks at the camera...

I press my eyes shut for a second and shake my head. I really, really shouldn't be thinking of his videos right now.

I almost say "sorry" but catch myself. "I guess it's a habit. I just don't want to offend anyone."

That scrumptious half-smile makes a reappearance. There's a flash in those gorgeous brown eyes. "Becca, you don't have to worry. I don't offend easily."

He leans back in his chair and sets his palm on the table. "So sexy videos?"

I clear my throat. "Yes. Sexy videos." I pull out a small notepad from the back pocket of my jean shorts along with a pen. "I jotted down some objectives."

"Objectives?" Gage asks with a lift of his eyebrow.

I nod. "Goals I want to accomplish." I flip to the first page.

"Okay, hold on a second. I want to make sure you know what you're getting into."

"What do you mean?"

"I watched most of your TikTok videos, and they're really cute. Wholesome, sweet, all that. You say you have a lot of kid customers too, right?"

"Yeah."

"Are you sure you want to transition to full-on sexy stuff? That could deter your current customer base."

"I'm positive. Look, I love all of my customers. But focusing on the wholesome stuff hasn't really been working out for me. I need to make more money—lots more money. And I know how cliché it sounds, but sex sells. At least it seems to."

Gage looks at me for a long second, like he's trying to process what I've said. "Nah, you're right. It does."

"Right now Sweet Cheeks is sitting at a few thousand followers. I'd love to hit half a million before the end of the summer, which is a month and a half away. I'm thinking if I upload three to four sexy videos a week, that could get us there."

I brace myself for Gage's scoff, for him to say that's a lofty goal for a tiny ice cream shop that's just over a year old.

But he doesn't. That focused stare remains on his beautifully chiseled features. "Seems doable."

"Really?"

He chuckles at the hitch in my voice. "Yeah, really. What about your goal of having your ice cream in stores and restaurants?"

I'm confused at what he's said, but then I remember my drunken DM.

I huff an embarrassed laugh. "Oh, that. That's more of a long-term goal. We can just focus on TikTok for now."

"Cool. Now what did you have in mind for sexy videos?"

I stammer, "Well, um, that's just it. I don't know. That's where you come in. I was hoping you could tell me what to do, I'd film it, then upload, and..."

"And ta-da, a half-million followers?" he says with a taunting smirk that makes me want to shrink in my chair.

"Well, um, yeah. But clearly you think that's ridiculous, so never mind."

I flip my notebook shut, but Gage reaches forward and gently stops me. "Hey. I didn't mean it like that." I look up at him and take in the shy look in his eyes. "I'm sorry. That was shitty of me to say it like that."

I glance down at his hand, taking in the spread of his

thick fingers, how his hand could cover mine. He pulls away.

I look up at him. "So *you* can say sorry?"

There's that half-smile again. God, it's hot.

"When I have a reason to—when I mess up, I say sorry."

Something in his gaze turns playful, but he blinks, and it's gone. I catch myself wishing I could see more of that playful side of him, but I quietly scold myself. I shouldn't be thinking of him in that way. I should be focused on the moment and the fact that he even agreed to come here and meet me.

"So are you going to be in these sexy videos?" he asks, throwing me off.

"Oh, um, no."

He frowns. "How's that gonna work then?"

"What do you mean?"

"Were you thinking of just filming metal scoops dragging through ice cream in slo-mo with porno music playing in the background?"

I cross my arms. "No. Er, um, maybe."

This time when he smiles, it reaches his eyes. And even though I feel absolutely ridiculous and completely out of my element talking to this guy who is sex on two very muscular legs, I also feel happy—proud of myself, even—for getting him to flash such a pure, giddy smile.

"You do some pretty suggestive things with the food in your videos. Always to some sexy slow jam," I say. "I've seen the way you...handle...certain ingredients. That thing you do with the grapefruit halves...how you run your fingers along the membrane really fast..."

The image of him practically fingering citrus fruit at lightning speed flashes in my mind. I almost choke.

"And remember that time you prepared that phallic

pastry thing with the mascarpone berry sauce that was clearly supposed to look like…like…"

Gage purses his lips together like he's trying not to laugh. "Like?"

My skin turns hot yet again. "You know what I mean."

"Why don't you want to be in the videos?" he asks.

I honk out a laugh. He looks at me like he couldn't be more confused.

I gesture along the length of myself while I sit. "I'm not exactly what anyone thinks of when they imagine sex appeal or superhot TikTok video."

The way he frowns, like he couldn't be more confused, throws me. Is that because he thinks what I've said is ridiculous? Is it because he thinks…that I could actually be sexy?

I shove away the thought. No way. A guy as off-the-charts hot and brooding would never think I'm sexy.

I'm the walking, talking human version of vanilla, remember?

"So what? You want me to do some sexy stuff with your ice cream and you film it for your TikTok?"

"Yes."

He shakes his head. "I can't."

My heart sinks. "Why not?"

"Because this isn't my shop. Yeah, I could be in some videos, serving up ice cream, but that might not get you the kind of traction you want. If I'm the only person people see in those videos, it might just drive them to my TikTok."

"Oh. I didn't even think about that."

"This is your shop, Becca. You own this place. You should be the face of your business. You should be in the videos, too, so people know it's your ice cream—so they know it's you."

Just the thought of doing what Gage does—act so

unapologetically sexy on camera over and over and over—makes all the nerves inside of me go haywire.

He must be able to tell because his expression turns sympathetic as he looks at me.

"What if we're in the videos together?" I blurt.

He squints slightly, like he's seriously thinking about it. "Okay."

"Really?"

He nods.

I squeal and clap for a solid three seconds before I realize what a loser I must look like. I stop and look over at him. "Thank you. Seriously."

He nods again, and I take a breath. "Okay. Now, how can I compensate you for your work?"

"What do you mean?"

"Well, I don't have much money to pay you. I was serious about the offer to give you free ice cream for life, if you want."

He chuckles. "You don't need to do that."

"I insist. I'm not taking your help for free."

"Why not? I'm offering it."

"Because that's what got me here in the first place." It's not till I say the words that I realize how pained I sound. It makes sense. It's only been a handful of days since my breakup—and just a couple days after finding out that Ben stole from me. The pain is still raw, and I'm reeling, but I don't want Gage to see what a mess I am on the inside.

I clear my throat. "Look, my ex used to help out at Sweet Cheeks when I first opened. I trusted him when he said he was happy to help me for free, but obviously he wasn't, given that after we broke up, he stole from me."

I glance off to the side, nervous about meeting Gage's gaze after spilling all that. Even though he seems like a decent guy, I don't know him well at all. What if he changes his mind down the line and wants something in return? Best to stop that from even being an issue.

I muster up the guts to look back at Gage. He looks like he wants to say something, but he stays quiet.

"I don't feel comfortable working with you unless you let me do something for you in return," I say. "It feels one-sided."

"Okay. How about this: my cousin is pregnant, and her biggest craving right now is ice cream. I'd score some major points if I surprised her with some pints from Sweet Cheeks."

I beam. "Done. Whatever ice cream flavor she wants, for the rest of her pregnancy, I'll whip up for free, and you can bring them to her."

"Really?"

"Absolutely. It's the least I could do. And if there's anything else that comes up that you can think of where I can help you, tell me. I mean it."

He grins wide. "Okay. Thank you."

"What's she craving now?"

"Chocolate chip cookie dough. And cookies and cream. And sherbert. Pretty much every flavor of sherbert."

"No problem." I hop up to the standing freezer behind me, open the door, and fetch half a dozen quarts. "Here you go."

Gage looks at the ice cream with wide eyes, then smiles. "She's gonna love this."

"You're gonna be her favorite cousin, hands down." I bag up the ice cream and hand it to him.

"I'll drop this off to her, then come back tonight."

"Tonight?"

"Yeah. We've got some sexy TikToks to film, remember?

We need to get started ASAP if you want to hit half a million before the end of the summer."

The smirk he flashes makes my throat go dry. Somehow, in the excitement of getting Gage to agree to help me, I forgot what I'll have to do: be sexy. On camera. With him.

He takes the bag from my hand and walks to the door. "Don't be nervous, Becca. This'll be fun."

Gage Grant winks at me. *He winks at me.* And then he's out the door, and I'm breathless.

I have no doubt he's right. The question is, will I be able to handle being sexy with Gage Grant?

Chapter 7

Gage

"You're nervous."

Becca aims her wide-eyed, crystal blue stare at me as she nods. I bite my bottom lip to keep from laughing.

I'm back at Sweet Cheeks, it's an hour past closing, and we're supposed to be filming a sexy video right now. But the moment I walked back in here, I could feel the nervous tension crackling off of Becca. Her shoulders are almost to her ears, and she can't keep eye contact with me for more than a few seconds without looking away.

It's not that I'm laughing at her or think she's ridiculous. She's not. She's actually the most adorable goddamn thing I've seen, even more so when she's nervous. I can barely take it as I watch those stunning blue eyes go wide and unblinking.

But I'm guessing she wouldn't want me, an almost stranger, going on about how cute I think her nervousness is.

So I refocus.

"Becca, I swear this is gonna be okay. It's really not a big deal, being so-called sexy on camera."

When she frowns, the bridge of her nose wrinkles the slightest bit. Holy shit, that's even cuter. Damn, does she even know what she looks like when she does that?

I shake my head slightly, annoyed with myself for where my head goes. I'm supposed to be helping her, not obsessing over how attractive she is.

"So-called sexy?" she says. "What do you mean 'so-called'? Gage, you're the definition of sexy."

I feel the smuggest grin pulling at my mouth. "You think I'm the definition of sexy?"

She presses her eyes shut and shakes her head slightly. Her peaches and cream complexion turns the same shade of pink as the cotton candy walls of her shop. "No, I didn't mean it like that."

"So I'm not sexy?"

"No, you are. I just meant..."

I finally let myself laugh. "Becca, I'm messing with you."

"Oh." She lets out a breath.

"I just meant that it never feels very sexy when I film my videos. It's actually pretty awkward."

Her shoulders lower the slightest bit. "Really?"

I nod. "I film by myself, and sometimes I prop my phone in the handle of my refrigerator. So whenever I flash a brooding expression or wink or smirk, I'm essentially eye-fucking my refrigerator."

Those bee-stung lips split into a grin, and she bursts out laughing. She has to grip the counter where she's standing, she's cackling so hard. I start to laugh too.

"Oh my gosh," she says after catching her breath. "The image of you doing that killed me."

She straightens back up, an easy and relaxed smile on

her face and the cutest fucking dimples on both of her full cheeks.

This woman. There's something about her that drives me wild in the best way. She's definitely different from the type of woman I've dated in the past. All of my exes and past hookups have been viciously confident ballbusters. I've always been a sucker for a hot girl with a brazen attitude. That kind of feisty flirting keeps me engaged and on my toes.

I've never gone for the sweet, innocent girls like Becca. I've always wanted to though. Just the thought of going after someone wholesome would be a damn good time. It would be fun as hell to corrupt an absolute sweetheart, to get her to go wild both in and out of bed, to show her just how fun it can be to be bad.

I haven't even heard Becca swear. What would it take for her to drop a curse word from those perfectly pink and plump lips? I blink, and an image flashes in my brain: Becca flushed from head to toe, her blonde hair mussed, her chest heaving as she pants and moans...

Jesus. That's enough, you creep.

I clear my throat and force myself to focus back on our conversation. "It's the truth. The behind-the-scenes is pretty silly and weird. Very, very unsexy." I glance around the darkened space. "Are we the only ones here?"

She nods. "I sent Tori home early so we could, um, have the place to ourselves."

"Great. Any ideas for Sweet Cheeks Creamery's very first sexy TikTok video?"

Becca hesitates before her cheeks go pink once more. "I mean, I don't think I can top that ice cream scoop with porno music you mentioned."

I chuckle. "It's okay. I've got plenty of ideas."

She looks relieved...until I show her the list of ideas that I brainstormed on my phone.

Notepad in hand, she falls into the chair at the table we sat at together this morning.

"You want me to slowly lick an ice cream cone?" She gawks up at me.

I sit down across from her. "That's how you'd normally eat ice cream, Becca. You lick it, don't you?"

She leans back in her seat, the look on her face adorably indignant. "Well, yeah. But to do it slowly would make it look all seductive..."

I tilt my head at her. "I thought that was the point."

Her expression falls. "Right." She skims the list again. "Licking an ice cream cone...licking my lips...licking ice cream off a spoon...okay, there's a lot of licking involved."

"Again, this is ice cream we're talking about here," I say, trying to hide the amusement in my voice.

"Eating a cherry. At least that's different. Dripping hot fudge on..." She makes a choking sound. I'm once again trying not to laugh. "Dripping hot fudge on your chest."

"You don't have to lick it off," I tease.

She frowns at the list and hesitates. "Licking whipped cream."

I roll out my shoulders to stretch and chuckle. "I know, I know. Too much licking."

"No, it's...that's fine." Her gaze fixes on my phone. A second later she looks away, and her expression goes shy and...embarrassed?

"You okay?"

She clears her throat. "Yeah. Fine. Let's do the first one on the list," she mutters before darting up and turning to the freezer.

I stand up and reach out to gently grab her arm. "Hey, wait. You're not comfortable with this, are you?"

"It's fine."

Her stiff body language and furrowed brows broadcast otherwise.

"Becca, I'm not here to make you do something you don't want to do. You clearly don't like my ideas. That's okay." I hope my tone comes off as easy and casual as I'm trying to convey. "What's something you'd feel comfortable doing?"

She hesitates for a second, but I notice her shoulders and arms are in a more relaxed position now.

Those saucer-like eyes fix on me, and she licks her lips. "I'm going to make a hot fudge sundae on camera. Then I'll slide it over to you, and you're going to lean down and lick it."

Well, shit. I wasn't expecting that. My mouth hooks up in a smile. Something inside of me ignites.

"Let's do it."

* * *

Twenty minutes later we're behind the counter at Sweet Cheeks. My camera phone is set up on a tripod, and I'm filming Becca as she dishes up the most delicious-looking sundae ever.

She's smiling down at the dish of ice cream as she drizzles some hot fudge, sprinkles nuts, and drops a cherry on top. Then, like we planned, she looks straight into the camera and makes a come-hither motion with her index finger. That's my cue.

She steps out of frame while I walk over, plant my hands on either side of the sundae, and lean down so my face is hovering right over it. And then I look up at the camera, quirk my eyebrow, and wait a beat. Then I wink, lower down even closer, and lick the hot fudge.

The warm, rich flavor coats my tongue. I swallow and step back, wiping my mouth with the back of my hand. When I make eye contact with Becca, she's beaming.

"Oh my god! Gage, that was incredible!"

I stop the video and walk back over to her to show her the footage. "That was pretty slick," I say. "I'll send it to your phone."

A second later it's on Becca's phone. She pulls up TikTok, and together we pick out music to play over it.

"This one," I say, choosing a remixed R&B slow jam.

Becca is nodding, biting her lip, and still smiling.

She uploads it to the Sweet Cheeks account, then turns to me. "What should the caption be?"

I'm about to offer a suggestion when she holds up a hand.

"Wait! I just thought of one."

She quickly types, then shows it to me.

When your ice cream sundae is almost as yummy as @gagegrant #icecream #sweetcheeks #icecreamdaddy #melt-inmymouth #yum #lick

My brow hits my hairline. "'Ice cream daddy'? That's an unexpectedly hot caption from a woman who was blushing at the ideas I brainstormed twenty minutes ago."

She bites back a smile. "I guess I just needed to dive in."

"I'm impressed. Especially with 'ice cream daddy.'"

That blush I like so much appears once more on her cheeks. Still grinning, she shrugs. "I thought it would be fun."

She uploads the video and looks back at me. She makes a shimmying movement with her arms. "Okay, I'm way too excited about this. I can't wait to see the response."

I grab my phone and post the video on my TikTok, but with a different caption.

Daddy wanted ice cream, so I hit up @sweetcheekscreamery and they knocked it out of the park

I show it to Becca, and she laughs. "We should eat that before it melts." She nods over to the sundae.

We stand by the counter and dig in.

"Holy shit," I say after a bite. "This is the best ice cream sundae I've ever had."

Becca flashes a shy smile. "Really? You're not just saying that?"

"Really. Seriously, Becca, this is incredible. How do you get your ice cream to taste so rich and flavorful?"

She tells me about a local organic dairy farm she sources her ingredients from and how she uses extra vanilla extract in every flavor.

"Not just vanilla ice cream flavors," she says after swallowing a spoonful of ice cream. "Putting extra vanilla in every flavor we make takes it to the next level. It makes the flavor richer and fuller."

I make an "mmm" sound as I help myself to a third heaping spoonful. "Damn. That must be it."

"Well, that and we let the ice cream sundae sit for a bit so it gets a bit melty. That's when it tastes the best, I think."

"Really?"

She nods excitedly. "Okay, so this is going to sound weird, but ice cream shouldn't be eaten when it's super, duper cold."

I smile when she says, "super, duper." I can't remember the last time someone said those words. It's cute as hell, just like everything else Becca does.

"Ice cream tastes the absolute best when you let it sit for at least a minute so it gets the tiniest bit soft. Not too soft though! You don't want a melty mess. That defeats the whole purpose of ice cream."

"Of course. That's just common sense." I nod along as I inhale my half of the sundae.

"Right?" Her eyes are practically sparkling. She is so damn giddy talking about ice cream, and I can't get enough of it.

"If it's too cold, you can't really taste the flavor. But after a minute, the chill mellows out, and that's when the flavors really burst. The cold cream hits your tongue, and bam! It's an explosion of sugar and fat and milk and vanilla and chocolate. So if you can, always, always, always wait a minute before digging in for the maximum ice cream flavor experience."

I drop my plastic spoon into the now-empty dish and lick my lips. Becca hands me a napkin. "I promise that from now on, I'll always wait a minute before digging into my ice cream. Unless I'm starving. Or unless it's a hot day and it's gonna melt."

She giggles. "Fair enough."

Just then her phone buzzes. When she looks at it, she gasps and cups a hand over her mouth. "Oh my god."

"What's wrong? Everything okay?"

She drops her hand to reveal the biggest grin. "Nothing is wrong. Everything is freaking fantastic. Look!"

She shows me her phone screen. It's the TikTok video she just posted to the Sweet Cheeks account. It's already gotten a thousand likes.

"It's been posted less than ten minutes," she murmurs at her phone screen. She playfully shoves my shoulder. "And it's because of you, you superstar. People are going nuts over you."

She shows me the comments.

OMFG ice cream daddy??!!

Holy shit is that @gagegrant?

Okay, I'm gonna need some ice cream now

Could I get a scoop of @gagegrant on my sundae kthxbye

Good lord would you look at that tongue

Can't tell if I'm turned on or just horny for ice cream

ICE CREAM DADDY YESSSS

"Holy crap..." She gawks at her phone screen. It's the first time she's kind of swore, even though "crap" isn't technically a curse word. But still. I like hearing Becca's sweet voice utter a borderline naughty word.

"We've gotten a thousand followers in the last ten minutes!"

I high-five her. "Well done."

She grabs my hand in hers. "This is happening because of you. Thank you."

Her tone turns soft. So does something inside my chest. She's so kind, so sincere.

"This is amazing," she says. "We should post another video soon."

"When do you want to film again?"

"As soon as possible. Tomorrow?"

"That works."

She hesitates. "I don't want to take up all your time though."

"You're not. I want to be here. I want to help you."

She grins. "Okay, great. Same time tomorrow night?"

"I'll be here."

Chapter 8

Becca

When Gage walks into my ice cream shop today, I'm nervous. Again.

Actually, nervous isn't the right word. More like a raging ball of anxiety.

Why, oh, why am I freaking out at seeing him again? I saw him yesterday, and I got over my nerves enough to film a sexy video that has earned Sweet Cheeks thousands of new followers and views. And on top of it all, we had a friendly chat over some ice cream. That was my favorite part of the evening, honestly. We clicked so well. It felt like talking to an old friend.

Maybe because he's Gage Grant and you still can't believe that this insanely hot TikToker and effortlessly cool dreamboat is here, in the flesh, working with you.

He flashes that devastating half-smile yet again, and my knees go weak. Yup. That's exactly why.

"We had triple our usual mail orders today," I blurt. "Because of, um, the video. On TikTok."

Wow. I could have said hello, but no. My weirdo brain decided to say the most random thing in the world.

Way to sound like a complete freak, Becca.

A chuckle falls from his perfect lips. "That's awesome. Congrats. You need help packing them up?"

I shake my head. "Tori and I came in early this morning to ship them all out."

"Which flavor was the most popular?"

"Unicorn swirl." When I realize I'm fidgeting with my hands, I force them to my sides.

Gage's dark brown gaze bounces from one of my arms to the other. "You nervous still?"

My shoulders slump before I can catch myself. "Yeah."

God, this guy can read me like a book.

"How could you tell?" I attempt a teasing laugh, but I end up snort-chuckling like the massive nerd I am. Fabulous.

But instead of wincing in pity, his half-smile turns full. "It's okay to be nervous. Don't worry."

He plops down at the same table we sat at last night and pats the table. "Come sit with me."

"But we have another video to shoot."

"Not just yet." He unzips the backpack he brought with him and pulls out a metal flask. He wiggles it at me. "How about some liquid courage?"

I start to smile. "Wait, did you bring that with you yesterday too?"

He nods. "I figured it would be good to have on hand in case we needed to relax a bit before filming. But you were a star yesterday."

"Unlike today." I grab two small paper cups and join him at the table.

"It's okay, Becca." Goosebumps flash across my skin even though it's ninety degrees out. That low, soft, coaxing voice is going to be the death of me. Gage could get me to do just about anything if he asked me in that sexy-as-sin tone.

"It's not a big deal," he says as he pours the amber liquor into both cups. "Nerves get the best of everyone."

"Not you. What is this anyway?" I ask when he slides a cup to me.

"Whisky. That okay?"

I nod even though it's been at least a solid year since I've downed a shot of whisky.

I hold up my cup, he holds up his, and we toast. I down the shot and instantly wince at the burn. "God."

Gage barely blinks as he knocks back his drink. "Not a whisky fan?"

I shake my head. "It's just been a while."

"I get nervous too," he says after a second.

"Not while you film your videos."

"Of course not. What's there to be nervous about when my audience is my refrigerator?"

I laugh, already feeling the effects of the whisky. My limbs are loose, and there's a hint of warmth coursing through my chest.

"I'm an odd duck, Gage," I say after a quiet moment. "I'll be bold one second, then lose my nerve the next. It's like my bravery is fleeting. I use all my energy to accomplish one thing that terrifies me, then I don't have the stamina to keep going. I have to build myself up all over again."

I glance up from my empty cup to meet his soft stare.

"You talk like that's a bad thing," he says.

I shrug.

"Thunderstorms freak me out."

I'm taken aback by his sudden admission. But then I realize: he's admitting this so that I don't feel as alone. He's telling me this to comfort me.

That warmth inside my chest spreads.

"They're legitimately scary," I say. "Thunderstorms are loud and dangerous and destructive. They lead to tornadoes sometimes. They make plenty of people nervous."

"It's different for me though. Ever since I was little, I get pretty bad stomachaches whenever there's a bad storm. I was hiking last year at Rocky Mountain National Park with my brother, and a thunderstorm moved into the area without warning. My stomach was cramping so bad, even walking was painful. By the time we made it to the car, I threw up."

"Oh gosh."

"You should have seen the way the other hikers looked at me while I was retching in the parking lot. Completely disgusted," he says. "That day freaked me out so much. Since then I refuse to hike if it's even a little bit cloudy."

He pours himself another shot of whisky and downs it. My chest squeezes as I watch him. His expression and body language are relaxed, but still. It means so much that he'd tell me something so personal, just to make me feel better.

He offers a small smile. "At least you're not letting your nerves stop you. You're still going through with the plan to film today."

His encouraging words send a jolt of determination through me. I motion for another shot. He looks surprised as he pours another. I down it and barely even wince this time. Screw my nerves.

I stand up. "Let's do this."

He stands up too, amusement tugging at his smile this time. "So what are we filming today?"

I take a breath. "Licking. Lots and lots of licking."

He bites his bottom lip as he grins. "Let's do it."

Ten minutes later, I'm holding a waffle cone with three scoops of ice cream between our faces.

He glances over at his phone, which is propped up on his tripod. He reaches over to press record, then looks over at me.

"Are you ready to lick?" he says with that killer crooked smirk.

I giggle so hard, I have to lean back and cover my mouth with my free hand. Thanks to the whisky, I'm feeling more relaxed and more prone to laughing fits. When I catch my breath, I nod at him. "So ready to lick."

A low chuckle falls from this mouth. Good lord, is everything this guy does ridiculously sexy?

I lick one side of the ice cream scoop stack while Gage licks the other. For the first few seconds, I have to hold back a laugh. This is so silly. And hilarious. Actually, it's not that funny. It's probably just because I'm tipsy.

A beat later Gage's hot breath hits my lips...and my tongue. And then I freeze. My legs wobble the slightest bit. My mouth waters.

Holy...Whoa...

Okay, I had no idea that the act of air leaving someone's lungs could be so damn sexy. But it is. And then I see it—his tongue.

Holy mother of god...

It's long. Like, much longer than the average human tongue length. I've seen it plenty of times in his videos, but in person, it's mesmerizing. And the way he moves it, slathers it along his side of the ice cream cone, makes me go hot between my legs. And then that telltale ache hits me in that exact spot.

What exactly is his tongue capable of?

The phantom pulse between my legs gives me a hint. If

Gage can move his tongue that deftly on an ice cream cone, I bet he's downright lethal when he kisses and does...other things.

Feeling Gage's hot wet breath hit my skin and lips and tongue *and* seeing his tongue this close to my mouth has my imagination doing a filthy, filthy loop.

Plus, the sound he's making. That low, faint grunt...

I force myself to play it cool, to take another slow lick of ice cream and blink and breathe. But then my filthy imagination takes hold. Suddenly the cone is gone, and Gage's hands are on my waist, pulling me against his body. His hot, firm body. His mouth is parted, and he breathes in, then exhales, his hot breath all over my skin and lips.

In my imagination, he leans forward and runs his tongue along my bottom lip. And then he flashes that sexy smirk.

"You want a taste, Becca?" he growls. "Because I'm dying for a taste of you."

And I know, without a doubt, he would taste a million times better than this triple scoop of mint chip...

Just then Gage quirks his head to the side, pulling me back into the moment. Eyes on me, he licks the smear of mint chip from his bottom lip. "How was that?" he asks.

"Great," I squeak out.

"You think we need another take?"

I shake my head so furiously that I almost drop the ice cream cone. "Um, no. I think we got it."

I stand there, hoping I don't look as guilty as I feel. Because here's Gage, focused on filming, on doing the best job possible to help me and my ice cream shop, while I've been mentally defiling him.

I clear my throat at least three times while he grabs his phone and shows me the footage.

I hold my breath as I watch it, hoping that my filthy thoughts aren't playing out on my face. Luckily I played it off somehow. I look normal—or as normal as I could look licking a giant ice cream cone with Gage Grant three inches from my face.

"Here." He takes the cone from me and sends me the footage. My phone buzzes. "You can upload it now if you want."

I silently nod, my heart beating at a dizzying pace as I fumble with my phone. I quickly type the first caption that comes to mind.

How many licks does it take till you get to the good part?

I show it to Gage, who's demolished half the cone. "Damn, that's good. You're a natural at this."

He nudges my shoulder with his, which snaps me out of my stupor. Well, that was a decidedly friendly gesture—and the perfect reminder. I need to get it together. No more fantasizing about Gage. One, it's creepy. And two, he clearly isn't into me, seeing as he just nudged me.

This is just the alcohol combined with being in the presence of a bona fide hottie. It's all warping my brain.

The heat inside of me dissipates, and I manage to smile at him. "I think I'm getting the hang of this sexy TikTok stuff."

He laughs and offers me the rest of the cone, which I finish while he checks his phone. The minute the video uploads, my phone is buzzing with notifications.

"I saw that Sweet Cheeks doubled its follower count since yesterday," he says.

"Yup. Almost ten thousand followers. Can you believe it?"

"Of course I can. We're a killer team." He walks back

over to the table, grabs his backpack, and slings it over his shoulder. "Same time tomorrow?"

"Absolutely."

"Any ideas on what we should film?"

I shake my head. "Not yet."

He flashes a knowing smile. "No worries. I'm sure we'll think of something."

He waves and heads out the door, and I let out the breath I'm holding. I check the video and see fifty comments already.

OH MY EFFING GOD

I now identify as a triple-scoop waffle cone

That girl is soooo lucky to share an ice cream cone with #icecreamdaddy

I'd pay good money to trade places with her.

I smile to myself, then spot a comment from Gage himself.

Okay beauties, we're taking requests. What do you want to see us do in the next video for @sweetcheekscreamery?

My mouth falls open as I skim the answers. Oh. My. God.

Chapter 9

Gage

A smile tugs at my lips as I walk up to Becca's ice cream shop. Last night I pulled one hell of a ballsy move. I don't usually leave comments on my TikTok videos. Sometimes I'll leave cheeky emojis as responses. But actual comments? Never.

I couldn't resist though. Filming and posting TikToks for Becca and her ice cream shop has turned into way more fun than I thought it would be. I mean, I'm accustomed to shooting sexy content. That's always a good time. But doing it with Becca feels different. It's more playful. And teasing. I want to see just how far she's willing to go.

When I walk into the store, she greets me with a shy smile and a knowing look.

"I saw what you did," she says.

"What did I do?" I can't help the hitch in my voice. She is the perfect combination of sweet and sexy.

When we shared that massive ice cream cone yesterday —when I realized just how close my mouth and tongue were to her mouth and tongue—my imagination went wild.

I swear, I could taste her breath, and it made my mouth water. She was so sweet and so wet...

And for a few seconds, I let my imagination take a dirty turn. I imagined what it would be like to taste Becca's perfect pink tongue and lips. And then my brain went downright filthy as I wondered how sweet she tasted in other places, specifically between her legs...

I clear my throat and silently scold myself for going there. Again. It's bad enough that I let myself think those sleazy thoughts about Becca even once. But again? Not okay. Really, really not okay. Especially since I can pretty much guarantee she wasn't thinking dirty thoughts about me. She was probably focused on her ice cream shop and saving her business. And there I was, standing less than a foot from her, fantasizing about the taste of her body.

I clear my throat and focus back on the moment. She's standing in front of me doing that endearing-as-fuck scrunched mouth thing I notice she does when she's working up the nerve to say something.

"Thanks to the comment you left on our video last night, we've gotten a lot of creative suggestions for today," Becca says.

"I saw."

"Some of them were pretty..."

"Pretty?"

"Suggestive." She bites her lip, and my knees buckle.

Jesus, dude. Get ahold of yourself. Becca's hot for sure, but she doesn't need you secretly lusting after her like some desperate creep.

I clear my throat. "I'm guessing you don't wanna film any of those."

Her full cheeks flush, and she shakes her head. "Of course not. But you sort of laid the gauntlet down when you asked for people to leave their thoughts. We can't just leave them hanging."

I sit down at our usual table and pat the seat next to me. "Let's scroll through the suggestions together and find one we can film. One that makes you feel comfortable."

She quickly agrees and joins me. She sets her phone on the table between us, and we sift through the hundreds of comments.

Becca's blue eyes bulge. "I had no idea people could make ice cream so...sexual."

"Anything can be sexual in someone's dirty mind."

"I guess that's true. Oh wow..." Her finger stops scrolling. "A human hot fudge sundae."

"Creative." I chuckle. "But not as creative as..." I squint at a comment. "Licking ice cream off of each other's faces."

Becca bursts out laughing. "That's ridiculous. And gross."

"Agreed."

"This guy is offering to pay us ten grand to fill a tub with ice cream and bathe each other in it. He wants to film us."

Becca rolls her eyes. "No way."

"We seem to be on the same page about what turns us off. Go us."

She chuckles. "This person thinks we should blindfold each other and feed each other different ice cream while trying to guess the flavor."

"Damn. That's some old-school stuff right there. Straight out of *9 1/2 Weeks*."

Becca aims a confused frown at me. "Nine what?"

"It's a movie from the eighties, an erotic thriller..." Her blue eyes go wide, making her look even more innocent and adorable. Of course sweetheart Becca hasn't seen it. "Never mind."

She focuses back on reading the comments. "I guess I missed the..."

I look up when she trails off. She's clamped her mouth shut, and her eyebrows are knitted together.

"What's wrong?" I ask.

She doesn't answer; her gaze is still fixed on her phone screen. I look back down at it.

Whipped cream bikini!

I roll my eyes. That's such a predictable suggestion.

I scoff. "Come on. At least be creative, right?"

I look over at Becca, whose shoulders are hunched over. Her cheeks are flushed yet again, but her expression is totally different now. Instead of playful and teasing, her eyes look shy, like she's ashamed of something.

"Everything okay?" I ask.

She starts to nod. "Yeah. Fine."

Her gaze remains glued to her phone as she swipes her finger across the screen so fast, I can't even read the comments.

"Becca, stop," I say gently. "What's wrong?"

"Nothing," she mumbles, still swiping so fast that the text is a blur.

I set my hand on her forearm. "Hey. It's okay. We can take a break."

She pulls her hand away and folds it in her lap, along with her other hand.

She's clearly upset, and it's because of me posting that stupid comment asking for video suggestions. I should have asked her first to make sure she was okay with this. But no, I jumped the gun and made a decision without her, and now, because of me, she's uncomfortable.

"I'm sorry," I say.

She looks up at me, bewildered. "For what?"

"Clearly my idea to ask for suggestions was a terrible one. You're uncomfortable."

She shakes her head quickly. "Gage, no. That's not at all how I feel. It's just that suggestion, with the whipped cream, it's, um..." She hesitates, then takes a breath. "This is going to sound ridiculous, I'm sure. But whipped cream is kind of a sore subject."

"How do you mean? If you want to talk about it," I say.

Her expression eases, and her shoulders lower. I'll admit, I'm curious as hell to find out what happened. But I also know it's none of my business. But maybe it would help if Becca talked it out. And I only want her to talk about if she feels one hundred percent comfortable doing it.

She leans back and tugs at her braid. "This is kind of embarrassing."

"I'm the king of embarrassing shit. Promise whatever you're about to say, I've done something that's ten times worse."

A tiny smile appears. My heart slingshots around my chest. It feels really fucking good getting her to smile.

"Like what?" she asks.

"I once got black-out drunk in college at a party, stripped all my clothes off, and fell out of a first-floor window. I landed in front of the girl I'd had a crush on most of the year and cracked my tailbone. She wasn't impressed," I say without missing a beat.

Becca honks out a laugh, then covers her mouth a second later. "I'm sorry. I shouldn't have laughed."

"Don't be sorry. I deserved to be laughed at. I was a dipshit who couldn't hold my alcohol. Lesson learned."

Her smile fades, and she glances down at her hands, which are folded in her lap. "I've actually done the whipped cream bikini thing. For my ex. Pretty recently." She swallows. I watch the slow movement down her long, delicate throat. "We had been in kind of a rut. We were both busy with work and hadn't had a date night in who knows how long, so I thought I'd spice things up and surprised him when he came home from work. And it backfired because that's the night he told me he had met someone else. So there I was, totally naked, covered in whipped cream, while my boyfriend confessed to cheating on me and broke up with me."

A weird surge of emotion crashes in my chest. Sympathy for Becca in that heartbreaking moment. Anger at her ex for being such a piece of shit. What kind of douchebag cheats on a woman like her? Yeah, I may not have known Becca for very long, but it's clear she's a kind person who works hard to keep her business going. I mean, Christ, she's forced herself out of her comfort zone filming sexy TikTok videos to save her ice cream shop. She's sweet and giving and charitable and generous. And this prick had the nerve to cheat on her?

Arousal is the third emotion that completes the weird-as-hell emotions cocktail inside of me. Is arousal even an emotion? Whatever, not important. I don't have the brain space to deal with that, not when I'm actively trying not to picture how sexy Becca would look with whipped cream all over her tits, between her legs, and across her perfect bubble butt.

Becca sighs, slumping forward. "And then a couple days after Ben broke up with me, he emptied our joint bank account." She aims her gaze at me. "That's the same day I got drunk and DMed you. I was desperate because I was heartbroken and had no money and no idea what to do. I felt so betrayed."

The anger inside of me has leveled up. I wanna cross paths with this Ben asshole so I can confront him and ask him what the fuck kind of low life he is to steal from and cheat on this angel.

A string of curse words rests on the tip of my tongue. But I hold back. Becca's in the middle of opening up about this personal and upsetting moment. I bet it was hard as hell to work up the nerve for her to do that, and I don't want to ruin it.

"I know it's silly, but that whipped cream bikini suggestion just brought back all those emotions from my breakup," she says. "It just reminds me of how I fell short—in my relationship and my business."

Her hand is in mine before I know it. I don't even remember making the move to touch her. It just happened. This primal need to comfort and protect her surges through me.

"Becca, I'm sorry for what you've been through. Your ex was a piece of shit for treating you like that." There's a bitter taste on my tongue as I speak of what that guy did to her. I want to spit it out, but I hold back the urge. "But I need you to know something: you didn't fall short. Not even close. He's the one who cheated. He's the one who stole from you. I hope he gets hit by a fucking bus for what he did to you."

She lets out a soft laugh. There goes that fluttering in my chest again. Fucking hell, it feels good to see her smile, to hear her laugh after seeing her so sad.

"You're incredible."

When she starts to shake her head, I gently squeeze her hand in mine. "You are, Becca. You're fucking amazing. You own your own business. You've been through all that shit, and instead of turning bitter, which you'd have every right to be, you're still one of the sweetest and kindest people I've ever met."

There's a dazed look in her eyes, like she can't believe what I've said.

It's then that I realize I've scooted closer to her. Our faces are barely a few inches apart.

"Your ex is the biggest dipshit on the planet. He had you waiting at home for him in a whipped cream bikini, looking hot as fuck, and he blew it."

The corners of her mouth quirk up in a shy smile. "Thanks for saying that."

"It's the truth."

I let go of her hand. She glances down at it for a long second.

A few quiet moments stretch between us. I notice the air feels different—thicker, almost.

I look back at her phone. "No whipped cream. We'll find something else to do."

"What about an ice cream body shot?" Becca says.

I look up at her.

She frowns, like she's attempting to refocus, and points to the phone.

Gage takes an ice cream body shot off of Becca! A dollop of ice cream, hot fudge, and a cherry! Delicious ;)

When I finish reading, my skin is hot, like I've been baking out in the sun for hours, even though it's nighttime and I'm indoors.

"Let's do it," I growl.

Minutes later Becca and I are on the floor. She's lying down, her T-shirt hiked up to just below her boobs. I'm kneeling next to her, perpendicular to her waist, a small bowl of ice cream in my hand.

I take in the expanse of perfect flesh in front of me. A few freckles are sprinkled across the left side of her stomach. A shiver moves through me, shaking me from the top of my head all the way to my hands and feet. Well, shit. She is beautiful.

I fixate on how smooth her stomach looks. So fucking soft.

A hard swallow moves down my throat. In a few seconds, I'm going to find out just how fucking soft Becca's skin is. I need to get my shit together.

She blinks, those mile-long lashes revealing a deep blue stare. "You ready?" There's a slight shake in her voice, and I can see the fabric of her shirt shuddering the slightest bit with each beat of her heart. She's nervous.

"You sure you want to do this? You sure you're comfortable?" I ask.

Without even blinking, she nods at me.

"I need to hear you say it, Becca." My voice is a low growl. I bet I sound like an animal, and it makes me embarrassed as fuck. I haven't even touched her yet, and I'm in shambles.

"I want to do this with you, Gage." Her words fall out in a single breath. Her chest heaves. She sounds like she's sprinted a mile.

The effect her raspy affirmation has on me is instant. A second later I've spooned a dollop of vanilla ice cream on her stomach along with a drizzle of hot fudge.

Her stomach sinks in, and her breath catches. "It's so cold," she whispers, like she can't believe it.

My eyes cut to her face. "Still okay?"

She bites her perfect bottom lip and nods at me. "Yes," she says a second later, like she remembers just how much her verbal confirmation means to me.

I set the dish down, but she stops me.

"Don't forget the cherry," she says.

I reach up and swipe the jar from the counter. With a shaky hand, I carefully set a maraschino cherry on the tiny mound of vanilla and chocolate. And then I lean over to hit record on my phone, which is set up a few feet away from us.

I don't say another word. My gaze connects with Becca's. With our eyes locked, I lean my face down to her waist. I lap up the ice cream in a single lick. But with even just that one swipe of my tongue, I take my time. I let my tongue linger for a couple of seconds, savoring the taste of the ice cream and Becca's skin.

She's sweet, just like I knew she would be. Not as sweet as the ice cream or the fudge or the cherry, but better. Different. She's soft and smooth, and there's a hint of salt on her skin, likely her sweat from earlier in the day, and fucking hell, even that tastes good.

So fucking good.

I feel a surge of pressure in my cock.

Fuuuuuck. Barely two seconds of my mouth on her stomach has me hard.

I lean up, swallow the ice cream, and wipe my mouth with the back of my hand. And then I dig my knuckles into the top of my thigh, the piercing pain a welcome distraction from the bastard in my jeans aching to get hard.

My gaze is still glued to Becca's. I can't look away, even if I wanted to. Even if someone offered me a hundred grand to look anywhere else, I couldn't. The sight in front of me is too perfect, too beautiful. Becca's eyes are wide and unblinking, her cheeks are rosy, and her chest is flushed, heaving up and down at what just happened—at what we've done.

Several seconds pass where we don't say a word. We just sit there, staring at each other, the sound of our shallow breaths the only noise between us.

And then she runs her tongue along her bottom lip. "How was it?"

I almost laugh.

Fucking incredible...Did you know you taste like candy? One lick of your skin, Becca, and I know without a doubt, you're the taste I'll crave forever...

I don't say any of that though, because I'm pretty sure I'd come off like a psycho.

"It was good," I say instead, my voice barely above a grunt.

"That's...good," she says through a breathy voice. She blinks a couple times, her gaze turning more focused. "You, um, have something. On your lip."

I wipe my mouth with the back of my hand. She shakes her head, stammering as she gestures to my face.

And then she sits up, putting our faces so close, we're almost touching noses. She wipes her thumb just under my bottom lip.

"You had some chocolate," she whispers.

"Thanks." I sound like I'm being strangled, but really, I'm just trying not to sound like a demon with the way that my insides are going haywire at Becca's touch.

A beat later her gaze falls to my lips. And then I know. We're going to kiss.

I lean even closer, my mouth hovering over hers. We're not touching yet, but I can feel her somehow. I can feel her breath on me, I can feel just how soft she is, how sweet she tastes.

And then my fucking phone rings.

We jerk apart. I land on my ass, then scramble up and

grab my phone off the tripod. It's then that I realize the video is still recording so I quickly hit "stop," and then answer.

"Hey. It's me."

I bite back a curse. Of all the times for my older brother to call me.

"Hope I'm not interrupting anything," he mutters.

I'm about to say that actually, yes, he's interrupting something really fucking important, but he speaks first.

"About the other day when I mentioned Dad. That was out of line. I was an insensitive dick. I'm sorry, man."

All the frustration simmering inside of me dissipates.

"Oh, um, it's okay."

"It's not okay. Look, you have every right to be pissed at Dad for what he did to you. I was an asshole for trying to talk you into seeing him."

From the corner of my eye, I see Becca aiming a concerned stare at me. I cover the mouthpiece of the phone with my hand and mouth, "My brother."

"Oh," she whispers, then nods and gestures for me to take the call. When she hops up, yanks her shirt down, and starts cleaning up, I want to scream out of frustration. Fuck. We were so damn close to what I'm certain would have been a hot-as-hell kiss.

"...and if you're not busy, I'm in your neighborhood with a six-pack of your favorite microbrew," Tyler says.

"What?"

"I was going to stop by and drop it off. And I can fix the water dispenser on your fridge too, if you want. I brought my tools."

"Oh. Uh..."

I hate how annoyed I am at Tyler in this moment. My brother is being decent as hell, trying to make things right and smooth things over with my favorite beer and an offer to help me. All I want to do is tell him to go away so I can salvage that moment between Becca and me.

But as the seconds pass, I know it's long gone. She's busy cleaning up. Tyler is on his way to see me as we speak. I just have to move on.

"Yeah, I'm on my way there now. See you soon."

I hang up and look over at Becca, who's standing next to the counter a few feet away.

"Is your brother okay?" she asks.

"Yeah, he's fine. He's on his way to my place. Surprise visit."

"Oh." I'm heartened at how disappointed she sounds.

"Well, you'd better get going then," she says quickly.

I'm taken aback, but she's right. I can't leave Tyler hanging.

"Here, I'll send you the video." It only takes a couple of taps, but I find myself trying to go as slowly as possible, just so I can have more time with her.

Becca looks at her phone and flashes a tight smile along with a thumbs-up. "Got it. Thanks again for your help."

"Sure."

The words aren't even out of my mouth before she darts off to the back. I stumble to my car, still half hard, my head in a fog.

Chapter 10

Becca

Tori locks the entrance to Sweet Cheeks when the last customer leaves, then spins around to me and pumps her fist in the air.

"Can you believe it? Sold out of every flavor!" she squeaks. She runs over and pulls me into a hug. "I can't remember the last time that happened. Can you?"

I shake my head. "Maybe our grand opening like a year ago?"

Tori breaks our embrace but keeps hold of my shoulders. "And we're shipping ice cream all over the country. We've never been this busy." She winks at me. "I think we know what we owe this success to."

She steps away and starts wiping down the counter. "I still can't believe Gage Grant licked ice cream off your stomach. God, you are the luckiest woman alive. Two days of that video being posted to the Sweet Cheeks' TikTok and look." She gestures to the empty containers of ice cream in the display case. "Brilliant marketing, Bec. You two are an amazing team."

Tori flashes a sly smile at me, and I feel my entire body

burn hot. I start closing out the register, but my focus is shot. It's been that way ever since the other night. That was the single hottest thing I've ever done in my life, and every time I think about it, I swear I'm going to combust.

For the past two days, Gage is all I've been able to think about. Actually, Gage's *tongue* is all I've been able to think about.

I still can't believe I had the guts to do that. I think back to that moment two nights ago.

What about an ice cream body shot?

I blink and see Gage's face. How his eyebrows lifted, how his mouth parted open, like he wasn't expecting me to say that. And then I remember how his expression shifted from shock to determination. I remember how his angular jawline bulged as he bit down and swallowed.

I remember how quickly he answered me.

Let's do it.

I must have called on some inner reserve of boldness I didn't know I had when I said those seven words to Gage. If someone asked me if I would ever proposition Gage Grant to lick an ice cream body shot off my stomach, I would have cringed or laughed hysterically. I've never asked anyone in my life ever to do such a thing—not Ben, not any guy I've dated. To think I propositioned a hot TikTok star who I've known for just a couple of weeks to run his tongue along my stomach is mind-blowing, to say the least.

But I did. Because I wanted his mouth on my body. I wanted his tongue on me. And he seemed completely into it.

It was also because I felt safe with Gage. I felt safe enough to tell him about that humiliating moment when Ben broke up with me while I was naked, covered in whipped cream. And the way he responded blew me away.

He was kind and supportive but also confused and upset on my behalf—and it was the most endearing thing ever, like he couldn't believe my ex could have broken up with me. Like Ben was nuts to leave me.

Your ex is the biggest dipshit on the planet. He had you waiting at home for him in a whipped cream bikini, looking hot as fuck, and he blew it.

Gage's words have been playing like a broken record in my mind these past couple of days. Yeah, maybe it's shallow, but god, it felt good to hear Gage Grant call me hot as fuck, to defend me, to insult my cheating and lying ex.

My skin is hot as goosebumps flash all over my body. Just like I have ever since the night it happened, I let the moment replay in my mind again and again. The soft grunts that ripped from his throat when he leaned his face down to my bare midsection. The intensity of his eyes as he raked his gaze from my face all the way to my stomach. How he made sure I was okay with what we were doing.

How heavenly his hot, wet tongue felt on my skin.

How he lingered a second longer than he needed to, as if he was savoring the feel of my skin, the taste of me.

How we almost kissed.

My brain goes fuzzy, almost like it can barely process what almost happened between Gage and me.

We were definitely about to kiss. And if Gage's brother hadn't called him and asked to meet up, I wonder just how far that kiss would have gone...

Gage's gloriously sexy tongue appears behind the darkness of my eyelids as I blink over and over. Between my legs, I start to pulse and ache. My knees start to shake.

Wowzers. If he can unravel me this much with a single swipe of his tongue on my stomach, I'd probably pass out if he ever made it between my—

"Bec!"

I yelp at the sound of Tori screeching my name.

"Damn. Where'd you go just now? I said your name, like, three times," she says.

"Oh, sorry. I was just thinking about how great it is that business is picking up."

"Mmmhmm. You sure it's not something else distracting you? Like a hot, jacked TikTok star with a penchant for licking your tummy?"

I scoff. "He doesn't have a penchant for licking my tummy. That was a one-time thing."

Tori tilts her head at me and props her hand on her hip. "Come on, Bec. I haven't pressed you because of how busy things have been at the shop, and I know focusing on that is your number one priority. But I can tell something's up. You've been starry eyed with your cheeks flushed for the past couple of days—ever since you posted that video to TikTok. Is it solely because of the belly lick? Or did you two get up to more?"

She wags her eyebrow, and I roll my eyes. "It was just the belly lick." I huff out a breath. "And um, we almost kissed."

Tori gasps. "What? Oh my god, I want all the details!"

I tell her everything—how I opened up to Gage about my breakup, how hot it felt when he defended me, how the heat between us amped up and up and up when he licked the ice cream shot off my body, how I was dying to kiss him. How our lips were touching the moment his phone rang and interrupted us.

"Whoa," Tori says in a breathy whisper. "Okay, yeah, you definitely were about to bone."

"Tori! We weren't!" I make a flustered huffy noise. "We would have just kissed. And made out. Maybe."

She quirks her eyebrow at me. "If you say so."

"It's not like it matters. The moment passed. It's long gone. I'm sure he's forgotten about it."

"You totally would have boned," she repeats. I groan and shake my head.

I move to wipe down the tables, crossing the spot on the floor where Gage and I were filming the other night...where we almost kissed.

My legs go tingly just crossing that patch of white tile. Would we have really gone at it on the floor? I've never thought to have sex anywhere but a bed or a couch or someplace soft and cushioned...

But the longer I let the thought linger in my head, the hotter it sounds.

Me on my hands and knees, Gage behind me...Gage lying on the floor, me straddled on top of him...

"Bec!"

I jolt up, dropping the washcloth on the floor. "God, Tori! What?"

Her head falls back as she laughs. "Oh my god, you're imagining having sex with him on the floor of the shop, aren't you?"

I make more huffy, flustered noises.

Tori chuckles and starts to fill the napkin dispenser. "The next time you guys film, you're definitely gonna make out. I'd put money on it."

I start to protest, but she stops me.

"Bec, you don't have to be so proper and buttoned up all the time. If the opportunity for a kiss presents itself, go with it. When are you two filming again?"

"Tomorrow night. He's coming here after we close."

"Perfect! You can film a sexy TikTok, get yourselves all worked up, then kiss!"

I roll my eyes at how she's talking like she's ticking off a to-do list.

She focuses on me. "There's nothing wrong with kissing Gage as long as you both are into it."

"So what, I'm just supposed to say, 'Hey, Gage, remember the other night when we almost kissed? Well, I can't stop thinking about how hot that was, and I think we should just kiss.'"

"Yeah." She says it like it's the most obvious thing I could say.

I make a scoff-laugh sound while mulling over her words. Maybe my best friend is right. Maybe it really is that simple.

Her expression turns playful, like she can read my mind. "It really is that simple, Bec."

"Tori, I could never say that to him. Not to, like, his face. Not without a few shots of alcohol."

She hops over to the counter and pulls out a bottle of bourbon we use to make our bourbon maple pecan ice cream flavor. She wiggles it in her hand, beaming.

I let out a laugh-groan. "You're the worst."

She sets the bottle on the counter, walks back over to me, and gives my shoulder a squeeze. "I'll just leave that out while you think about what you want to do."

The rest of the evening as I clean and close down the shop, I can't stop eyeing that bottle of bourbon.

Chapter 11

Gage

My lungs are on fire as I gasp for air. I pump my feet faster and faster against the treadmill until it feels like they're about to fall off. Then I punch the button, slowing it to half the speed.

As I ease to a walk, I rest my hands on my hips and catch my breath. Sweat drips down my face. My entire body is aching, but it's exactly what I want—what I need. The discomfort is a distraction from what I actually want to be doing, which is kissing the hell out of Becca.

My mind drifts back to that night at her ice cream shop when we almost kissed. Even now her sweet and salty flavor dances on my tongue. God, she tasted amazing. And for the past two days, I've been wondering if her mouth tastes as good.

As soon as that thought takes hold in my head for the millionth time, I shove it away. Here I am, fantasizing about this sweetheart, like some deviant. I've had to up the frequency and intensity of my gym workouts to twice a day just to keep myself from thinking about her.

I check the time on my phone. It's just past ten o'clock

the night before I'm due to meet her at her ice cream shop and shoot more videos for TikTok. My stomach is one massive knot. As excited as I am to see her, I have no idea what the hell I should say.

Hey, Becca. How have you been? I haven't been able to get the taste of your perfect skin out of my mouth, and I've been fantasizing about your lips and tongue nonstop for the past forty-eight hours. Wanna make out?

I scoff at myself and wipe the sweat from my face with my forearm. File that under "borderline creepy shit I should never say to Becca."

But it's the truth. I can't get her out of my head. And if I'm being totally honest, I've been drawn to her from the moment I met her. That ice cream body shot and that almost kiss just amped things up. Becca is beautiful, funny, sweet, and sincere. *And* sexy as fuck.

Just then my phone buzzes. I'm surprised when I see it's a text from Becca.

Hey! So!! How are you??? Okay, um, I have a secret.

I chuckle softly to myself as I watch three gray dots appear, then disappear, then appear, then disappear again. Even when she texts, she's freaking adorable.

Instead of waiting, I text her back.

Me: *What's your secret?*

Becca: *Okay...so here's the thing...*

Becca: *I've been thinking about our kisssss*

Becca: *Oops sI meannnt kiss**

Becca: *Ugh I'm not texting so well LOLLL*

Becca: *Err, um, almost kiss, I guess, since we didn't actually kiss.*

Becca: *And the ice cream shot too. That was crazy hot, right? Like, super duper hot.*

I'm grinning wide as I read her string of texts.

Me: *I agree, it was crazy hot. And I've been thinking about that almost kiss too.*

Becca: *You have???*

Me: *Of course I have.*

Becca: *That's good! Because I have an idea. What if when you come over tomorrow night, we kiss? Just to get it out of our systems.*

I stop walking on the treadmill and almost fall off, I'm so shocked. I definitely wasn't expecting sweet Becca to be so direct. My dick strains in my gym shorts. I really, really like it.

Me: *I'd love to kiss you.*

She sends back seven party emojis, and I laugh so hard, the guy on the treadmill next to me jolts and loses his balance. I mutter, "sorry" as I turn off the machine and head to the men's locker room. I plop down on a bench and skim her reply.

Becca: *This is fantastic! I'm so glad we could be adults about this. One kiss, get it out of our system, then get back to being filming buddies and friends.*

A small sting hits me straight in the chest. It catches me totally off guard, until I realize what it is—the thought of only having one kiss with Becca.

Slow your roll, dude. You're lucky she wants to kiss you even once. Don't get greedy.

Me: *I agree*

Five smiling emojis. I grin at my phone.

Becca: *Okay! Tomorrow it's happening! Here's our schedule: 1. Film a sexy TikTok 2. KISS!!*

I double over laughing. God, she's hilarious. My stomach does a flip. Damn, when was the last time that happened?

I refocus, relishing that feeling inside of me.

Me: *Can't wait ;)*

* * *

When I walk into Sweet Cheeks, I don't see Becca standing behind the counter, cleaning up after closing, like usual. The place is empty.

"Hello?" I call out. No answer.

I notice a massive glass bottle of bourbon sitting at the counter. It's nearly full. It looks like someone took a couple of shots from it though.

I smile to myself, thinking about the string of texts Becca sent me last night. I wonder if she had a few slugs of the hard stuff before she texted me, proposing that we kiss.

While I walk over to the bottle, the door to the back swings open, and in walks Becca.

Her doe eyes go wide for a full second before she starts to smile. "Hey." She sounds breathless, and something about makes the skin on my arms go hot.

Is that what she sounds like when she's writhing against another body? When she's turned on? When she's so aroused, she's aching to burst?

I clear my throat and bite down so hard, my jaw aches. Jesus, I really, really need to get ahold of myself. I can't be thinking such X-rated thoughts. She's standing three feet from me.

"Hey," I say, my voice strangled. I gesture to the bottle. "Are we incorporating a new ingredient into today's video?"

Becca chuckles and shakes her head. "I needed a bit of liquid courage. For later. For when we, um..." She fidgets with her hands. "When we, you know..."

I can't help the wide smile that pulls at my mouth. "Kiss?"

84

She nods quickly, her pale cheeks flushing ruby red.

I rest my hand on the counter, leaning forward. "Say it with me: kiss."

She laughs as we say it together.

"Funny how you could text the word 'kiss' so many times to me last night and you can barely say it now," I tease.

She crosses her arms, her cheeks fading to pink. She glances at the bourbon. "I had a few gulps of that to help me build up the nerve." She looks back over at me. "And it's a lot easier sometimes to write something than to say it. And then to actually *do* that thing..."

I take a step back to give Becca more space. Clearly she's nervous, and I don't want to crowd her.

"Listen, if you changed your mind, Becca, that's perfectly okay. We can forget the other night ever happened. And we can forget about our text conversation." My tone is light as I speak. As disappointing as that would be, I'm not about to kiss Becca if she's uncomfortable.

She frowns and shakes her head quickly, like she's upset at the idea of us not kissing. It sends a tiny thrill through me.

"No, I definitely still want to kiss you, Gage. I'm just a really awkward and nervous person." She lets out a flustered laugh.

"You're not. You're fucking adorable."

She smiles before biting her bottom lip. "You're too kind."

"Nope. Just speaking the truth."

Her smile fades, and a whole new expression takes over her angelic face. She looks like she can't decide between lunging at me or kissing me.

That thrill from seconds earlier resurfaces, only this time, it throttles me.

Becca wants me. She's turned on by the thought of kissing me.

For a moment all we do is stare at each other. We exchange a quiet knowing look that has me buzzing from the inside out. I take in the way her chest heaves up and down, the way her gaze on me has turned hungry.

I swallow hard, feeling my heartbeat kick up. This kiss is going to fucking destroy me.

She blinks, and it's like some silent gauntlet is thrown down. That shy smile of hers transforms. The corner of her mouth quirks up. It turns her face from innocent to naughty —like she can't wait to wreck me with her mouth.

Well, fuck. I am so ready.

"We should probably film the video first, right?" she says in that breathless voice before clearing her throat.

I grunt and nod quickly, then pull out my phone and tripod from my bag. My hands fumble as I set it all up.

"What do you want to film me doing?" I say as I finish getting everything together.

When she doesn't answer at first, I look up and see her putting together a small dish of ice cream behind the counter.

"You'll see," she says in a teasing tone. And then she winks at me. I almost choke. God, she's like the perfect balance of angel and devil, and I can hardly take it.

"Come here," she says when she's finished.

I hit record on the camera on my phone and walk over to her. She glances over at my phone and moves so she's in frame. She points for me to stand in front of her so that we're facing each other. She holds a small scoop of some rainbow flavor. It's topped with whipped cream, which makes me smile. I think that means she's not letting that bullshit with her ex bother her as much anymore.

"What flavor is that?" I ask.

"Rainbow cotton candy." She runs her tongue along her perfectly pink bottom lip.

I take a slow, silent breath in and out. We're not even touching, and I'm turned on. I can feel myself getting hard, so I discreetly dig my thumb into the side of my thigh. The sharp pain helps me to deflate.

Before I know it, Becca dips her index finger into the whipped cream and touches it to the tip of my nose. She smiles, then I smile. And then she leans forward and licks the whipped cream off me.

A strangled noise rips from my throat. I grit my teeth, not because I'm mad—the exact opposite, actually. Fuck me, that was playful and shocking and hot. My dick is aching in my pants at the feel of her soft, wet tongue on my body.

That move she just pulled? It's like foreplay. Sweet, candy-flavored foreplay.

She steps back and sets the ice cream on the counter. That's when I notice her entire chest is as pink as her cheeks. She touches her hand to her mouth before resting it at her side. "Was that okay?"

I don't answer her. I can't. I'm not capable of formulating any words right now, not when my entire body is pulsing with heat and need, all from the touch of her tongue on the tip of my nose.

I just nod my head, rest my hand on her hips, and pull her against my body.

"Okay?" I grunt.

She nods quickly. And then I crash my lips against her mouth.

It's barely a second before I'm moaning. Fucking hell, she tastes like sugar. And she's soft. Her skin, her lips. *So fucking soft.* It's barely two seconds into this kiss, and I'm about to lose my mind at how fucking heavenly her lips and tongue are.

She moans too as she moves her lips against me. I catch myself smiling as she pushes back against my mouth. Yeah, Becca is shy and sweet, but her kisses aren't. She moves like she's starving and I'm the meal she's after.

A second later I feel the sharp pull of her hands tugging through my hair. I growl. It always, always drives me wild when a woman gets rough with my hair—especially someone like Becca. I don't know what I expected she'd be like, but this? I really, really like this. A little sweet, a little shy, a little feisty and feral and rough.

My hands are digging into the fabric of her jean shorts. She presses harder into me, like she wants to be closer. I hook my hands under her thighs and lift her up. She instantly wraps her legs around my waist. I quietly marvel at the smoothness of both our moves, how it seemed to happen almost instinctively.

Still kissing, I walk the few steps to the nearby counter and set her on top. Her legs don't budge. They stay wrapped around my middle, tight and snug, like she's gripping onto me for dear life. And then I wonder if Becca would do the same with her legs if I were kissing her pussy instead of her mouth...

My dick is rock-hard at just the thought of her thighs turning vise-like around my head.

I slow our kiss in an attempt to pace myself. Thankfully, Becca doesn't seem to mind as she moans against my mouth. Her mouth and tongue turn teasing. She laps that candy tongue of hers gently, lightly against mine, and oh shit, there goes my dick again. It's practically steel in my jeans.

She leans back, breaking our kiss. "You taste way, way

better than the whipped cream. Better than the ice cream too," she pants.

I gently grab her chin in my hand and lead her mouth back to mine. "So do you," I say against her mouth.

With my other hand, I grip her lower back, pushing her harder against me. I feel the heat between her legs and between mine. It's then I realize how perfectly we're aligned. My dick is pressed up against the seam of her shorts.

Becca's head falls back as she gasps. "Oh my god...Gage..."

Both of her hands grip my shoulders as she presses her bottom half firmer against me. She shifts slightly, then starts to move back and forth against the bulge in my pants, harder and harder. That's when I go still so I can take in what's happening.

I savor the visual of her flushed face and neck and chest, the way the strap of her tank top falls down her shoulder, revealing a hot pink bra strap. I savor the way she grabs at my body, like she can't get enough of me, the heat between her legs as she rubs against me harder and harder.

She leans forward, wraps her arm around my neck, and buries her face in my shoulder. With her other hand, she grips my bicep. As she grinds against me, she moans into the meaty part at the top of my shoulder.

"That's it," I growl against her skin. "Use me to get yourself off."

I feel her nodding her head as she grinds harder and faster. I trail soft kisses down her neck and along her shoulder. Her hands dig deeper into my skin and muscle. My eyes roll to the back of my head. It's hot as hell feeling this girl lose all of her inhibitions and work herself to orgasm all over me.

"Holy shit," she mutters in a disbelieving tone.

I smile against the impossibly soft skin along the side of her neck. "I think that's the first time I've ever heard you cuss."

She exhales and chuckles before groaning. She sinks her teeth into my skin, and I nearly lose it. Fuck fuck fuck, that's hot.

"I can't help it," she murmurs. "You feel amazing."

"Then keep going. Work yourself all over me."

Becca does exactly that, gripping me tighter as she grinds even faster.

"Gage, I...I'm almost..."

I run my tongue along her collarbone, then gently scrape my teeth along her impossibly soft skin.

She yelps and completely falls apart against me. I wrap my arms around her as she convulses and thrashes through her orgasm.

A dozen seconds later, she comes down. She pulls her arms away from me, her chest heaving, the look on her face dazed and shocked, like she can't believe what just happened. She cups her hands around her cheeks as she aims her cloudy gaze at me.

She blinks. "Wow, um...That was..."

"Hot?"

She blinks again. This time her eyes are shy. "Um, yeah. Something like that."

She hops off the counter and rests a hand on her hip. The other hand covers her mouth. Then she shakes her head and looks up at me, her eyes wide. "I don't do...that."

"What do you mean?"

She gestures between us, then the counter with flailing hands. It's so awkward and cute that I start to laugh but stop myself when her expression turns panicked.

"I don't grind myself to orgasm on my ice cream shop countertop with a guy I barely know, I mean."

A weird punch hits the inside of my chest. Wait, is she upset about what just happened? And what does she mean by "guy she barely knows"?

"It's okay, Becca. You don't need to freak out about this."

She frowns. "I'm not freaking out," she says, her voice pitchy.

"Clearly."

Her frown turns into a scowl. My attempt at a joke failed miserably. She opens and closes her mouth a few times but never says a word.

She closes her eyes and shakes her head. "Sorry, I guess I just need a minute."

"That's okay. You don't have to apologize for that."

When she opens her eyes, she zeroes between my legs. I'm still rock-hard, and it's obvious. "And um, I don't know if I can help you with that. Sorry if you assumed that I should, um, do that for you because of what you did for me..."

All the muscles in my torso tense at what she's saying.

"Becca, hold on." I have to pause around the bitter taste in my mouth before saying more. "First of all, stop apologizing. And second, we need to get something straight. I'm not assuming or expecting anything. You don't need to do a single thing for me. Ever. I wasn't thinking that or assuming that or expecting that."

When she blinks, she looks the slightest bit relieved, which makes my body go cold. Jesus, does she think she owes me sex or something just because she had an orgasm with me? What would make her think that? Did the guys she date in the past put that fucked-up idea in her head? Was her ex like that?

Fury and repulsion sitting in the pit of my stomach like a boulder, I swallow back the feeling and refocus on her.

But she speaks before I can say anything.

"I need to close up." When she crosses her hands over her chest, my shoulders sink. She's closing herself off to me. I should leave and give her space.

"Of course. I'll take off." I quickly grab my phone and tripod. I send the video to her and walk out the door, that boulder burning a hole in my stomach the rest of the night.

Chapter 12

Becca

"I have no idea what got into me. I can't believe I did that."

As soon as I finish talking, I take a long sip from the margarita Tori whipped up for me, then I look over at her sitting on the far end of my couch. Her eyes are wide, and her jaw is on the floor. I cough. Wow. I don't think I've ever rendered my best friend speechless before.

She finally blinks and closes her mouth. Then she shuts her eyes and shakes her head. "Okay, wait. I need a moment to process what you just told me."

She leans over and grabs the bottle of tequila from my coffee table and downs a shot.

"But what about your drink?" I motion to the margarita in her hand.

She shakes her head as she swallows. "Nope. I need something stronger. Three nights ago you and Gage made out in the ice cream shop, and then you rubbed yourself all over him until you came."

My face heats. "Yup."

93

A second later, Tori bursts out laughing so hard, the couch shakes.

"You think this is funny?"

Tori leans over and grabs my hand. "I'm not laughing at you, Bec. I swear. I'm just shocked," she says while trying to catch her breath. She stops laughing. "It's so out of character for you to do something like that. But it's also fucking awesome. So fucking awesome."

When I don't say anything, Tori sits up and looks me straight in the eye. "Bec. Do you realize what a legend you are? You got to make out with Gage Grant, the TikTok hottie. He made you come. Gage Fucking Grant gave you an orgasm."

Hot goosebumps flash across my arms at the memory of what Gage and I did the other night. It doesn't matter how many times I think about it—my body always reacts the same way. That dip in my stomach, that kick in my heartbeat, that hitch in my breath, the way my skin feels like it's on fire. My body has committed to memory those insanely sexy minutes I spent kissing and touching and grinding on him.

"You got to make out with the guy that millions of people lust after. The TikTok hottie that millions of people fantasize about gave you an orgasm."

Her eyes go wide as she says "orgasm."

"Okay, yeah, it was super hot," I say quickly. "But it was so out of character of me to do that."

Tori doesn't even blink. "So?"

"What do you mean 'so'?"

"Bec, I love you. But you don't always have to overthink things. So it was out of character for you to shed your inhibitions and have a hot-as-fuck make-out with a TikTok star. Who cares? Did it feel good?"

"Of course it felt good. It felt amazing."

"Did you enjoy it?"

"Yes."

"Great! That's all that matters."

"Not all that matters," I mutter. Tori gives me a look, and I spill about how the night ended with me sputtering to Gage about how I had never done that with anyone before and how even when he reassured me that it was all okay, I awkwardly hinted that he should leave.

"Oh." Tori's expression falls. She pats my hand.

I take another sip of my margarita. "He was amazing, Tori. Like, not only is he an incredible kisser with a jacked body and is sweet and funny, but he's also supportive and nonjudgmental. Once our kiss started getting more and more heated, he let me lead things. I mean, he practically coaxed me through an orgasm, no thought for himself and what he needed to get off. He was so cool about everything that happened between us. And the whole time, he was turned on. Like, majorly turned on."

Tori's brown eyes bulge. "I need details."

"He was rock hard. And, um, well...judging from his hardness, I could tell that what he has between his legs is likely...very impressive."

Tori's eyes practically sparkle. "I knew it! I knew Gage was packing! I mean, he's got that big dick energy. I could tell from the moment I met him. It's obvious in his videos too, but to really gauge it you have to be in person, and..."

She trails off as soon as she takes in what I'm sure is my incredulous stare.

"Never mind. That's not important right now," she says.

"God, I'm the worst." I groan and lean back against the arm of my couch. If I hadn't freaked out and made things awkward, we could have kept going. And I could have...

I trail off as the memory of Gage all hot and panting and turned on clouds my brain. In a split second, I'm propped on the counter of Sweet Cheeks, my legs wrapped around his waist, my fingers digging into his sculpted back and shoulders and biceps. I can taste his mouth again, how soft his lips were, how firm his tongue was as he teased and tasted me.

I can feel how hard his dick was against my thigh, how it throbbed as he shifted and settled between my legs. How good it felt. How just pressing myself against his body turned me on. How fast I was able to orgasm.

"I've never come like that before. I mean, I've never come so hard or so fast with my clothes on," I mumble to Tori.

Her brow flies up.

"Before the other night with Gage, I've always needed to be naked with a toy or have a guy's mouth or fingers work my clit. I-I've never been able to be fully clothed and just rub myself on someone and have an orgasm."

Tori downs more straight tequila. "Damn, he's good."

"He really is. And I blew it."

She coughs on her sip. She wipes her mouth. "Bec, don't tell me you're going to give up. Clearly this dude has a huge boner for you. Don't let this be a one-time thing."

"*Had* a huge boner. I'm sure it's long gone now, given I practically kicked him out after making things excruciatingly awkward."

"You're not even going to try and start things up again?" she asks, ignoring what I've said.

I shake my head.

Tori aims a pointed stare at me. "I wish you wouldn't give up so easily."

"What am I supposed to say to him? 'Hey, Gage. Sorry

about kicking you out of my shop with a raging hard-on the other night. Feel like hooking up again?'"

"Sure. Why not?"

"No way. Look, obviously I'm not ready to hook up with anyone or do anything even remotely sexual. I'm not even a month out of my breakup with Ben. I can't even handle one kiss with a guy. Look what it turned into: a total mess. It's best if Gage and I move on as friends and pretend this never happened."

She pins me with a deadpan stare. "You can't pretend your way out of this, Bec. You know you still have to film a ton of sexy videos with this guy, right? That means you need to actually talk to him."

I cover my face and groan. "I know. God, it's going to be so freaking awkward."

Tori leans forward and tops off my margarita with more tequila. "Well, you've been through awkward situations before, so..."

I toss a pillow at my best friend. She chuckles before aiming a sympathetic stare at me. "It'll definitely suck, but you'll survive."

I guzzle more of my drink. "I hope so."

Chapter 13

Gage

I hit the doorbell at my cousin's house in Lakewood, just a few miles outside of Denver. A ding-dong version of the theme song from the movie *Halloween* echoes so loud, I can hear it through the door.

"Coming!" Millie yells. Ten seconds later she answers, her face red.

"You okay?" I ask. I start to reach for her, but she waves me away.

"I'm fine." She palms her massive belly. "Now that I'm carting around a bowling ball in my stomach, it takes me longer to get places. And god, does it drain me."

I lean down and hug her. "Are you ever going to change your doorbell ring?"

"No way. It's creepy enough that it scares away all the missionaries that come to our door. It's staying forever."

"You're ruthless."

"Damn straight. You brought me ice cream, right?"

I laugh. "Of course I did."

I hand her the paper bag full of a half-dozen pints of Ben and Jerry's. Her deep brown eyes brighten immediately. She rips open the bag as I walk inside and shut the door behind me. She's grinning so wide, you'd think she's being presented with the keys to a new car and not six pints of ice cream.

"Gage, you're the best cousin in the whole wide..." Her expression falls as she looks at the pint in her hand.

"What's wrong? I thought you loved Chubby Hubby?"

Her shoulders sag. "I thought you were bringing more Sweet Cheeks ice cream."

"Oh..." I hold back a flinch at just the mention of Becca's ice cream shop.

It's been three days since we kissed, since we shared that insanely hot few minutes when I got to watch Becca shed her inhibitions completely and do the hottest thing I've ever seen. I got to see her go from shy to sex kitten as she worked herself against my dick all the way to orgasm.

And it's been three days of radio silence since then. No text, no phone call, no drunken TikTok DM. She hasn't even posted the video we filmed to the Sweet Cheeks Creamery TikTok. I've checked every day since that night and still nothing.

It's clear she's still freaked out about what happened and needs space. And that's exactly what I've been trying to give her every time I fight the urge to text or call or DM her. She clearly doesn't want to hear from me.

That realization makes that boulder in my gut scrape deeper. She wants nothing to do with me.

I clear my throat and focus on my cousin's disappointed stare. Now that Becca and I aren't even speaking to each other, I wasn't about to run to her shop for more ice cream.

"Sorry, I haven't been by Sweet Cheeks in a while," I tell Millie.

"I figured. I haven't seen you pop up in any of their TikToks."

I grab the bag from her and walk past her into the kitchen.

"I swear I don't watch the sexy videos of you on the Sweet Cheeks TikTok, just like I don't watch the videos on your own TikTok account. I just watch the preview on the main page of the Sweet Cheeks account. When I see a glimpse of you, I know you'll be in the video, so I don't watch it. Promise."

"Great," I mutter as I shove the pints of ice cream into the freezer.

"Hey, leave one out."

I frown at her. "You were just complaining that you didn't want this ice cream."

She shakes her head and shoves her wavy black hair out of her face. "I did not. I said I thought you'd bring me Sweet Cheeks ice cream, which I much prefer. I never said I don't still want the ice cream."

I roll my eyes and hand her a random pint. She rips off the lid and starts licking the top of the ice cream.

"Can't you wait two seconds for a spoon?" I fetch one from a nearby drawer and hand it to my cousin. She plops down on a barstool at her kitchen island.

She scoffs and shoves a spoonful of Cherry Garcia into her mouth. "Did you seriously just tell your pregnant and ravenous cousin to wait for food?"

She sticks her tongue out at me. The frustration inside of me melts, and I chuckle.

"You are insufferable when you're pregnant, you know that?"

She nods, grinning. "Yup. My tiny body is growing a

massive baby. Soon I'm going to have to push it out of my vagina. I'm allowed to be insufferable."

I groan. "Jesus."

"Why don't you make yourself useful and eat the leftover *pansit* that Peter cooked yesterday?" she says before inhaling more ice cream.

I pull the Tupperware container out of the fridge, dish up a plate, and heat it in the microwave. "You're sharing leftover *pansit* with me? Has hell frozen over?"

Pansit has been Millie's favorite food since we were kids. Anytime there were leftovers, she always laid claim to them. If anyone tried to eat them before she got to it, she'd unleash hell.

"Pregnancy hormones," she says around a mouthful of ice cream. "I can't stand the taste of pork right now. Third trimester is all sorts of fun."

I nod and dig into the leftovers.

"So how come Sweet Cheeks hasn't uploaded a video in a while?" Millie asks.

I shove a massive forkful of *pansit* into my mouth and take my time chewing. I'm only a year older than Millie and her twin brother Austin. My siblings and I grew up next door to them here in Lakewood. Our moms are sisters, which means that our families spent almost every day together for most of our childhoods. Even now that we're grown and she's married and living across town from me, we still see each other at least once a week. We're as close as siblings, and she can read me like a book. She's always been able to. Sure, I can brush off her questions or feed her some lie, but she'll see right through it.

"We're having some creative differences," I finally mutter.

She arches her eyebrow so high, it almost hits her hairline. "What did you do?"

I roll my eyes. "Nothing. Like I said, creative differences."

"Do you honestly expect me to believe that?"

I think back to when I told Millie about my deal with Becca and Sweet Cheeks, how I'm helping her create sexy content to boost her social media following and her business. I kept it brief, but like always, my nosey and intuitive cousin knows when more is going on.

"So I was scrolling through Sweet Cheeks' earlier posts on TikTok," she says as she scrapes her spoon against the cardboard cup. "I saw some blonde girl. That must be Becca, right?"

"Mmmhmm," I say while chewing.

"She's just your type."

I frown at her when I finish chewing and swallowing. "What exactly is my type?"

"Hot," Millie says without missing a beat.

I laugh despite the frustration caused by my nosey cousin.

She pushes aside the empty carton of ice cream. "Okay. I'm full and happier now and done with the snippy comments," she says. "For now."

I go back to my food.

"What's really going on, Gage?" she asks, her tone gentle this time. "I can tell something is bothering you."

I feel myself soften. I pick at the pile of noodles on my plate. "Look, I appreciate that you care, but I'm not gonna talk about this with you."

Her gaze on me narrows, then her brows lift suddenly. "Oh, damn. Something went down. Something...romantic maybe?" Her voice hitches up.

"I swear to god, if you keep at this, I'm leaving."

She holds up a hand. "Okay, okay. I'm sorry." She rests her hand on my arm. "Really. I know I shouldn't pry, but I can't help it. You've been so secretive ever since...well, you know."

"No, I don't. Explain it to me."

She leans back at the hardness in my tone before exhaling. "You've been this way ever since you fell out with your dad, Gage. Don't think I haven't noticed."

I can feel all the muscles in my torso tighten as I brace myself for whatever my cousin is about to say.

"I know you hate talking about it, so I won't. I promise. But I just want to say that ever since then, you've been really secretive about your work. You don't talk about it. And you don't talk about anything personal either. You've really clammed up. And when I press you on it, like the stubborn brat you are, you clam up even more. And I get it, I do. But I also want you to know that you don't have to be like that, not with me. You're like a brother to me. I don't give a shit what you do for a living or what you do in your relationships, as long as you're not hurting anyone. I just want you to be happy." She grabs my forearm and squeezes, melting the invisible armor I just threw on.

"Thanks, Millie."

I help her off the stool. She's standing at the open fridge door, surveying the contents, when I finally speak.

"You're right. I guess you could say it's a romantic issue with Becca."

She spins around to look at me.

"I'm trying to figure it out. I'm not sure how it'll pan out, but I'll be okay. Promise."

"Can you make up with her soon? I'm gonna need you to go back and get me more Sweet Cheeks. Ben & Jerry's is good, but going back to that after eating Becca's heavenly ice cream is like going back to ground chuck after you've had Wagyu beef," she says.

I start to chuckle. "I'll do my best."

She stands there with an expectant look on her face, clearly waiting for me to say more.

"That's all I'm going to tell you, Millie. I don't care how close we are, I'm never, ever talking to you about my sex l—"

She shrieks and cups her hands over her ears. "Gage! Earmuffs! I didn't mean *that* sort of stuff. Please, for the love of god, never tell me about your sex life. I can't even stomach watching your TikToks."

I cackle at the horrified look on my cousin's face. "Hey, you asked."

"Well, there goes the rest of my appetite." She winces and rests a hand on her stomach. "And now I have to pee."

She disappears down the hall. I hear the front door open. Austin walks into the kitchen with his husband Declan.

Austin smiles when he sees me. "I didn't know you'd be here."

"Millie had an ice cream craving," I explain as I hug him and Declan.

Austin rolls his eyes, laughing. "Guess who she roped into hanging the artwork for the nursery?" He and Declan point at themselves.

"Man, she's really putting all of us to work, isn't she?" I say.

Declan walks over to my plate of *pansit* and helps himself to a bite. "If I had known I'd be tapped for free labor for the rest of my life, I'm not sure I would have married into this family."

"Oh, please. You absolutely would have. First of all,

you're crazy about me. And second, you get delicious free food for the rest of your life. That's more than a fair trade."

Austin takes the fork from his husband's hand, ruffles his fiery red hair, and takes a bite.

"Help yourselves, guys," I say. "Not like I was eating that or anything."

"You're too kind, cuz," Austin says around a mouthful before feeding Declan another bite. I laugh.

"Oh hey, guess who I heard from?" Austin pulls out his phone and shows me a selfie Maya texted him. She's making a peace sign and sticking out her tongue next to some weird-looking cactus.

"She's staying in a yurt on a mindfulness retreat near Joshua Tree National Park."

"I don't know what any of that means," I say. Declan laughs. "Figures you'd hear from her before me, her own brother."

It really doesn't bother me that Maya would rather text our cousin than me or Tyler. She and Austin have been best friends ever since they were little. I'm just glad she's keeping in touch with someone from the family.

"You know how your sister is," Declan says. "She does things according to her own schedule. She hates it when we nag her about keeping in touch."

Millie walks back into the kitchen and beams at her brother and brother-in-law. "You're finally here! Here, let me show you where I want you to hang the paintings."

Austin holds up a hand. "Not till we get some food in our bellies."

"So demanding," Millie teases before telling them to help themselves to the leftovers.

"But if you touch any ice cream, I will murder you."

Austin and Declan each flash her a thumbs-up.

Millie groans. "I have to pee again."

She shuffles down the hall. My phone buzzes in my pocket.

When I see it's Becca calling me, I can't believe it.

Nerves crackle inside of me. This is probably going to be one hell of an awkward conversation.

I answer anyway. "Hello?"

"Hey. It's me. Can we, um, talk?"

I can hear her nervousness in her strained tone. I wonder how long she spent working up the nerve to call me.

"Yeah, of course. Hang on a sec." I walk down the hall into Millie's darkened office. "Sorry, I'm at my cousin's place. I just needed to find a quiet spot."

"I'm sorry for interrupting. If you need to go, that's totally fine."

I smile at the care in Becca's tone. "It's okay, really. I could use a second away from her busting my balls."

"Oh." She lets out a surprised laugh. "Wait, is this your cousin who you brought ice cream from my shop for?"

"Yup. That's Millie. She had an emergency craving tonight, and since her husband is at work, it was up to me to deliver. And I failed miserably."

"What happened?"

"I brought her Ben & Jerry's. She thought I was bringing ice cream from your shop."

Becca's light chuckle echoes in my ear. I can feel my muscles loosening as the tension leaves my body. It feels good to laugh and talk like this about something fun and easy.

"I have to side with your cousin. My ice cream is much better," she teases. I can tell she's smiling on her end of the line, and it makes me grin wider.

"I definitely agree. I just wasn't sure that it would be

okay if I strolled in your ice cream shop asking for more pints of ice cream after, uh, we kissed."

"Right."

There's a stretch of silence after Becca speaks. I press my eyes shut and grit my teeth. Way to stall the conversation.

"That's the reason I called, actually," Becca says. "I regret the way I left things with you the night we kissed."

"It's okay," I say.

"It's not." She sighs. "Look, you were really sweet, the way you handled everything after I, uh…well, you know."

My brain flashes back to when Becca rode my boner to orgasm. My skin goes hot.

"Um, thanks?" I say after a second. To my surprise and relief, she chuckles.

"God, I'm making this so awkward. Again."

"It's okay, Becca."

"It's not though. I practically kicked you out of my shop."

"If that's what you needed to do to make yourself comfortable, that's fine."

She stammers. "Okay, you're handling all of this really well."

"I swear, it's not a big deal. We kissed, and shit got intense. It happens."

"Has this happened to you a lot before?" She sounds mystified.

"What do you mean?"

"I mean, do women get excited around you like I did?"

I take in her adorably worded question, how she sounds curious and shy all at once. "Yeah."

She lets out a breath. "Oh my gosh, of course they get

excited around you. Duh! It's *you*. You're handsome and hot and confident and sweet."

I can't help the flush working its way up my cheeks. Even though Becca sounds like she's reading off a grocery list, it still feels good to hear her name the qualities she finds attractive about me.

"So it really wasn't a big deal? What, um, happened between us?" she asks, her tone hesitant. "Because honestly, I was so embarrassed that I just completely let myself go in front of you. That doesn't happen for me."

She sounds so flustered as she speaks, which ignites a slew of questions in my brain. Does she normally have a hard time having an orgasm? Is this something she deals with when she's alone or only when she's been with a partner? If it's a partner problem, is it yet another instance of some mediocre man who's too selfish in bed to care about making her come?

I hold back from asking. That's none of my business, and I've got no right to ask her any of that.

"I didn't want to give you the wrong impression either," she says quickly. "I'm not even a month out of my last relationship and definitely not ready to start anything romantic with anyone, and I didn't want you to think that I wanted to start something up with you, like you're some rebound or that I was using you to get over my ex or..."

"I promise, it wasn't a big deal," I say. "You didn't make me feel like that at all. The moment got heated, that's all. It's happened to me before."

"Okay," she says as she exhales. "I was also nervous that I hurt your feelings when I kicked you out."

"Becca, it's really okay. I appreciate you being concerned about my feelings, but I promise, I'm good. My feelings aren't hurt at all." I speak with a smile and a gentle tone, hoping she believes me.

"Okay." This time when she says it, I can hear the smile in her voice. "Thanks for being so cool about this."

"It's all good. Really."

"So we can move on? As friends?"

"Of course we can."

"I'm so glad you said that." She lets out a breath. "And hey, maybe we should do other activities together in addition to filming sexy TikToks with each other. Like, more friend-type activities. That's probably why I, um, got all hot and bothered the last time we were together. I mean, the kissing amped things up for sure, but it probably doesn't help that the times we've hung out, it's always been in this sexy vacuum of us filming erotic TikTok videos."

I bite back a laugh at her wording. "That's fair. We can brainstorm some friend activities."

"Do you feel like coming to Sweet Cheeks tomorrow and shooting another video? I'll get you stocked up on ice cream for your cousin. Just text me whatever flavors she wants."

"That sounds perfect. Millie will be thrilled."

We make plans for me to come over after she closes, like normal.

"Can't wait," she says.

We hang up, and I walk back out to the kitchen, where Millie is chowing down on pickles dipped in queso.

"Where'd Austin and Declan go?" I ask.

"I put them to work."

I let out a low whistle. "You run a tight ship, cuz."

She winks at me before taking another bite of pickle. "What's that smile for?" she asks.

I didn't even realize I was smiling. I scratch my fingers

through the stubble along my jaw and clear my throat. "What flavors of ice cream do you want from Sweet Cheeks? I'm heading there tomorrow night."

She drops her pickle. "You and Becca are good again?"

"Yup," I say.

I brace myself for another interrogation from my cousin, but she must be too excited at the prospect of more of her favorite ice cream because she just yelps and claps and lists off all the flavors she wants.

"Why don't you just text me a list?" I tell her as I grab a pickle from the jar she's eating out of.

She whips out her phone, her fingers flying across the screen. "On it."

I cough when she texts me a dozen different flavors. "Jesus."

Millie points to her bump. "The baby wants dessert after every meal. Even breakfast. And ice cream is the perfect dessert."

I laugh, then text Becca Millie's list.

Me: *I'm sorry for that embarrassingly long list of flavors. My cousin is a monster.*

Becca: *LOL it's not a problem at all, I'm just so flattered that my ice cream is her biggest craving.*

"Damn, I don't think I've seen you smile like that in a long time," Millie says when I put away my phone.

I roll my eyes, but my smile doesn't budge.

Chapter 14

Becca

"How's this look?" Gage asks as he stands in the middle of my ice cream shop with no shirt on.

I frown at his bare chest, then spray another dollop of whipped cream over his left nipple. "There. Now you're perfect."

He looks down and frowns at his chest. "Perfect definitely isn't how I would describe myself right now, but I'll take your word for it."

I laugh and press record on his phone, then swipe the tub of rainbow sprinkles from the counter. "You ready?"

"As I'll ever be."

I take a handful of sprinkles and toss it over the whipped cream smiley face adorning Gage's chest. I aim for the two whipped cream circles covering his nipples first, which make up the eyes of the smiley face. Then I toss a handful of sprinkles over the whipped cream mouth that runs along his washboard stomach.

He barely flinches as the sprinkles hit his body. He stares straight ahead with a smoldering scowl on his face. When I finish, he looks down. A grin splits his face, and the most satisfied feeling comes over me. It feels really, really good to make Gage smile.

"Wow. I look like a unicorn jizzed all over me."

I almost fall over, I'm laughing so hard. The low rumble of Gage's laugh sounds above me.

"I think that would make a pretty good caption for this video, don't you?" he says.

I hold up a hand until I catch my breath. "No way. The Sweet Cheeks account would get banned for sure."

I walk over to where his phone is set up and stop the video.

"How is it?" he asks.

"It's perfect! People are gonna go crazy when I post it."

He glances around. "Can I grab a towel or something from you?"

I look up, realizing that he must be eager to clean up. "Oh, right! Sorry." I grab a stack of paper towels and hand it to him.

Yesterday we cleared the air over the phone. I expected us to take longer to get back to how we were, but things feel surprisingly natural between Gage and me. I was a nervous wreck, of course, up until the moment he walked into Sweet Cheeks, that easy smile on his face. He asked how busy the shop was, what flavors I was featuring for the day, normal conversation stuff. At that moment I felt completely at ease. It was exactly like Gage said: no big deal. We could move past our kiss and my moment of utter madness. We could be friends.

I even felt comfortable enough to suggest an idea for today's TikTok video, which entailed him being shirtless and covered in whipped cream and sprinkles. And it didn't feel weird at all.

While Gage cleans up, I upload the video to TikTok and add some effects.

"Wanna take a look?" I glance up at him and my eyes go wide at the sight of all the muscles in his chest and abs flexing as he reaches to toss the paper towels in the nearby trashcan.

"You okay?" he says with a smug half-smile.

I blink quickly and shake my head. "Yup. Fine. Totally fine."

"Did I miss a spot?" he teases, gesturing to his bare chest.

"Nope. You did an excellent job cleaning yourself up." My skin goes hot. I guess seeing muscles flex in real time triggered something in my lizard brain.

Gage chuckles as he pulls his T-shirt back on. Together we watch the slow-motion video of him standing still, a sexy scowl on his face, painted with a whipped cream smiley face. Rainbow sprinkles crash against his beautiful bare chest. In the background, a frenetic remix of a popular EDM song plays.

Gage reads the caption. "'Taste the rainbow sprinkles.' Nice."

I upload the video, and my stomach does that familiar flip it always does when I upload a new video to Sweet Cheeks' TikTok account.

"We're so close to one hundred thousand followers," I say as I scroll down the main page. "And it's only been a few weeks of posting sexy videos with you. I honestly think half a million is possible."

"Of course it's possible." He flashes that killer grin, the one that makes him look devilish and handsome all at once. I could swear I feel tingles in my tummy. I shake it off. He's my friend. I really, really shouldn't be getting tingles from looking at my friend.

He's your friend who gave you one hell of an orgasm.

I shove aside that thought and refocus on the moment. That was a one-off. Gage and I are strictly friends now, and I shouldn't be lumping him and orgasms in the same thought.

I start to clean up, then remember the ice cream flavors that I set aside for his cousin.

"Okay, so I've got cookies and cream, mint chocolate swirl, spice cake, s'more, and then—"

"Holy shit," Gage mumbles.

I spin around. "What?"

He holds up his phone to me. "Sweet Cheeks just hit one hundred thousand followers."

"What?" I drop the pint I'm holding, then quickly grab it and shove it back in the freezer before running over to him.

"Are you serious?" I grab the phone from his hand.

"Dead serious."

"But I just looked not even five minutes ago, and we were a few hundred past ninety-nine thousand. That's almost a thousand new followers in minutes."

"It must be the new video you posted."

I look and see the video has garnered thousands of views and comments. Loads of those comments are people saying how they're planning to order a shipment of ice cream from Sweet Cheeks. Even more people say they're going to road trip to Sweet Cheeks so they can try the ice cream and take photos and videos to post on their social media accounts.

"Holy cow."

"You did it, Becca. One hundred thousand followers." Gage beams at me.

I pull him into a hug and chatter about the orders that are about to come in and how the lines will be even longer when we open tomorrow. I stop myself and lean back so I can look at him. "Gage, there's no way I could have done this without you. Thank you."

His smoky brown eyes turn tender. "It's my pleasure. But hey, it's not all me. Your ice cream is what's winning them over."

"Yeah, but you're the famous face who's bringing them in."

He raises an eyebrow. "You're getting busier and busier because customers love your incredible ice cream. Give yourself the credit you deserve, Becca."

That tingle from earlier hits me again, only this time, I can feel it all over my body.

"I did it," I say in a quiet voice.

Gage, whose arms are still wrapped around me, gives me a squeeze. "Louder."

"I did it," I say again.

He tilts his head at me. "Come on. You can do better than that."

I take a breath. "I did it!" I yell.

Gage laughs. "Hell yeah you did." He steps back and high-fives me. "Now we need to celebrate."

I check the time. "But it's late. It's past ten already, and I'm planning on getting up early so I can fill the online orders before we open..."

Gage shakes his head. "I won't keep you out late, I promise. Just one celebratory drink. One hundred thousand followers is a huge milestone, Becca. You gotta celebrate.

You deserve to celebrate yourself and all the hard work you've done."

He's right. "Okay. Let's go."

Ten minutes later we're walking through the LoHi neighborhood. Even on this weeknight, there are dozens of people dining and drinking along the outdoor patios.

"Where to?" I ask Gage as we walk along the crowded sidewalk.

He points to the right, and I follow him into an unassuming brick-front building that looks more like an old library than somewhere to get a last-minute drink. When we walk in, I'm immediately hit with the heavenly smell of roasted garlic. It's a dimly lit place with a dozen wooden tables on one side and a long bar on the other.

"What is this place?" I ask. He leads us to two empty stools at the end.

"I used to work here years ago as a line cook," he says. "They have the best garlic bread. And the best champagne."

"Sounds expensive."

"My treat."

"I can pay for myself."

He narrows his gaze at me, and my stomach flips. It's that scowl I've seen in his TikTok videos but a bit softer. And god, is it hot. "Nope. We're celebrating your success, and the proper way to do that is with a glass of champagne. On me."

I swallow back the drool that's suddenly pooled in my mouth. "Okay."

The bartender comes over, and Gage orders garlic bread and two glasses of champagne.

"So is this where your passion for food started?" I ask, taking in the old school décor.

It looks like a classic family-run Italian restaurant. The

color scheme is all deep browns and blacks and reds with white tablecloths. The wall at the far end boasts a dozen framed photos of rolling hills and vineyards, along with black-and-white photos of smiling folks. Members of the family who own this place, I bet.

"Kind of. It was my first job as a high schooler and first job in the restaurant business," Gage says. "But I've been cooking since I was a kid. My mom is an amazing cook. Everyone on her side of the family is, actually. I grew up in the kitchen."

I picture baby Gage helping in the kitchen and hold back an "aww."

"So that's where all of your gourmet inspiration started?"

Gage chuckles. "The food my family cooked and taught me how to cook growing up was the exact opposite of gourmet. And I mean that in the best way possible. They're all about satisfying, home-cooked, simple, from-the-heart recipes. Not at all pretentious. My mom's family emigrated from the Philippines to the US when she was little, and cooking their family recipes was how they stayed connected with their roots. Whenever we cook those recipes, it always feels like so much more than just food. It feels like love."

I take in the warm look on his face as he talks about his family and how passionate they are about food.

He shakes his head, his smile turning shy. "I'm just now realizing how weird that sounds."

I rest my hand on his arm. "It doesn't. At all. What you said was beautiful, Gage. It's so cool how food holds such meaning for you and your family. I wish it did for my family."

His gaze turns worried as he looks at me. "Did you and your family struggle with food or something?"

"Oh gosh, no. We were totally fine, thankfully. But my parents were terrible cooks. So am I. We mostly ordered food or made simple stuff, like sandwiches or salads."

"That's cool though. Sandwiches rock."

"Not as much as home-cooked food. Or ice cream."

"Obviously."

"Ice cream is the love language of my family. That was always how we showed our love and celebrated. If I got straight As or my parents got good news at work, we'd go out for ice cream. When I was little, they'd have my birthday parties at an ice cream shop. When I graduated high school, instead of a standard sheet cake, my parents got an ice cream cake to celebrate. They both travel a ton for work, but whenever they're home here in Denver, the first thing I do is run over their favorite flavors from Sweet Cheeks."

Gage grins. My stomach flips. I'll never, ever get tired of seeing him smile.

"Maybe it's silly, but that's why opening Sweet Cheeks was so important to me—and why keeping it in business is too. It's more than just ice cream. It reminds me of all the happy times I had with my parents growing up. For us, ice cream is love and joy."

Gage rests his hand against his heart. "Damn, that's beautiful."

I playfully shove his shoulder.

"I'm serious," he says. "Home-cooked Filipino food is the heart and soul of my family. Ice cream is the heart and soul of yours. They're both equally beautiful."

I beam at how perfect his words are.

The bartender returns with two glasses of champagne and garlic bread. "Sorry about the wait on these." He huffs out a breath. "We're short-staffed tonight."

I glance around at how crowded the bar has gotten. I didn't even notice. I was so engrossed in talking to Gage.

"No worries, man," he says.

The bartender flashes a grateful smile at us both before darting off to help more patrons. Gage and I grab our glasses. He raises his. "To Sweet Cheeks being a massive success."

I clink my glass against his. I take a sip and moan. "Oh my god, that's the most amazing thing I've ever tasted."

"Told you it was good."

I'm about to take another sip when someone bumps me from behind. I spin around to see two flushed-faced college-age girls staring at me, wide-eyed.

"We're so sorry," she says sweetly. "It's these damn shoes." She kicks up her leg to reveal a killer stiletto.

I smile and shake my head. "It's okay. I've been there. That's why I stick to these." I kick up my sneaker.

She chuckles and glances past me. A second later her eyes go wide. "Oh my god."

Her friend gasps. "Holy shit, are you Gage Grant? That hot guy on TikTok who cooks?"

I turn around to Gage. He clears his throat and offers a tight smile. "That's me."

The two college girls glance at each other and squeal, then scurry over to him.

"You don't mind if we take a selfie with you, do you?" Stiletto girl pulls out her phone and leans close to Gage before he even has time to answer.

"Hey, would it be okay if you FaceTime our friend Brianna?" the other girl asks. Just like her friend, she doesn't wait for Gage to answer before running up to him and pulling out her phone. "You're her celebrity crush." She glances up at him and licks her lips. "And you're my hall pass."

My jaw drops as she waggles her eyebrows at him and moves even closer to him.

Gage frowns and leans back, but there's nowhere for him to go. He's flanked on either side by two aggressive women who don't seem to notice or care that they're making him uncomfortable.

"Uh, actually," Gage mumbles, "I'm busy at the moment with my friend, and I don't really—"

"Aww, come on!" Stiletto girl runs her hand on his chest. "We're huge fans of yours. We watch your TikTok every day, since the very beginning. We've always thought you were so sexy."

"Yeah, can you show your abs? My friend would die if I sent her a picture of your abs."

Gage frowns. "That's not something I'm interested in doing."

Hall pass girl pouts at him. "Come on, one pic of those gorgeous abs!"

Gage pulls away from her. "Look, I appreciate your support, but I'd like to just have a quiet night with my friend."

"God, you don't have to be a dick about it," hall pass girl mutters.

And that's when something inside of me snaps. I've watched in disbelief as these two strangers invade my friend's space and violate his boundaries. It stops now.

"Hey," I bark, jumping off my stool. Hall pass and stiletto girl whip their heads at me. "Both of you stop touching him right now."

Their eyes go wide as they stumble back.

"I don't care how sexy his TikTok is, that doesn't give

you the right to grope him. That's so fucked up. Can't you see how uncomfortable you're making him?"

Both of their faces turn beet red. They back away from him and exchange an embarrassed glance.

"He told you 'no' multiple times. He's clearly not interested. Leave him alone."

They stumble away, muttering apologies. It's not till then that I realize just how quickly my heart is beating.

I turn to Gage and gently touch his arm. "Are you okay?"

He doesn't answer me right away. He's dazed as he looks at me, like he's trying to make sense of what I'm saying. I start to second-guess what I just did. Maybe I crossed the line by lashing out on his behalf.

"Yeah. I'm good."

"Are you sure?" The need to comfort Gage in this moment is overwhelming, but I hold back. I glance down at my arm and am surprised when I see that I'm not shaking. A second ago it felt like my entire body was buzzing with fury and adrenaline.

He starts to smile. "I'm sure. Thank you for what you did."

"You don't have to thank me. They crossed the line. I'm so sorry they did that to you."

He shrugs before grabbing his champagne glass and taking a long sip.

"Wait, does that happen to you a lot?" I ask before sitting back down.

"Not a lot. Most of the time if I get recognized, people are cool about it. Sometimes they ask for a selfie, which I'm cool with. But every once in a while, I get people like them who think that just because I do sexy stuff on TikTok, that entitles them to my time or my body."

My stomach churns. "That is so messed up."

"It is what it is."

"It's not, Gage. It is never, ever okay for anyone to touch you without your permission or make rude comments about your body."

He stares at me for a long second, almost like he needs the extra time to fully soak in my words.

When he blinks, he looks down at the bar top. "I guess I never thought of it that way. I mean, it definitely makes me uncomfortable when people treat me like that. But people kind of dismiss it if you're a guy. Like, they think it's impossible that a guy wouldn't like to be felt up by an attractive woman."

"That's ridiculous. Men can be groped and sexually harassed. Anyone can. It doesn't matter your gender."

That dazed look in his eyes starts to dissipate. He nods. "You're right."

For a minute we quietly sip our champagne and eat the garlic bread.

"You were a fucking beast, by the way," he says. "It was awesome to watch."

I look up at him. "Really? I was afraid you'd think I was a psycho for going off like that."

"Not even close." He smiles and drains the last of his drink. He checks the time on his phone and shows me. "We should get you home."

Chapter 15

Gage

I walk in the direction of Sweet Cheeks and Becca's apartment building in a daze.

Holy shit.

Seeing Becca like that, all pissed on my behalf and standing up for me, blew me away. It's not that I thought she was meek or anything like that. Clearly, she's a strong person who's been through a lot, what with her breakup and her douchebag ex stealing from her. And I've seen her work hard and hustle day after day. But to see her literally stand up for me and cuss out those women was incredible.

And pretty fucking hot, if I'm being honest.

I set aside that thought and focus on how good it felt to know that Becca had my back, how she was willing to shed her sweet personality and turn into a beast to defend me. And then for her to check on me, comfort me, and go out of her way to make sure that I felt safe and validated...

I glance over at her as she walks beside me. She offers that shy, sweet smile that's become my favorite of hers.

My stomach does that flip thing again. Becca is amazing. I mean, I've thought that about her since the day I met her. But she's a truly good person who isn't afraid to stand up for what's right. That's something I don't see often—not on social media and definitely not in a world of people willing to screw others over to get ahead.

"Hey, um, I don't have to head back to my apartment just yet," Becca says.

"I thought you didn't want to stay out too late."

"I changed my mind."

She smiles, the look in her eyes bright and eager, like she doesn't want to end the night just yet.

Her gaze falls to the ground. She starts to fidget while we continue walking, and she shoves her hands in her pockets.

"I guess my adrenaline is still pumping a bit from earlier." She laughs softly before looking up at me. "And I'm having a nice time with you. I don't want to say goodnight just yet."

I smile at her. "I don't want to either."

We round the corner of the block, and Sweet Cheeks comes into view.

"Let's sit on the bench out in front and enjoy the quiet," she says. "It's always so busy during the day with the traffic and people coming in and out. I never get to sit outside of Sweet Cheeks and just take it in."

"Let's do it."

We plop down on the wooden bench off to the side of the entrance.

I reach my arms over my head to stretch and peer over at Becca. "Adrenaline still pumping hard, is it?"

She chuckles. "A little."

"Gotta say, I was blown away when you dropped an f-bomb back there."

Becca wrinkles her nose as she smiles, like she's embarrassed. "I only swear when I get super pissed. It's pretty uncharacteristic of me."

"I like that. A lot. So many people swear all the time. Like me. It takes the punch of cuss words. They're supposed to shock, but if you say them all the time, they lose their shock value."

Becca chuckles. "That's a good point. I never thought of it that way."

"I appreciate your use of profanity," I tease. "You don't say it unless you mean it."

"Precisely." She aims a finger gun at me, and I'm pretty sure my heart explodes right in my chest. Goddamn, I can barely handle how cute that was.

"I can't picture you getting pissed very often," I say. "It seems very un-Becca-like."

"It is." She looks ahead, her gaze turning thoughtful. "You know, the last time I swore before tonight was the night my ex confessed that he was cheating on me."

I feel that squeeze in my chest again. Just thinking about her ex hurting her like that has me tense.

"I did something else that night that was pretty out of character."

"What was it?"

She sighs, her delicate shoulders falling with the movement. "I threw his clothes out of the window of our apartment—well, *my* apartment now—when he confessed that he'd been cheating on me."

I lean back, shocked at her admission.

She twists her head to look at me, her eyes shy. "That's horrible, isn't it?"

"No. I think a lot of people in your situation would have done what you did."

125

"It doesn't make it right." She kicks at the concrete with the tip of her sneaker. "I was just so pissed. And I swear I wouldn't have done it, but the way Ben was talking was just so hurtful. He kept saying that we'd been drifting apart for months and that I shouldn't be surprised that he found someone else."

I grit my teeth. This fucking guy.

"I just snapped. I felt so humiliated."

"Hey." I grab her hand in mine. "He's the one who should feel humiliated. He had you—an incredible, stunning, and sweet woman. And he lost you because he was a selfish prick who couldn't keep it in his pants."

She starts to smile, but there's still sadness in her eyes. "I just feel disappointed in myself. Yeah, it was wrong of him to cheat, but I shouldn't have lost my cool. I should have been the bigger person and stayed respectful and calm."

I shake my head. "That's impossible. Becca, you're human. It's a very human thing to get upset when you find out that your partner is cheating on you. It's not fair to expect yourself to react calmly when you're thrown into a high-stress situation like that."

She blinks a few times, like she's soaking in what I've said. "I guess that's fair."

"And come on, it's not like you ran the guy over with your car. Now *that* would be overreacting."

A soft chuckle falls from her lips. "That's a good point. Can I get some sort of credit for that? Maybe put that on my resume? Or etch it onto a plaque? 'Didn't run over my cheating ex.'"

I laugh. "Absolutely. And besides, he stole your money on top of cheating on you. He's a piece of shit and deserved at the very least to have his clothes thrown in the street."

She sighs. "Maybe you're right."

I can tell she's still bothered by what she's done, even though she has no reason to be. That cheating prick got off easy. He betrayed Becca's trust *and* stole her savings out from under her. If anyone had done that to me, I'd lose it. But that's just how truly good Becca is. She doesn't crave revenge like other people. And she feels bad about getting upset. That's how kind-hearted she is.

The urge to comfort her digs at me.

"I've done some pretty out of character things too. Hurtful things," I say after a second. "Worse than what you did, Becca."

Her eyebrows crash together, concern radiating in her expression. "What do you mean?"

I take a second. "For a long time, my dream was to be a chef like my dad. He's pretty famous in the culinary world. He owns a couple of high-end French restaurants here in Denver, and a bunch of others in California and New York. He's been on TV too."

Becca's crystal blue eyes practically bulge out of her head. "Oh my gosh, your dad is chef Andre Thomas Grant?"

I huff out a breath and nod. "The one and only."

"I had no idea. I mean, I've seen him on TV when he's been a guest judge on cooking shows, but I would have never guessed the connection. You two don't look anything alike."

"I look like my mom. My brother and sister do too. We took after her features. The only thing we inherited from our dad was our height."

I notice I'm tapping my foot against the leg of the bench, I'm so anxious talking about my dad. But I want to get this out. I want to open up about this to Becca.

"He was always so focused on building his gourmet

empire, ever since I was a kid. He wasn't around a lot. My mom raised my siblings and me, while my dad was busy traveling to promote his restaurants. And even when he was around, it felt off. When he'd play with me as a little kid or try and talk to me, it always felt so forced. I could tell he was uncomfortable being a dad. From the get-go I felt disconnected from him because of that. He and my mom split up when I was in elementary school, and I saw him even less. But I loved him. I wanted his approval, just like every kid does."

I swallow hard as I work up the nerve to tell Becca the rest. "That's why I got into gourmet cooking. I always loved cooking, but when I was a teenager, I started focusing on gourmet meals specifically. It was the one thing my dad and I could connect over—the one thing that made me feel close to him. I didn't get to see him much growing up after my parents split. He was traveling constantly and would only be in town one weekend every month or two months. But the weekends that he was around, I'd spend with him at his restaurants here in Denver, learning the ropes of cooking. It felt so good to be around him when he was in his element and acting natural. It was never awkward or stilted like it was when I was little. Gourmet food was our common bond.

"And honestly? I wanted to impress him, show him that I was building my skill set as a cook. That I wasn't expecting him to pull strings for me or hire me to his restaurant. I wanted to show him that I could make a name for myself. That's why I started my TikTok a couple years ago, to practice my cooking skills and build a fanbase for my food. I started out like so many other people on that app, posting videos and getting a small amount of attention and likes. But I was persistent and eventually built a decent following.

I realized that the sexier the content was, the more attention the videos would get. Like you said before, sex sells."

When I glance up at her, she's smiling softly. "It's true."

I let out a soft laugh. "I gained followers pretty quickly. I was able to make money too. Tons of kitchenware companies, online grocers, and meal prep delivery companies started reaching out to me and offered to pay me to use their products and ingredients. I couldn't believe it, but I was pumped. I could make a living with TikTok. Yeah, it's not the conventional way to get started in the culinary world, but who cares? The world is changing, and social media can be a powerful tool if you use it strategically. So that's what I did."

Becca's expression is a mix of rapt and sympathetic as she gazes at me. I can feel the muscles in my neck and shoulders tense. "My dad approached me last year and asked if I'd be interested in taking over a sous chef position at his restaurant. I was thrilled and said yes, of course. I was working there a month when he took me into his office and..."

Becca looks at me, concern etched in her frown. I swallow back a bitter taste in my mouth.

"He found my TikTok. He was pissed. And embarrassed. He said he was disgusted that I would post such degrading videos of myself. And then he fired me."

The hot sting of tears burns my eyes. I blink them back quickly. "He said I was no better than a porn star. That I was trash, that I was tarnishing his name in the food and restaurant industry, that I was ruining everything he had spent decades building."

Becca grips my hand in hers. "Gage, that's awful. I'm so sorry."

I shake my head. "It's classic Andre Thomas Grant.

Obsessed with appearances. Thinks that there's only one way to do something: his way. Any other way is wrong. Always freaking out about what people think of him and his impeccably curated image. Terrified that me, his son, would ruin his reputation as a top-tier chef because I'm a trashy, sex symbol thirst trap."

Becca squeezes my hand. "Don't say that. You're not any of those things. You're brilliant. There's nothing wrong with what you do, Gage."

The conviction in Becca's tone makes my chest squeeze. I can tell she means every word she says.

"That's what I said to my dad, that I wasn't ashamed of my TikTok, that it made me the cook I am today, and that because of my success, I can support myself doing what I love. And then I told him that if he was ashamed of me, then I no longer wanted him in my life. I told him I never wanted to see or speak to him ever again. I was so angry I couldn't even think straight."

Becca's eyes shine with unshed tears.

"I know that cutting my dad out of my life is terrible. I'd never done that, cut off contact with a family member. Family means everything to me," I say. "But I realize now that my dad never saw me as anything other than an extension of himself—a way to make himself look good to the world. And yeah, maybe it's harsh, but I don't want anyone like that in my life, even if that person is family."

I look down at our joined hands. The feel of her soft skin and how her light complexion contrasts with my dark tan send warmth through me. The knot of nerves inside of me starts to loosen.

"Gage, I...I don't know what to say. I'm so sorry that happened. You deserve to be loved and accepted by your dad. I'm sorry that he's so caught up in things that don't matter."

"Me too," I say through a breath. "But the rest of my family is loving and accepting. My mom and relatives are all supportive of what I do. My brother and sister tease me from time to time, but that's our normal sibling dynamic. I give them shit too. I can feel how much they love me despite how we bicker and tease. And they have my back no matter what. That's what matters."

Becca offers a soft smile. There's still a gleam of sadness in her eyes as she looks at me though. "It sounds like you have the most amazing family."

A long moment of quiet passes between us. I realize that we're still holding hands. I catch her looking down at our hands. She lets out a nervous laugh. "Sorry, I guess I got a little carried away."

"Don't be sorry," I say before squeezing her hand. "I needed that."

As painful as it was to talk about my dad, it also felt good to tell Becca. She listened patiently while letting me talk, making me feel supported and comforted.

"I didn't mean to turn this into a therapy session." I slip my hand out of hers.

"You didn't. We're friends. I'm happy to listen to you, Gage. Always."

She gazes at me with something extra in her eyes, something I can't quite place or name.

"I wanna cook for you." It's not until the words are out of my mouth that I realize how weird and random that sounds. But I want to spend more time with Becca. I want to see her outside of her ice cream shop. I want to do more than just film sexy videos together. I want to make her feel comforted and cared for and doted on.

I swallow hard, my nerves crackling inside of me as I wait for her to say something. I brace myself for a "what are you talking about?" or a "no, thanks." But instead, she beams at me and says, "I would love that."

Chapter 16

Becca

When I arrive at the door of Gage's apartment, I stop myself and take a deep breath.

I don't know why I'm so nervous. We're friends. Friends invite each other to their places. Friends cook each other meals. I do this with Tori all the time.

You're not sexually attracted to Tori.

And *that's* the difference. Gage is my friend, but there's no denying how attracted I am to him. And the fact that he gave me a mind-bending orgasm a handful of days ago that I still think about...still fantasize about.

Just this morning before getting out of bed, I was so turned on thinking about riding Gage's rock-hard dick that I had to break out my vibrator. I've never come that quickly before while pleasuring myself.

This is more than just sexual attraction though. It's how he opened up to me last night about his dad. Just thinking about how his dad lashed out at him sends a wave of anger and frustration through me. I can't believe he would be so narrow-minded. Gage carved out a culinary career for himself using TikTok. So many parents would be thrilled to have a kid like him who is brilliant, talented, and industrious.

That anger and frustration inside of me are eclipsed by pure warmth. The fact that Gage chose to tell me something so personal and painful means everything. It means he trusts me. It means he cares about me.

God, this guy. He is freaking *amazing*. He's handsome and physically perfect. But he's also sweet, thoughtful, kind, hardworking, supportive, and nonjudgmental, with a killer sense of humor. I bite back a laugh, remembering his unicorn jizz joke. If I could build a dream guy, it would be Gage.

I shake my head, banishing those thoughts, and refocus on the moment. I can't be thinking about my friend like that.

I swallow and knock on his door. A few seconds later he answers, flashing that killer crooked smile. His eyes fall to the bottle of wine in my hand. He raises his eyebrow at me. "I told you not to bring anything."

"You're doing all the cooking," I say. "It's the least I could do."

He chuckles and thanks me while gesturing for me to come in. He takes the wine bottle, and I kick off my sandals. He gives me a quick once-over.

"You look really pretty." His voice is raspy and low when he speaks. It makes my knees weak. "I don't think I've ever seen you in a dress."

I play with the hem of the mint green sundress I'm wearing. "That's because you've only seen me in my ice cream shop. I dress for comfort when I'm at work."

"And outside of work, you dress to kill."

My face goes hot, and I bite my lip. "You're very smooth. And very kind."

He doesn't even blink. "Just stating the obvious. You're stunning, Becca. No matter what you wear."

Maybe it's the low rumble of his voice or how close we're standing to each other in his narrow hallway, but something in the air between us changes. It's thick and hot and very, very un-friend-like. Gage licks his lips, and for a second I think I'm going to faint. But then he spins around and starts walking into his apartment.

"I'll pop this open," he says.

I mutter a "sounds good" and follow him into his apartment. The kitchen and living room are an open space, with a granite island and bar stools serving as the unofficial barrier.

"I love your place," I say as I gaze around and take in the exposed brick walls and massive floor-to-ceiling window on the far side. "It's so hip."

"Is it?" Gage chuckles as he pops off the cork.

"Definitely." I plop on one of the wooden barstools at the island. "This is exactly how I'd picture the apartment of a cool, early-thirties guy with better-than-average taste in décor."

His chuckle turns into a full-on laugh. He grabs two wine glasses from the floating shelf behind him and pours the wine. "Do I get points deducted if I tell you that my sister and my cousin helped me decorate it and picked out all the furniture?"

I laugh and shake my head. "Nope. That means you're smart *and* resourceful."

He hands me a glass and raises his. "Cheers to that."

We clink our glasses and take sips of the wine. My gaze

lands on Gage's throat as he swallows, mesmerized by how his Adam's apple bobs with the movement. I blink, and the visual of me wrapping my fingers around his neck appears. I bet he'd feel hot and thick and hard...

God, Becca. Stop objectifying your friend, will you?

I gulp more wine and try not to think about how sexy the contrast would be between my pale fingers and his tan, thick neck...

"I'm not a wine expert," I say quickly. "So, um, sorry if it's not very good. The guy at the shop said it was from a really good vineyard though."

Gage makes an "mmm" sound as he takes another long sip. "It's delicious. This Malbec will go great with dinner."

He winks at me before spinning around and checking the metal pot simmering on his stove. As he moves, his back and shoulder muscles bulge under his cotton T-shirt.

"It smells amazing, by the way." I inhale the aroma of roasting meat and vegetables. My mouth waters.

Just focus on the food and not the fact that you're aching to devour Gage.

"I made a rack of lamb with roasted potatoes and rosemary shallot gravy, and homemade sourdough bread."

"Oh my god," I say into my glass. "You're spoiling me. That's way fancier than my normal sheet pan dinners I throw together."

He spins around. "Nothing wrong with a sheet pan dinner."

When he bends down to open the oven, my eyes go wide. Oh my good god, his ass is beautiful. My brain short-circuits wondering how exactly he got such a perfect backside. Does he do a lot of squats? It's clear he lifts weights given how cut he is, so that's probably part of—

I press my eyes shut, halting my inner thoughts. *Stop.*

I spin around on my stool and fan myself, thankful that Gage's back is to me. I focus on the first thing I see.

"Wow, what a cool palm tree!" I blurt and immediately regret it. I sound like such a loser.

Gage spins around, brow furrowed in confusion until I point out the framed photo on the wall of him standing with a guy and a woman around his age—his siblings, I'm assuming. They're decked out in swimsuits on a beach, posing next to a massive palm tree.

"Oh, that." He leans against the kitchen island. "That's my brother and sister and me in Boracay in the Philippines a few years ago. We were visiting our mom's family."

I stand up, glass of wine in hand, and walk over to get a better look. Gage's sister and brother are as gorgeous as he is. "You and your siblings got all the ridiculously good-looking genes."

Gage booms out a laugh before refilling his wine glass and joining me. "I'll be sure to relay the compliment. It'll make their egos even bigger."

I chuckle and take in how all three of them have the same gorgeous deep brown eyes, brown-black hair, and tan skin.

"Who's the oldest?" I ask.

"Tyler. But only by a couple of years. Then me. Then our baby sister Maya. She's three years younger than me."

I observe how Tyler is a couple of inches taller than Gage, with a leaner builder and a shaggier haircut. He looks like a surfer. Maya stands at just under Gage's height and looks like a literal model with her perfect complexion and flawless skin. She's flanked by her hulking brothers in the photo.

Gage tells me Tyler lives here in Denver, but Maya moves constantly.

"She moved to Los Angeles a handful of months ago. Before that she was working as a professional house sitter in Seattle. And before that she worked as a pet nanny for some friends of hers in Portland."

"What's a pet nanny?"

Gage shakes his head. "I have no idea."

"She sounds like a free spirit."

"She definitely is."

"And your brother Tyler?"

"He's a douchebag."

I chuckle and playfully shove Gage's arm. "Come on, don't say that about your brother."

"If you ever meet him, you'll understand. I love him, but I also want to strangle him half the time we're around each other."

"Aww come on, he can't be that bad."

"He absolutely is that bad. He's thirty-two, and half the time we see each other, he tries to greet me with a purple nurple," Gage mutters.

"A purple what?"

He frowns at me. "You don't know what a purple nurple is?"

I shake my head. "I'm an only child. This sounds like something rambunctious siblings do to each other."

He nods. "That's true, actually."

He goes quiet and takes another sip of wine.

I playfully smack his arm. "Well, are you ever gonna tell me what it is?"

"No. Too embarrassing. I shouldn't have said it in the first place."

I roll my eyes and laugh. "Okay, well, you have to tell me now."

"Nope."

"Oh, come on. We're both adults."

When he doesn't say anything for a few seconds, I assume his stubborn streak wins out. But then his cheeks go red. He looks at me for a long moment without even blinking. "It's when you pinch someone's nipple and twist it."

"Oh..."

Gage's gaze drops to my chest for a split second before he redirects it back to my eyes. For a fleeting moment, I wonder if he's imagining my nipples.

I hope so.

That thought makes my nipples go hard. I cross my arms over my chest.

He clears his throat and blinks away that dazed look. "Dinner's ready. Are you hungry?"

That low rumble betrays the reined-in look on his face. Gage was definitely thinking about my nipples. And that thought makes my entire body go hot.

"I'm starving," I rasp.

Minutes later I'm sitting at the kitchen island while Gage dishes up the food. He sets an impeccably plated dinner in front of me: a trio of medium rare lamb chops with a pile of roasted potatoes on top of a pool of gravy.

"This looks incredible." I gaze down at the small sprig of mint that sits atop the lamb. When he spins around to me, I smile at him. "Even the smallest detail on the plate is flawless." I tap the mint with my fork. "You're so talented, Gage."

A flustered smile pulls at his lips as his cheeks flush pink. "Thanks."

A roaring sound rips from my stomach. Gage's eyes go wide. I shrug. "I guess I'm pretty hungry."

We both laugh. I can feel the tension from all that nipple talk from minutes ago dissipate.

He sits down next to me with his own perfectly plated dinner.

"Just warning you, I haven't eaten much today in preparation for your gourmet dinner," I say, picking up my knife and fork. "I'm going to inhale this. Don't judge me."

He chuckles. "We'll see. That first bite determines everything. You won't inhale it if it doesn't taste good."

I tilt my head at him. "Just smelling this dish has me drooling. There's zero chance it will taste anything less than amazing."

I slice a chunk of the perfectly pink lamb, spear it with my fork along with a slice of potato, and drag it through the gravy. When I pop it in my mouth, I moan. It's an explosion on my tongue. The fat and salt of the lamb, the buttery starch of the potato, the smoothness of the gravy—even the bit of mint is perfect. The sharpness and freshness of the herb are the perfect complement to this rich bite of food.

My eyes roll back, and my head dips. I cover my mouth with my hand as I chew, moaning the entire time.

"Oh. My. Freaking. God. Gage!"

I turn to him and see him smiling as he chews. "It's good then?"

I shake my head. "Good is not a sufficient word. We need a new word to describe the deliciousness of this meal."

I rip a hunk of the sourdough bread loaf sitting on a plate between us and dip it in the small plate of olive oil, roasted garlic, and herbs that Gage prepared.

I make an "mmm" noise that echoes through the apartment.

"Okay, that's the best bread I've ever had, hands down."

"Really?"

I nod at Gage with wide eyes to convey just how good it is. "Yes, really."

I dive back into the meal like a shark in the middle of a feeding frenzy. The flavors are so perfect, so well balanced, and I can't get enough of everything.

By the time I finish, Gage is only halfway done with his dinner.

"Whoa." He chews quickly and dabs at his mouth. "You ate that impressively fast."

"Never question my speed when I'm hungry."

He holds up a hand, laughing. "Noted."

I lean back on the barstool, shaking my head in disbelief. I'm in some post-meal daze that only comes when you've had a perfect meal.

I down the rest of the wine in my glass. "That was orgasmic."

It's not until a few seconds later that I realize what I've just said. My eyes go wide. "That was a pretty weird thing to say."

I bite my lip and hazard a glance at Gage, who just looks amused as he finishes the last couple bites of lamb and potato. "Orgasmic, huh?"

"Mmmhmm," I mumble behind my water glass before taking a long gulp. "I guess I got a little carried away."

Gage smiles down at his plate before his eyes cut to me. "No worries. Shit just got intense."

He winks at me while he chews, and my mind rockets back to the day we talked through our kiss and my orgasm.

Shit got intense. It happens.

I'm tingling and hot all over all at once. I hop up and grab our empty plates. "Let me clean up."

I head straight for the sink despite Gage telling me not to.

"Hey, no way you're cleaning up."

I flip on the faucet, relishing the feel of the water splashing over my skin. It's cooling me off, and I really, really need that.

"I insist." I wipe the plates with a sponge. "You cooked, so I should clean."

"Becca, come on." I can hear the smile and the playful frustration in Gage's tone as he walks up behind me. "Let me clean up."

"Nope." I grab a pan and squirt some dish soap on it.

He huffs out a breath. "You're not gonna make this easy, are you?"

There's a hitch in his voice that amps up the determination inside of me. I can't help but smile.

"Nope," I repeat. "I'm a stickler about stuff like this, and I always have been. Whoever cooks shouldn't have to clean. That's the rule."

"It's my apartment, my rules."

"Nice try. Still no."

This playful teasing dynamic I've got going with Gage has me feeling like my whole body is on fire.

"Fine." His arm shoots from behind me, shutting off the faucet. A half-second later his hands are on my waist and he's flipped me around to face him. I'm holding back a laugh as I attempt to spin back around to the sink, but nope. His grip on me is too firm. I move to grab his forearms, but in a split second, his hands move to my wrists.

Gage quirks his eyebrow at me. "My place, my rules."

When his ridiculously sexy, low growl hits my ears, my breath catches. It's always hot to hear Gage speak like this, but when he's clutching onto me, pinning me between his muscled body and the counter, I turn to putty. All I can do is stare at him, my chest heaving, and try not to melt.

I swallow as I take in how his burnt sienna gaze goes from focused to fiery the longer he looks at me. Our faces are barely an inch apart now. I'm so close I can taste his breath. My brain slingshots back to the night of our kiss and how good he tasted.

"So stubborn," I rasp.

"Always," he rasps back.

My eyes fall to his lips. His perfect plump lips. Lips that I'm dying to sink my teeth into and tease.

"I want to kiss you," I admit in a shaky voice. "I-I know that I shouldn't...I know that I said I wanted to be friends, and, um, friends don't—friends *shouldn't* kiss each other..."

Gage's grip on my wrists loosens. His hands fall to my hips, and he grips me hard. I moan. I can feel just how much he wants me in the way he digs his fingers into the fleshy part of my hips.

He closes his eyes for a long second. "I'm fucking dying to kiss you, Becca."

My skin is on fire, and I'm trembling, shaking with need. Every part of me wants to kiss Gage.

He opens his eyes. "But I only want to kiss you if that's what you really want."

My heart thunders in my chest. Between my legs, I'm aching, just like I was the night we kissed.

"I want to kiss you, Gage. But..."

I take a second to swallow and feel his grip on me loosen.

I close my eyes as I work up the nerve to say this. "But I know that I won't be able to stop at just a kiss. I want you. So, so bad. I want you, but I don't think I'm ready for you."

His hands fall away from me, and he takes a step back.

His expression is curious and confused all at once. "What do you mean?"

I swallow, the heat and arousal inside of me shifting to nerves. "I'm a month out of my last relationship. I need to get my head on straight and learn to be alone before I jump into anything romantic. You're a dream guy, Gage. A literal dream guy. And I'm too nervous to even kiss you right now. I'm afraid I'll screw it up because I didn't take enough time to be alone and process things after my breakup."

He rubs the back of his neck, taking in what I've said.

"I don't want to screw up our friendship or a potential romantic relationship by moving too fast."

"So you just need some time?" he asks.

I nod and cross my arms, bracing myself for what he'll say.

"Okay."

I stammer at his quick response. He looks completely laidback about it too. "Seriously?"

He starts to smile. "Yeah. Look, I like you, Becca. A lot. And I'm really, really attracted to you."

"You are?"

He squints at me like he's confused before he laughs. "Of course I am. You're the sweetest and kindest person I've ever met. You're adorable and funny. And you're fucking hot."

I giggle nervously. "Wow, um, no guy I've been with has ever said that to me before."

He shakes his head like he's in disbelief. "Those guys were dipshits. You're incredible, Becca. And if friendship is all you want right now, I'm good with that. I'm happy to be your friend. But if you ever want more, I'm ready."

I'm speechless at how straightforward Gage is, how simply and clearly he's managed to explain his feelings, how calm he is during what could have been an excruciatingly awkward conversation.

Maybe things between us really can be that simple, that easy.

"I love being friends with you, Gage. I love making sexy TikToks with you too."

The corner of his mouth quirks up. "Same."

"You're really okay with just being friends? I don't want it to come off like I'm leading you on or anything like that."

He shakes his head and moves closer to me. "You're not leading me on. You've been clear about your feelings and what you want. So have I. It's okay for us to be friends who are attracted to each other, who also aren't quite ready to take it to the next level. There's no rule that says you have to be friends forever or get into a relationship right away if you feel an attraction. We can take our time and do things the way we want. And if nothing ends up happening, that's okay too."

His words halt the nerves swirling inside me. I smile up at him. "You're so effortlessly cool about everything, you know that?"

"Not dishes though. Don't ever try to clean up in my kitchen again, okay?"

I burst out laughing.

"How about dessert?" he asks.

"You made dessert?"

Instead of answering, he steps over to the fridge, opens the door, and pulls out a lemon tart. My mouth waters.

"I always make dessert," he says with a wolfish smile.

For the next hour we chat and laugh over dessert and wine. I notice the sun setting through the massive window.

"I should get going," I say.

"I'll walk you to your car."

"You don't need to do that."

He shoots me a look. "No way you're walking to your car alone when it's getting dark."

There's a flutter in my chest at the protectiveness in his tone. We walk out of his building together and down the block to my car.

"So, um, how should we end this?" I ask as I stand in front of my car. "Hug? Kiss?"

A naughty smile tugs at Gage's lips.

I roll my eyes and laugh. "I meant a kiss on the cheek."

"Definitely that."

I laugh again and press a kiss on Gage's cheek, relishing the roughness of his stubble and how soft his lips feel on my cheek.

When we pull apart, I catch the tail end of a dazed look in his eyes before he blinks it away.

"Thank you for dinner."

"It was my pleasure."

We linger for a few seconds before he opens my car door for me. "Drive safely, okay? Text me to let me know you got home, will you?"

That chest flutter hits once more. "I will."

As I drive off, I look in my rearview mirror and see him watching me.

Gage is my friend—my hot friend who I'm aching to kiss and do a million other filthy things with.

"You can't jump his bones, not yet," I say to myself.

That night in bed, I check my phone and see Gage's latest video pop up on my TikTok FYP.

It starts with a shot of a slice of that lemon meringue tart sitting on his kitchen counter. Then he leans into frame and slowly flicks his tongue along the merengue topping before licking his lips.

When I read the caption, I nearly burst.

TFW she says the dish you made her was orgasmic.

I squeal into my pillow, still processing the fact that Gage Grant and I are attracted to each other. Now I just have to figure out a way to take things to the next level without totally screwing it up.

Chapter 17

Gage

"I say we go out for a drink."

I look up from my phone, which is set up on my tripod. "This is getting to be a tradition, isn't it? Going for a drink after we film a TikTok video?"

Becca grins at me, her blue eyes sparkling. I don't understand how she can work such long days at her ice cream shop, film TikTok videos with me in the evenings, and still look like a fresh-faced angel.

"I like that we have our own tradition," she says, tugging at the hem of her jean shorts.

I can't help the smile that pulls at my lips or the giddy feeling coursing through me. It's been a week since I had her over for dinner at my place, and I was this close to kissing the hell out of her—and then some.

Part of me wishes it had happened. Every time I'm at my kitchen sink washing up, I think of that moment when my hands were on her hips. We were so close I could taste her sweet breath, and she was looking at me like she wanted to attack me.

No doubt sex with Becca would be mind-blowing. But

when she put a halt to things because she felt she wasn't ready, I understood completely. As attracted as I am to her, that's not the only reason I like her. She's also become a good friend to me in the nearly six weeks we've known one another. I've never developed a friendship so quickly, and that's not a fact I take for granted. Yeah, I'd be psyched if Becca changes her mind someday and wants to date me. But right now what she needs is a friend, and I want to be that for her.

"You know I'm always up for a drink," I say. I send the video we just filmed to Becca and break down my tripod.

"How about that champagne bar down the street?" she says. "I'm in the mood for bubbles."

"Sounds perfect."

Fifteen minutes later we're waiting at the hostess stand at a place called La La Lina's. The hostess greets us with a dazzling smile. "It'll just be a moment. We're clearing off a table for you," she says.

"No problem," Becca says cheerily. "Oh, I forgot to tell you. I mixed a new ice cream flavor for your cousin to help with her cravings."

Something warm pools at the center of my chest. "You didn't have to do that."

"I wanted to. She's growing a beautiful baby in her body, and that's no easy task. She should have her every whim catered to and every craving satisfied."

"You are officially Millie's favorite person ever."

Becca laughs before pulling out her phone. "You said she was craving pretzels and spicy food, so I mixed dark chocolate ice cream with pretzels, a peanut butter caramel swirl, and flecks of cayenne pepper. I know that sounds weird, but I swear, it's delicious. Tori and I spent the past few days taste testing, and we're certain of it."

She shows me her phone screen. When I make out the image, I'm speechless.

"Millie's Mix," I say, reading the label of an ice cream pint.

Becca nods excitedly. "Cute, right?"

"So damn cute. Millie is going to love it. She'll probably cry tears of joy."

Becca claps softly in excitement. "Yay! Tears of joy are the reaction I strive for with every gift and surprise I ever plan."

The hostess returns and says a small table in the back is ready. We follow her through the winding path of the restaurant, which is laid out in a giant circle. I reach over and touch her arm as we walk. "That was so thoughtful of you, Becca. Truly. You're amazing for doing that."

Her skin ignites in a pink blush as she smiles shyly at me. "I'm just trying to do a little something for her."

"This is more than a little something. It's amazing, and I have no doubt she's going to love it."

Becca's grin goes wide. The hostess shows us to our tiny table, and we sit down. I start to lower myself into the chair when someone bumps into my back.

"Crap, sorry," a tall guy with blond hair says.

I wave a hand. "It's okay. This place is kinda crowded."

He yanks at the suit of his jacket and offers a polite nod to me. And then he looks past me, and his eyes go wide.

"Ben?" I hear Becca say. I whip my head to her and see a bewildered look on her face, like she's disgusted and shocked at the same time.

It takes a second for me to register Ben's name in my memory. When I finally do, a boulder-sized knot lands in my stomach.

This fucking prick. This thieving, cheating motherfu—

"Becca." He sounds like he's been punched in the gut when he says her name.

For a split second, I wish I could have punched my fist into his stomach. This is the guy who broke Becca's heart, who made her doubt how amazing she is, who stole her money. I squeeze and loosen my fist at my side over and over.

"What are you doing here?" she says.

I take in how Ben doesn't answer right away. He just stands there, his nostrils flaring, biting down so hard, I can see the muscle in the side of his jaw twitch.

"Just out with a friend," he mutters.

Bullshit. This prick is lying. And I bet I know why.

Just then a tall brunette walks over. "Hey, are you gonna pay with the Black Amex, or..."

She goes quiet as she takes in the scene. I turn to Becca to check on her. Her facial expression is almost unreadable. Her mouth is a straight line, her eyes are focused, and she's not outwardly reacting to what her ex has just said. The pain in her eyes is crystal clear though.

"Black Amex, huh?" A bitter laugh falls from her lips. It makes my chest sting. "That's a pretty-high rolling credit card, Ben. Where'd you get the money for that?"

She looks him straight in the eye as she speaks, her tone steady and pointed. The guy tugs on his tie, the look on his face like he's contemplating strangling himself to get out of being questioned by Becca.

"That's none of your business," he finally says.

The woman he's with—his girlfriend, I'm assuming—bounces a confused stare between him and Becca. "Do you two know each other?"

When Ben starts to shake his head "no," I see red. This

fucking asshole. Is he seriously going to lie while he's standing between his ex and his current girlfriend?

Becca's eyes go wide with disbelief as she witnesses her ex deny her existence while standing right in front of him. But she doesn't lash out at him like I expect—like he deserves. Instead, she looks around him to his girlfriend.

"Yes, we do know each other actually. I'm Becca, Ben's ex-girlfriend. He broke up with me last month when he confessed to cheating on me. And two days later, he emptied my bank account. He stole twenty thousand dollars from me."

The woman gasps before her gaze darts over to Ben. "What the hell? Is that true? Were you seeing me when you were still with her? And god, you took her money too?"

"Don't you dare lie," Becca bites.

Ben's shoulders sink when he exhales, his jaw tight. "There are two sides to every story," he says to the woman next to him.

Becca's jaw drops. I realize I'm clenching my hands into fists. I force myself to loosen them.

This guy. Fucking unreal. Yeah, I'm sure Becca wasn't perfect in her relationship. No one is. But she didn't cheat on him. She didn't steal his money. And she's not telling outright lies about him while he stands in front of her. She's a million times better than this guy is.

This prick is a piece of work and deserves a punch to the face. My hands stay at my sides though. This situation is bad enough as it is. Becca is clearly hurt at seeing her ex and having to witness him lie about her. As satisfying as it would be to kick the shit out of this guy, it would only make things worse.

My focus needs to be on supporting Becca.

I notice the woman with Ben furrowing her brow, like

she's processing what he's just said. "So wait, does that mean you *did* cheat on her and steal from her?"

Ben turns red. She starts to step away from him, but he reaches for her. "Chrissa, baby, I can explain."

Becca scoffs. "God, Ben. I can't believe you would stoop this low."

Her voice shakes as she trails off. I look down and notice she's trembling. I take her hand in mine and feel her instantly still. Her pained stare softens the slightest bit as she looks at me like she's grateful for my support. Like she's relieved I'm here.

Protectiveness surges through me. I turn to the woman. "Chrissa, right? Becca is telling the truth. Do yourself a favor and drop this guy."

"Who the hell are you?" Ben glares at me before looking at Becca's and my joined hands.

"A friend," I spit.

"Why the hell are you chiming in? This conversation doesn't involve you."

He takes a step toward me and straightens to his full height, which is a couple inches taller than me. I let out a laugh. This dipshit. So predictable. Posturing like a peacock, trying to intimidate me into backing off.

Fat fucking chance.

I let go of Becca's hand and step forward and into Ben's space. He stumbles back a step. This jerkoff might be taller than me, but a few inches of height doesn't mean shit if he can't back it up with muscle and skill. I've got at least fifteen pounds on this guy. And the way his eyes widened when I stepped up to him tells me he's all talk.

"It absolutely involves me," I say to him, "because you're telling lies about my friend. You're the asshole, Ben. You cheated. You stole. Be a fucking grown-up and take responsibility."

Out of the corner of my eye, I see Chrissa shaking her head. She crosses her arms as she glowers at Ben. "We're done."

She looks past me to Becca. "Thanks for the warning." When she looks at me, her gaze turns focused before her eyes go wide. "Oh my god! You're that sexy chef guy from TikTok! *That's* where I recognize you from!"

I'm thrown off by her reaction. "Uh, yeah. That's me."

Chrissa looks at Becca once more. "You traded up, honey." She twists to Ben. "Go to hell."

She marches toward the exit. Ben runs after her, pleading for her to stop and hear him out. But before they even make it to the door, she grabs a nearby glass of water, spins around, and splashes him in the face. "I said, we're done. Leave me alone."

A chorus of gasps from the nearby tables follows. Chrissa walks out of the restaurant and hops into a rideshare. Ben stands there, his face dripping wet. A guy sitting at a nearby table hands him his napkin.

"Ouch, dude. I think you better cut your losses and go home."

Ben rips the napkin from the guy's hand and scrubs it over his face, muttering profanity. He walks out of the champagne bar and stomps off down the street.

When I turn to check on Becca, there's a punch to my gut. Her eyes are misty, and she's still shaking.

"Hey," I say softly. "It's okay."

She shakes her head. "I need a drink."

I hold back a wince. She's clearly upset. Distraught, actually. I don't know if downing alcohol is the smartest way to cope.

"How about some water?"

That dazed look fades. She looks determined now. "No. I need something harder than what this place has to offer."

"Becca, I don't know if drinking is the best—"

She holds up a hand, cutting me off. "I just ran into my ex-boyfriend with another woman. I had to stand there as he looked me in the eye and lied about me. I deserve some hard alcohol." She glances around the dimly lit space. "This place is too romantic." She gestures at the décor: the candles, the low mood lighting, the white rose centerpieces. Most of the tables look like they're couples on dates.

I sigh. "Fair enough. There's a dive bar next door. Let's go."

* * *

Becca stumbles forward as I walk her back to her apartment. "God, what a dick Ben is," she slurs.

A trio of people walking past us stops their conversation to glance at us, probably because the volume of her voice is a hair under a shout.

I wrap my arm around her waist and pull her close to me to help steady her as she walks. "I agree. That guy is the biggest dick I've ever met."

She looks up at me, her crystal blue eyes glazed over from the three tequila shots and two cocktails she downed in the last ninety minutes. "You know what wasn't that big? Ben's dick."

I help her stay steady while walking along the sidewalk. She stops suddenly and turns to look at me. Her eyebrows crash together, and her expression turns worried. "Oh gosh, that was so mean, wasn't it?"

I shrug. "It's not mean if it's true. It's just stating facts."

Her expression turns thoughtful, and she nods to herself. "Okay, truth? Ben's dick was actually a good size. It's just that he acted like such a massive dick tonight—way, way bigger than the dick he actually has."

I laugh. "That's a fair assessment."

We continue walking. "It's not like the only thing I care about is size. It's not. I swear. Girth is just as important. And technique. And open-mindedness. He hated that I used a vibrator. Can you believe that?"

I make a choking sound, but Becca doesn't seem to notice. Christ. Just the thought of Becca using a vibrator on herself is enough to make my head explode. An image of her writhing in bed, face flushed, moaning and panting as she presses a vibrator between her legs sends a wave of heat to my dick. I swallow and force myself to look at the pavement below. I focus on the grainy texture, how it's more of a brown-gray color than a true gray—anything to keep my mind from wandering to that filthy place.

I clear my throat. "That's too bad he was so insecure."

"So very insecure," she mumbles before hiccupping.

We round the block, and the storefront of Sweet Cheeks comes into view. Becca stumbles, and I stop her.

"Hey, are you okay?" I ask her.

She wrinkles her brow like she can't believe I asked. "Of course I'm okay. I'm fantastic."

She marches ahead, then trips on a crack in the sidewalk. I reach out and catch her by the arm to keep her from falling.

"Yup. Fantastic, for sure." I spin her to face me. "I'm going to carry you the rest of the way, okay? It'll be easier."

Her face brightens instantly. "Yay! No one ever carries me! I love being carried."

I chuckle, then lean down and throw Becca over my shoulder.

"This is how sexy firefighters carry people out of burning buildings, isn't it?" she says.

"I'll take your word for it." Again I'm chuckling. When we arrived at the dive bar and she requested a shot of tequila to kick things off, I was worried she'd end up crying and even more upset than she was when we ran into him. But all she ended up doing was vent about Ben.

"I just...God, I can't believe I was ever with him. That I ever loved him. That I ever trusted him. That I ever lived with him and shared a life with such a lying, cheating, deceptive—oh! A lucky penny! Wait, stop!"

I halt and glance down at the ground. A tiny shiny copper circle winks up at me in the brightness of a nearby streetlight.

"It's face up! That means it's good luck! Here, put me down so I can grab it."

I do as she tells me. She crouches down and plucks the penny from the concrete, then tucks it into the side pocket of her shorts.

She holds her arms out. "Okay, I'm ready to be carried again, pretty please."

I grin down at her before hauling her over my shoulder again.

"You know, Gage, you could totally be a sexy firefighter."

"No, I couldn't. I don't have the proper training."

"Oh. Good point. Well, you could play one on TV."

She directs me to her apartment. I make it to the door that leads to her place upstairs, which sits to the left of the entrance of Sweet Cheeks. I set her down on her feet but support her with my arm. "I'm gonna need your keys to get in."

She fumbles with the zipper of her purse before getting it open and digging out her keys.

"Ta-da!" she sings as she holds them up to me.

Laughing, I take them from her and unlock the door. I guide her inside, shut the door behind me, and feel her tug on my hand. I twist around to see her smiling with her eyes closed, holding her arms out, like she's expecting a hug.

"Carry me please," she says in a sing-song voice.

I'm sure the grin on my face is goofy as hell. But I can't help it. Becca is ridiculously adorable when she's drunk.

I lean forward, crouch down, and throw her over my shoulder once more.

"Wee!" she says as I take the first flight of stairs.

"What floor are you?" I ask.

"Third. All the way at the end. Sorry."

I chuckle. "No worries. This is when I get to put all that weightlifting and cardio to practical use."

There's a snapping noise behind me. "I knew it! I knew you weightlifted."

As I make my way to the second flight of stairs, I feel her pat my ass.

"Squats, right?"

I laugh. "You guessed it."

"Seriously, you've got the perfect squat butt. Your butt could be in magazines. And damn, you're not even breaking a sweat while carrying me up these steps. Wowzers, Gage. Like, major wowzers."

I'm laughing so hard, I have to stop walking and grip the railing right before hitting the third floor. Hearing sweet Becca talk about my ass so matter-of-factly is the most precious and wholesome thing I've ever heard, and it's freaking hilarious given she'd never, ever talk about what my ass looks like when she's sober.

"Shoot, am I too heavy?" she says.

"No," I say through a laugh. "You're making me laugh so damn hard with all your talk about the perfect squat butt. I need to catch my breath."

"Oh." She giggles.

"One more flight of stairs. You ready?"

"I'm ready. Promise I won't talk about your butt anymore."

When I reach the third floor, I set her down. I unlock the door to her apartment and watch as she kicks off her shoes and drops her purse on the ground. I leave my sneakers next to hers, then follow her into the kitchen.

"I need a snack. Then bed."

She wobbles as she walks to the refrigerator, so I gently grab her hand and lead her to sit on a stool by her kitchen counter.

"Why don't you let me make you something?"

She blinks, her eyelids droopy with fatigue. "Mmm, yes, okay."

I fetch her a glass of water. "Drink this first."

She guzzles the water while I dig through the contents of her fridges.

"Just to warn you, I don't have anything fancy in there. Nothing that you could cook one of your famous gourmet meals with."

"No worries. I'll figure something out." It's slim pickings in Becca's fridge: loads of condiments but not much else. Just half a loaf of bread, butter, cheese, some celery, half a tomato, coffee creamer, and something in a Tupperware container that looks like it should have been thrown out days ago.

I twist around to check on her. "Grilled cheese?"

In a blink her eyes go from sleepy to wide and bright. She grins and nods.

Five minutes later I set a crispy and hot grilled cheese in front of her. Before I can even sit down with my own sandwich, she's taken two giant bites out of hers.

"Oh my gahhhh, Gage!" she says with her mouth full. "Best grilled cheese ever! Why have I never thought to add sliced tomatoes to my grilled cheese sandwiches before?"

"Now you know." I take a bite of my sandwich and swallow.

"This is the only way I want to eat grilled cheese now."

"With tomato?"

She quirks her eyebrow and shakes her head. "You making them for me."

There's a strange feeling in my chest. A fluttering sensation. I let myself imagine what it would be like to do this—to cook for Becca, to make her favorite grilled cheese sandwich after a long day of working at her ice cream shop, to cuddle with her on her couch while watching a movie together.

That fluttery feeling morphs into an ache. Fuck, I want that.

Becca hiccups, jerking me out of my little fantasy. I hop up and refill her glass and hand it to her. I take in just how tired she looks.

"Hey, do you have any aspirin?" I ask.

"Bathroom. Medicine cabinet," she murmurs.

I grab a couple of aspirin, quietly admiring how very Becca the décor is: there's a fuzzy, hot pink bathmat on the floor, and the shower curtain boasts a pastel floral design. It reminds me of the vibe and aesthetic of Sweet Cheeks: so pretty and cute and warm and welcoming.

I hand the aspirin to her. "You should take that now so you won't have a headache in the morning."

"Good idea."

She downs it with more water, then closes her eyes and falls into me. "So, so tired, Gage."

I help her up from her stool and prop her against me. "Let's get you to bed."

I walk her to her bedroom, which is decorated just as prettily as her bathroom: white plush comforter and pillows on the bed, gray wood dresser and nightstand, a pastel pink armchair in the corner with a paisley print decorative pillow.

She falls face-first into the bed and moans. "So comfy."

I'm about to wish her goodnight, but she flips on her back and fumbles with the zipper of her jean shorts. I turn to leave and give her privacy, but she stops me.

"Wait, Gage. Help. I'm too tired." Her arms flop to her sides, like she's given up completely on undressing herself.

A hard swallow moves through my throat. "Becca, I'm not sure if that's such a good idea."

Real talk: I'd be lying if I said I wouldn't like to see her undress given I'm ridiculously attracted to her. But I'd also feel like a creep.

She pins me with those doe-like eyes that are swollen with fatigue. "Please?"

I clear my throat. She's asking me for my help. And this wouldn't be the first time I've helped a friend undress when they were too drunk to do it themselves. Hell, I've helped most of my male friends and my own brother put on or take off their clothes when they've been shit-faced.

"Okay." I walk over to Becca. With shaky hands, I unzip her jean shorts. She shimmies her hips slightly as I start to slide them off. When I see that she's wearing hot pink lace panties, my eyes bulge out of my head. My gaze quickly darts to a random spot on her comforter, and I drop her shorts on the floor.

She leans up on her elbows, a satisfied smile on her face. "Now my bra."

I choke. "Um, Becca, I don't feel comfortable helping—"

She giggles. "I know. I can get this myself. Watch."

My eyes go wide as she reaches both arms behind her to unhook her bra over her top. She slides one hand under her shirt sleeve and pulls her bra strap off, then repeats that same movement with her other hand.

She pulls a hot pink bra out of her shirt sleeve and tosses it on the floor. "Pretty slick, huh?"

I blink, mesmerized by the sexy-as-hell way Becca just undressed herself in front of me while remaining mostly clothed.

"Yeah, actually."

Another giggle falls from her mouth. "Let's go to bed."

I nod quickly. "You're right, I should get going. Goodn—"

"What? No," she whines, leaning forward and catching my wrist in her hand. "You gotta stay and cuddle me."

I almost choke on my tongue. "You want me to cuddle you?"

She smiles and nods, her stare sleepy.

I rub the back of my neck. "Becca, I want to. Believe me, I want to. But you're dr—"

With a surprising amount of strength I didn't realize she had, she yanks me forward, and I fall onto her bed.

She pulls my arm around her waist and maneuvers so that I'm spooning her. "I'm drunk, but I still know what I want. And I wanna cuddle with you," she murmurs into her pillow.

I can feel her relax against me. It takes a few seconds for me to process the shock of what is happening, but when I do, I start to relax. I can't deny it—cuddling with Becca in bed feels really, really good. Closing my eyes, I savor the warmth of her body, how soft her skin feels against mine.

So damn soft.

"You should take those off," she says, patting my jeans. "It's way more comfortable to cuddle in your undies. I would know." She giggles.

I laugh. God, I adore her. I do what she says and slip out of my jeans, leaving me in just boxers and a T-shirt. After I wrap my arms back around her, it's not even a minute before her breathing turns deep and steady. She's asleep.

And something about that—something about how quickly she was able to relax with me—hits deep. Becca feels comfortable enough to invite me into her bed, to fall asleep pressed against me.

My heart rams against my ribcage. Fuck, holding her feels incredible.

It's not long before I start to feel tired. Before I know it, I'm fast asleep.

Chapter 18

Becca

When I wake up, I'm smiling. Eyes closed, I let out a soft chuckle. This doesn't happen often. I can't remember the last time I woke up with a grin on my face.

But it's probably because I feel so well-rested and cozy and warm. I hum softly into my pillow, pulling my comforter tighter around me.

I won't be able to fall back to sleep, but that doesn't stop me from keeping my eyes closed, relishing this cozy moment. I don't even have a headache despite how much I drank last night.

Last night.

My eyes fly open as I remember what happened.

Heading to that champagne bar with Gage...running into Ben and his new girlfriend...feeling hurt and angry at how he refused to admit how he wronged me...dragging Gage to the nearest dive bar so I could down enough alcohol to forget that jerkoff Ben...

Gage.

I go warm and fuzzy at the memory of him carrying me

home over his shoulder and how doting and caring he was as he cooked for me and made me drink water and aspirin to avoid that godawful hangover headache.

And then my stomach flips when I remember undressing in front of him and pulling him into bed with me.

I hear the soft sound of snoring behind me. I twist my head around and see Gage sleeping soundly next to me, a respectable few inches between us.

I turn slowly away, cupping my hand over my mouth. I press my eyes shut, but that grin pulls at my mouth once more.

Gage is in bed. With me.

Like a perfectly timed highlight reel, I think back to the moment we both hit my bed and how good his massive, muscled arms felt around me, how I sank into his firm body, how cuddling him felt so natural, so easy.

Yeah, I should probably feel embarrassed at how I acted last night. And I am, a little. When I get drunk and I'm around someone I like, I tend to get very touchy-feely. But drunk me managed to do something that sober me has wanted to do but didn't have the guts to do: get close to Gage.

I press my eyes shut as that telltale ache pulses between my legs. Crap. Hangover horn. I should have known it was coming.

Thankfully, due to the aspirin Gage had me take last night, I've been able to skip the hangover headache. But I'm not able to skip the horniness that follows me the morning after a night of heavy drinking.

I feel Gage stirring behind me. Slowly, I turn over to face him right as he opens his eyes. He blinks a few times, his rich brown eyes swollen from sleep. His hair is mussed, and the scruff along his jawline somehow looks even sexier in the morning.

The corner of his mouth hooks up. "Morning."

A giddy feeling courses through me at hearing just how low and gravelly his morning voice is. "Good morning. Thank you for taking care of me last night."

He rolls to his left side, facing me. We're not even a foot apart now.

"My pleasure."

"Was it?" I bite my lip. "I was pretty drunk, and I'm remembering what a handful I was."

His half-smile turns into a grin. "It was absolutely my pleasure to take care of you, Becca."

His words combined with that pointed look in his eyes have my stomach doing somersaults.

"I'm sorry I made you sleep in my bed with me." I bite my lip. "In addition to sending rambling DMs, I, um, get really affectionate and handsy when I'm drunk. I hope I didn't make you feel like you had to stay in bed with me." This is the thing I'm most embarrassed—and most nervous —about. As much as I loved falling asleep cuddled with Gage, I need to see how he feels the morning after it happened.

"I'm not sorry." I watch his Adam's apple bob as he swallows. "You don't have to worry, Becca. I liked cuddling you. I liked sleeping in your bed with you. A lot."

There's a flash behind his eyes that makes the ache between my legs throb even harder.

I bite back the Cheshire grin splitting my face. "You're an excellent cuddler, by the way. Ten out of ten cuddling. I fell right to sleep."

A low chuckle falls from his beautifully thick lips. "I remember. You were out like a light."

I tap my fingers against the fabric separating us. Gage must notice me eyeing the space between us because then he asks me, "Do you want to cuddle again?"

I'm grinning and nodding as I scoot toward him, settling against his chest. His arms wrap around me, and I'm instantly warm.

I hum against him, closing my eyes, relaxing fully against the sexiest, most comfortable human body pillow.

"Um, Becca?"

"Yeah?" I say through a breath.

"Do you, uh, realize that you're grinding against my leg?"

My eyes fly open, and I instantly stop moving. I didn't even realize...

I bury my face into his chest and groan-laugh. "I'm sorry. I, uh, should probably explain that."

Gage rests his head on top of mine. "It's nothing to be ashamed of."

"I just, um okay, so here's the thing. Sometimes, the morning after I drink, I can get pretty, um, turned on."

"Hangover horn," he says without missing a beat.

"Exactly."

"That's okay. Like I said, it's nothing to be embarrassed about."

I can tell he's smiling as he says it. I relax against him even more. When I lean back and look up at Gage, I notice his gaze has gone full-on fiery, like he's turned on by what I've said. Like he can feel the heat burning inside of me and is burning up too.

Like he wants me just as much as I want him.

And that's what gives me the nerve to do what I do.

I press a kiss to his throat. "Gage." I'm breathless when I say his name. "Will you fuck me?"

167

A garbled grunting noise rips from his throat. I kiss his rough, stubbled skin once more, savoring the slow movement as a hard swallow glides down his throat.

He shifts to look down at me. "Becca, you have no idea just how badly I want to fuck you. But I want to make sure we both know what we're getting into."

I glide my hand down his chest, anxious to find out what it feels like to do this same movement against his bare skin.

"You said before that you weren't ready for anything romantic," Gage says with his eyes closed, like he's summoning the power to talk while I touch him. "You said your breakup was too recent..."

"I did say that." I press a kiss to his chest. "But I feel differently now. Seeing Ben last night made me realize how done I am with him. I'm done letting my past with him dictate what I choose to do with my life now."

His eyes open, and he looks down at me.

"I like you, Gage. I'm so attracted to you, it's nuts. And I want you. Right now."

I slip my hand underneath his shirt. My eyes nearly roll to the back of my head as I feel the heat of his soft skin and the firmness underneath.

His mouth curves up, and he runs his tongue along his bottom lip. "I've been wanting this—wanting *you* for so long, Becca. Pretty much ever since I met you."

I lean up and dust a kiss to his lips. Something wild flashes in his eyes. It's like the touch of my lips sets him off. In a split second, his hand falls to my waist, and he pulls me against him so I'm flush with his body. And then he kisses me, his tongue diving into my mouth like he's dying and the only way to stay alive is to kiss me over and over and over.

My hands fly to his hair. I tug the thick, black-brown

strands like I'm holding on for dear life as our tongues tease and lick and tangle.

We pick up right where we left off during our first kiss. This time, there are no tentative, slow touches. Our tongues go full-on filthy.

"Grind on me again," Gage growls against my mouth. "I want you to work yourself all over me."

I moan into his mouth as I hook my leg over his hip so that my crotch is pressed against his thigh. Against my other leg, I feel that unmistakable hardness. He's rock hard. My mouth waters in anticipation of seeing, tasting, and feeling that part of him very, very soon.

I do what he tells me—what I've been aching to do for so long. I move back and forth against his thick, muscled leg, the ache inside of me deepening despite the fabric barrier of my panties and his boxers.

Gage cradles my face with his hand as he kisses me so hard, I can barely breathe. He digs his fingers into my hips as I move faster and harder against him.

"Do you know how many times I've fantasized about you? About you doing this? You rubbing your perfect pussy against me, making yourself come..."

I nip at his bottom lip, and he growls. "Probably as many times as I have."

His grin turns devilish as he leads me to his mouth once more. When his grip slides from my hip to my butt, I groan in approval.

"You're gonna come so hard on me, Becca. And then I'm gonna make you come even harder with my mouth. And then even harder on my dick."

I gasp as a sizzling wave of pleasure swells inside of me. Just like the first time we did this together, Gage's words get me insanely hot. I can feel the intensity build and build to an inevitable peak. I work myself faster and harder against his leg, burying my face in his shoulder as I groan and whimper. Between my legs, the pleasure throbs hot. My clit is pulsing so hard as I sprint toward climax, I can barely take it.

I turn feral, biting the meaty part of Gage's shoulder. He growls, then laughs.

"Bite as hard as you need to. Use me. Leave your mark on me. I fucking love feeling you get rough with me."

His words are like a flame dropped into a vat of fireworks. My orgasm takes hold, and I explode. I writhe and shake against Gage, muffling my screams against his shoulder.

He licks and kisses and lightly bites the side of my neck while I come. My entire body is tingling and throbbing at once. The pleasure is too much. Waves of ecstasy crash through me, leaving me shuddering against Gage.

When I loosen around him, he leans back, his hands still holding me by the waist.

A satisfied smile pulls at his lips. "Good?"

"So good."

In one smooth movement, he rips his shirt off before sliding me on my back and hovering over me. When he kisses each of my breasts over my T-shirt, I shiver.

"H-how are you so good? You're making me go wild, and you're not even touching my skin."

A smug grin is his answer. He slowly pulls my shirt over my head, lowers his head to each of my breasts, and repeats the slow teasing kisses from seconds ago. I make a hissing noise. It feels so freaking good.

Gage takes his time, his tongue moving slowly, softly, firmly. As soon as he starts to kiss down my stomach, all the muscles in my torso tense in anticipation of what he's about to do. His hot, wet breath sheets across my inner thighs and between my legs. Gage hasn't even touched me there yet, and already I'm vibrating with pleasure, with the need to feel his tongue on me.

He presses the softest kiss inside my left thigh, then my right thigh. My mouth falls open.

"Gage..." His name falls from my mouth in a desperate, ragged whisper.

"Do you like that? My lips on your thighs?"

I nod and whine instead of answering. I close my eyes, savoring the teasing way he dusts those whisper-soft kisses on my skin.

"Where's your vibrator?"

My eyes fly open at his words. I lean up on my elbows and look at him. "What?"

He lifts his head from between my legs, and that devilish half-smile reappears. "Your vibrator. I wanna use it on you. Would that be okay?"

My mouth is open, but I'm stammering. I'm physically unable to formulate words. I need a second to process, to collect myself, because just the thought of Gage using my vibrator on me is almost too much. My brain feels like it's buzzing.

"Um, that definitely would be okay. That would be more than okay. That would be freaking fantastic."

A light chuckle falls from Gage's mouth. There's adoration in his gaze as he studies me. He leans up and crawls over me, kissing the tip of my nose. "You are fucking adorable. Now where's your vibrator?"

There's a twitch between my legs at the firmness in his tone and the hungry look in his eyes.

"My nightstand. Top drawer."

He reaches over and fishes it out. He settles on his knees

between my legs, his gaze scanning the bright purple silicone. "The famous Rabbit model, huh?"

I bite my lip and nod. "It's, um, my favorite. Of the ones I've tried."

His eyebrows tick up, and he shifts slightly, pulling at the elastic waistband of his boxers. "What others have you tried?"

"Um, well, I had a vibrating wand for a while. That was fun. The bullet vibe I had was nice too, but not my favorite. Not a ton of power. And it broke soon after I ordered it. This one though..." My heart thuds as I look at my sex toy in Gage's hand. "That's my favorite by a long shot."

Gage's jaw is bulging as he looks between me and my vibrator, like he's biting down hard. He clears his throat.

"You okay?" I ask.

"Hearing you talk about the different sex toys you've had and imagining you using them on yourself is hot as fuck, Becca. I'm trying my hardest not to come in my pants like an amateur."

His admission has me soaring. Just knowing that someone as sexy and confident as Gage finds me so hot that he's in danger of coming too soon is the confidence boost of a lifetime.

I lean up and kiss him. "I'm dying for you to use my vibrator on me. Will you make me come hard?"

I've never seen Gage's eyes go that wide. Another wave of confidence bursts through me. I've never felt comfortable enough to speak so bluntly about my pleasure with anyone I've been with before. But with Gage, it's different. He makes me feel secure in a way I've never felt before. I can be completely myself around him, and not only is he cool with it, but he also thinks it's insanely hot.

He wraps his free hand around my thigh and yanks me

farther down the bed. The sudden movement has me flat on my back again.

"So fucking hard," he rasps.

He leans his face to the crotch of my panties and runs his tongue roughly up and down my slit. I gasp at the ceiling, in awe of how good his tongue feels when he hasn't even made contact with my skin yet.

That ache inside of me amps up. He licks again and again. My clit throbs harder and harder. I'm gasping and shaking already.

He sits up and slides my panties down my legs before holding my vibrator up to me. "Get this wet for me."

That throb between my legs turns into a throttle. Good thing I'm lying down, because a line like that would have me collapsing, it is beyond sexy. My toes start to curl as the wave of pleasure inside of me kicks up. I take a breath to steady myself. If Gage's growled command can send me to the edge of climax, I need to prepare myself. This is going to be an insane orgasm.

I lean up and lick along the shaft of the vibrator. Gage groans, and I smile. A second later he slides it inside of me. For a second he holds it there, and I relish that feeling of being filled up. He turns it on, and I hear that familiar buzz. I close my eyes, humming as it throbs and pulses inside of me. A second later, his silk tongue laps at my clit.

I fall back down on the bed and moan. It feels like a lightning bolt of pleasure is striking between my legs.

"Oh my...oh my...oh my..." I can't even finish my sentence before the pleasure and the sensation amp up. Gage must have adjusted the vibrator, because in addition to his tongue, I feel those glorious rabbit ears flick against my clit.

His tongue moves in perfect tandem with the vibrator. I

didn't think anything could feel better than Gage's tongue, but I was wrong. Paired with my vibrator, the pleasure is insane. Mind-bending. Leg-shaking. Earth-shattering.

The intensity is unlike anything I've felt before. Like pleasure but times one thousand. Like being overstimulated, but in the most glorious way possible.

My jaw falls open as I gasp for breath. "Gage..."

He hums against my clit, and one of my calf muscles spasms. Holy crap. That...that's even better. I fist the bedsheets with both hands as that lightning bolt strikes again and again. Heat and pleasure collide between my legs. I silently order myself to take slow, deep breaths. This is pure ecstasy, and I want it to last as long as possible.

Somehow the pleasure keeps amplifying. It builds higher and hotter. The muscles in my thighs and calves twitch and shake uncontrollably. I'm a woman possessed by the pleasure given to me by Gage's tongue and my vibrator.

"Gage, please...I'm not gonna last...It feels so, so good..."

Somehow, even though I knew it was coming, my orgasm sneaks up on me. It hits, and it absolutely rattles me. It is beyond powerful. Actually, powerful isn't even the right word. More like all-consuming and overpowering. Pleasure floods me. I can feel this orgasm in every muscle and bone in my body. I've never, ever felt anything this strong, this *good*.

I scream Gage's name so loud my throat aches. When he finally turns off the vibrator and pulls his mouth away, I stop thrashing. All I see are stars. My hearing is fuzzy.

After blinking a dozen times, I finally make out Gage's smug smile. He licks his lips, devouring me with that fiery gaze of his.

I try to speak, but all that comes out is garbled nonsense.

Wow. Gage has given me an orgasm so powerful that I can't even form words.

He touches my thighs, but I hold up a hand. Finally the words come out. "Wait. Just...wait."

His eyes go wide. "Are you okay?"

I nod. "More than okay." I close my eyes and laugh as I roll my head back. "I just need a minute. You just blew my mind. Like...whoa..."

Gage's low rumble of a laugh hits my ears. I open my eyes. "I'm serious. I've never had a vibrator used on me during oral and...um...well..."

"It was okay then?"

I lightly shove his shoulder. "It was mind-bendingly incredible."

He lowers his face to the inside of my thigh and presses a soft kiss to my skin. "It's a shame no other guy has tried that with you. It's one of my favorite things to do."

I reach down and run my hands through his thick, wavy, ink-black hair. "Well, now it's one of my favorites too."

He smirks at me, that devilish gleam in his eyes. "Good. But I'm not done with you yet."

Chapter 19

Gage

As I catch my breath, I take in the scene in front of me: Becca splayed out naked on her bed, chest heaving, her skin flushed and dotted with sweat, her beautiful blue eyes dilated and dazed from the orgasm I've just given her.

My dick throbs in my boxers. I run my tongue along my teeth, savoring her sweet flavor as it lingers in my mouth.

Holy fuck.

I've never seen a hotter, more stunning sight.

This woman.

I've had plenty of incredible sex in my life, but being with Becca is something else entirely. There's something so addictive about her. Maybe it's that sweet girl nature of hers. Maybe it's knowing that when I kiss her and touch her, this good girl completely unravels. Maybe it's hearing her curse while I've got my face buried between her thighs because she's too aroused to think straight. That's one of the sexiest things I've ever witnessed. Maybe it's that every time I taste her, my mouth waters.

My heart throbs in my chest and not just from all the

foreplay we've been engaging in. Yeah, I'm hot for Becca, but this feeling is so much more than physical attraction.

It's the fact that this absolute angel is into me and wants me just as much as I want her.

It's the fact that I get to see sweetheart Becca shed her inhibitions and allow herself to be as dirty as she wants to be in bed.

It's the fact that she makes me feel happy in a way that I haven't felt in a long time.

I've gotten the pleasure of seeing Becca come three times, and I feel like the luckiest motherfucker on the planet. But that's not enough though. Right now, I want to blow her mind.

I slide off my boxers and reach down to the floor for my jeans. I fish out my wallet from my pocket and pull out a condom.

Those gorgeous blue eyes sparkle. Her grin grows wide.

"See something you like?" I tease.

"Oh yeah. You're really, really big. And thick."

"Am I?"

She nods quickly. "That's, like, the perfect combination."

I chuckle, letting myself relish the ego boost from her compliment. "I guess we'll find out."

Smiling, I start to rip open the condom wrapper with my teeth, but Becca reaches up to stop. "Wait."

I immediately still. "What's wrong?"

"Nothing. I just..." She licks her lips and directs her gaze to my cock. "I want to taste you first."

I have to take a second to steady myself. Just the thought of Becca's sweet mouth and tongue working me over sounds like heaven. But it can't happen.

"Believe me, I want that. So bad," I tell her. "But I won't

last long if you do that. And I need to be inside of you. I need to make you come again."

She lets out a shuddery breath, and her smile takes on a smug edge, like she's just now realizing how much power she holds over me when I'm around her.

"Just one taste? Please?" she asks, her tone and smile coy.

My head falls back as I groan. There's not a chance in hell that I'll be able to say no to her.

"Fuck yes," I growl. She quickly sits up, her perfect little tits bouncing with the movement. My dick aches even more.

She leans down and glides that soft, wet tongue up and down my shaft. Heat and pleasure rocket from my balls to my dick. I have to bite down as hard as I can to keep from howling, she feels so fucking good.

When she starts to work her mouth up and down my length again, I thread my fingers through her hair and stop her.

"Becca. Your tongue...that feels...I won't last," I grunt.

She pulls away, her smile on the edge of mischievous. "I only wanted a taste."

My legs are twitching as she falls back on the bed. A fire ignites inside of me, and I grab her by the thighs and move her so she's flush with my body. I slide on the condom and line myself up with her perfect pussy, which is still wet.

I slide in and pause, savoring just how fucking good she feels.

Becca's gaze turns dazed once more. Her eyes roll to the back of her head, and her legs start to shake. "Oh my god," she whispers. "Gage, you feel so, so good."

"How does this feel?" I grunt as I lean forward, deepening the angle between us and slowly glide in and out of her.

She doesn't speak right away; all she does is gasp. After a few minutes I grab her vibrator, turn it on, and hold it against her clit. Her eyes fly open, and her jaw drops. She fists the bedsheets until her knuckles turn white.

"Tell me how this feels."

She starts to shake her head. "This isn't possible."

"What isn't?"

Her stare turns unfocused as she gazes up at the ceiling. She looks like she's hypnotized.

"This doesn't happen." Her chest heaves. "I-I don't come this much, this fast."

I grin down at her and pick up my speed. "How close are you?"

She inhales sharply and reaches a hand to my arm. When she digs her fingers into my bicep, a growl rips from my throat. Seeing and feeling Becca start to unravel around me is the biggest turn-on.

That ache in my cock intensifies. Heat spreads through my body. I steady my breathing and flex the muscles in my thighs to keep from coming. Becca needs to come first before I do.

"Really close," she sobs.

I kick up the speed of her vibrator and watch as that familiar panicked look flashes through her eyes. I feel her flex around me as she starts to come. I bite down so hard, the base of my skull starts to ache. But that's exactly what I want. The flash of pain is enough to hold off my orgasm just a little bit longer...

When Becca breaks a few seconds later, it's so fucking beautiful. Her entire body thrashes, and she's screaming so loud, my ears are ringing. When I realize she's screaming my name, something in my chest rattles. She digs her nails so hard into my skin that I'm certain she's going to leave scrapes and bruises. And that turns me on even more. I'm driving this angel wild and rabid with pleasure.

The ache inside of me intensifies, and it's not long before I lose it too. With my free hand gripping her hip, I thrust hard and fast until I blow. For several seconds, all I can do is kneel there and catch my breath. When I finally pull out and lean back on my heels, I'm dizzy. Fuck, that was amazing.

I take a few seconds to steady myself before ripping off the condom and tossing it into the nearby trash can. She's still clutching my arm; I'm still clutching her hip. I turn off the vibrator and toss it to the side.

For a while we stay in that position: me hovering over her on my hands and knees, her legs wrapped around my waist and her hand gripping my arm.

We stare at each other, dazed and gasping for air.

"That was..."

"You are..."

We both laugh. She reaches up and pulls me to lie on top of her. We kiss, and I roll over next to her.

"Wow... just...wow..." she muses as she cuddles into my chest.

"You took the words right out of my mouth," I say. "I'm a ruined man because of you."

She giggles and traces her fingers along my chest. The light touch sends tingles through me.

"You've done the same to me," she says. "We're definitely going to need to do that again. And again. And again."

I laugh and start to kiss down her neck. "I think I can manage that."

* * *

"Ice cream for breakfast? Are you kidding?" I shake my head at Becca, but I'm also grinning like a goofball.

She licks caramel ice cream off her spoon, a naughty smile on her face. "I never kid about ice cream. It's my livelihood. And my passion." She winks at me.

It's been a week since Becca and I first slept together, and we haven't been able to keep our hands off each other since. During the day, we work on our own, then every night I end up at her ice cream shop, and we film TikToks for Sweet Cheeks. And every single night we've ended up at her place, doing filthy things in her bed.

This morning we're at my place though because last night I felt bad about always crashing at hers. When I mentioned wanting to cook a late dinner for her at my apartment and having her stay over, she looked like I was offering the moon to her.

I glance at her sitting at my kitchen island, wearing one of my T-shirts and a pair of my boxers. My shirt hangs off her shoulder since it's about three sizes too big for her, and holy shit, is it cute.

I could definitely get used to this—waking up next to Becca every morning, seeing her wear my clothes as pajamas, teasing each other over breakfast...

My heart feels like it's swelling in my chest. And that's when I realize just how long it's been since I've had *that* feeling—the feeling of wanting to be with someone all day, every day. Of wanting to be in a relationship. Of wanting no one else but them.

Easy, tiger. She's fresh off a breakup and made it clear that she doesn't want anything serious right now, just a good time. Don't ruin a good thing by letting yourself catch feelings and get too serious too fast.

I focus on the moment, on having a fun and carefree morning with Becca.

"All that sugar first thing in the morning is too much for me," I tease.

"Aww, you're too healthy for your own good, Mr. Green Smoothie."

I laugh as I finish blending my usual breakfast, a shake made of kale, banana, Greek yogurt, frozen berries, oat milk, and vegan protein powder.

I down half the drink in a few gulps. "I gotta offset all those decadent meals I cook and all the ice cream I've been indulging in lately."

Becca licks a dollop of the ice cream she brought over last night from her spoon. Her blue eyes are on me as she teases the head of the spoon with her tongue. My dick aches as I watch her work her tongue just like she did on me last night...and earlier this morning.

She swallows, then smiles at me. "Come on. You know you want a taste."

I round the corner of the kitchen island and walk up to her. I plant one hand on her waist and cup the other over her cheek, then kiss her until she's moaning and breathless.

We break apart, and I lick my lips, savoring the mix of flavors on my tongue: the sweetness from the strawberry ice cream and the heavenly taste of Becca's tongue and lips.

"Delicious," I hum as I lick and nip at her bottom lip.

Becca laughs against my mouth. "Me or the ice cream?"

"You. Always you."

Her cheeks and chest blush the same shade of pink as her strawberry ice cream. It's hot as hell seeing how much of her body flushes when she gets turned on.

She reaches down and palms the bulge in my boxers.

She quirks an eyebrow. "I'm craving something different now."

"Is that so?"

She bites her lip and nods. A split second later, I haul her to sit on the edge of the counter and step between her thighs. She wraps her legs around me, kissing me as she claws at my shirt.

I kiss the hinge of her jaw, relishing how she shivers and moans softly.

"I changed my mind. I'd rather have you for breakfast," she says, her voice breathy as I kiss down the side of her neck.

I lightly nip at her collarbone. My dick is getting so hard, it hurts. Hearing Becca go from sweet to talking dirty is the biggest turn-on. I fucking love it when a good girl gets filthy—and I love it even more when I'm the reason for it. I'm the one who makes her comfortable enough to shed her shell a bit and give in to all those naughty thoughts and feelings.

She yanks my shirt over my head and moves to kiss my chest. I close my eyes and groan. And then my phone blares, jolting us both.

Becca almost loses her balance on the kitchen island counter, but I hold her in place.

I look over at my phone and see it's my cousin calling. Cupping her face with both my hands, I press a kiss to her lips.

"Ignore that," I say.

The ringing ends, but then it starts back up a second later.

I lean my head back and groan. "I'm going to kill my cousin."

Becca chuckles. "You should answer it."

I grab my phone and pick up the call. "What?"

Millie scoffs. "Well, hello to you too, sunshine. What a lovely way to greet your cousin."

"I'm in the middle of something, and you're interrupting."

"Ah okay. In all seriousness, I'm sorry for bugging you. But I need your help."

"What's wrong? Is everything okay?"

"Not really." Millie lets out a long exhale, like she always does when she's frustrated and upset. "My mom, your mom, and pretty much all of our aunties are pissed that I'm not having a traditional baby shower. They're upset that I want to go to Thunder From Down Under and are refusing to come."

"Uh, isn't that a good thing? Do you honestly want to get a lap dance with Auntie Patty looking on?"

Millie makes a disgusted sound. "Of course not. But I don't want half of our family to be mad at me." Another heavy sigh. "I just wanted to do something for me, you know? Something that would be fun for me. My mom and our aunties practically planned my and Peter's wedding and all the events leading up. I wanted one thing that was mine."

I soften at the sound of Millie's dejected tone. As loving and supportive as our family is, Millie is right in that they tend to meddle in our lives. I remember how stressed she was dealing with everyone giving her their opinions when it came to her bridal shower, engagement party, and wedding.

"You're right. You deserve to celebrate your baby shower exactly how you want. I'll make sure of it."

"You're the best, Gage. Thank you. I just think we need to plan something else, maybe the weekend after Thunder From Down Under, to appease the family."

"I think that's a good idea." I tug a hand through my hair and lean against the kitchen island.

"Something proper and more traditional. With fewer naked dudes."

I laugh. "What, like a tea party? Is that wholesome enough?"

Millie laughs. "Something like that yeah."

"Or wait, how about an etiquette class?" I joke. "Or an ice cream social."

Becca pauses from sipping her coffee and looks over at me. "What's going on?"

I tell Millie to hold on and explain the situation to Becca.

She smiles. "Let's do it."

"Do what?"

"An ice cream social baby shower."

"Really?"

"Yeah. I'd love to do it. We can even have it at Sweet Cheeks and decorate with flowers so it looks like a proper shower. I'll set up an ice cream bar with different toppings." She's smiling as she speaks, like she's excited at the idea. "I mean, if that's okay with your cousin. I don't want to step on anyone's toes or anything like that." She scrunches her lips like she's unsure.

I lean down and kiss her. "You're incredible, you know that?"

She blushes and shakes her head. "Just trying to help, like you helped me with Sweet Cheeks. I wouldn't have the social media following that I currently do without your help, Gage."

Just this morning Sweet Cheeks hit four hundred thousand followers. I woke up to Becca squealing in bed and showing me the follower count on her phone. We promptly celebrated with morning sex.

"You helped save my business. Without you, I wouldn't have a line out of my shop every morning that's three blocks long, I wouldn't be busy from open to close, I wouldn't be shipping ice cream all over the country," she says. "I want to do this for you and your family. It would mean so much to me."

I press a soft kiss to her lips. "Let me run it by Millie, but I'm certain she's going to love it."

I don't even finish before Millie blurts yes.

"Oh my god, are you serious? Gage, that would be freaking amazing! Tell Becca thank you for me. I'll tell her in her person, of course, but please relay to her just how much this means. Seriously, she is so generous for offering to do this. And hey, can I take home some pints after the shower? I'll pay for them of course."

"Of course you can."

"You have to bring her to Thunder From Down Under, okay? If she's going to do all that work for my shower, she deserves to come out and have a good time with us."

"I'll be sure to invite her."

"Cuz, I seriously owe you and Becca! You're the best!"

We say goodbye and hang up. I turn back to Becca. "Millie loves the idea."

Becca claps her hands and grins wide. "Yay!"

"She also wants to invite you to her Thunder From Down Under baby shower."

"Really?" Becca's eyes go wide before a shy smile pulls at her lips. "I mean, I don't want to impose."

"You're not imposing. She wants you to come." I wrap my arms around her. "I want you to come too. If you want to. And if the idea of watching a bunch of dudes strip off their clothes for the most outrageous baby shower ever doesn't turn you off completely."

She chuckles. "No, I'm definitely into it. It's just...Your family will be at Sweet Cheeks for your cousin's shower, right?"

I try to decipher the uncertain look in her eyes. "Yeah, my brother, all my cousins, and aunts and uncles will be."

"I'll be meeting them. And well, I guess I'm not sure how you want to...or if you want to..."

She closes her eyes and shakes her head. She frowns up at me. "Sorry, I'm not making a whole lot of sense."

I kiss the wrinkle between her eyebrows. It disappears instantly. She smiles up at me.

"Are you nervous about meeting my family?" I ask.

"It's not just that. It's..." She hesitates for a second. "I love where you and I are at right now, just, um, enjoying ourselves, no pressure and all that. And I know I said I wasn't ready for anything serious...but meeting family is kind of a serious thing to do..."

Dread pools in my stomach. Becca is getting cold feet about us at the thought of meeting my entire family. Damn it, why didn't I think of this?

I try to smile at her, but I can feel the tension in my face. "I can just tell them we're friends, Becca. It's no big deal."

"Oh. Okay."

That wrinkle in her brow is back.

"What's the matter?"

She looks at me, her gaze steady, almost like she's gearing up to tell me something important. "I thought that's what I wanted, to just be friends. But the moment you said it, it didn't feel right."

My stomach twists. I'm not sure where this is going. "What feels right to you?"

She opens her mouth, then quickly closes it. She flashes a tight smile. "Never mind. I don't know what I'm babbling about. I'm not making much sense."

She starts to turn away, but I catch her hand in mine. "Hey," I say softly. "Talk to me."

When she doesn't say anything right away, I gently squeeze her hand. "Becca, you can tell me anything. I mean it. Whatever's on your mind, I want to hear it. I promise I won't get upset."

She hesitates before taking a breath. "This is probably going to sound insane given that we've only known each other not even two months. I know we went into this with no expectations, but I really like you, Gage. And I...I want to be more than friends with you."

I grin wide. "I feel the same way. And I want that too."

Becca lets out a breath and flashes a relieved smile. "Really?"

I cup her face in my hands. "Really."

"So, um, how do you want to introduce me to your family?"

"As my girlfriend." I don't even blink when I say it. Yeah, things are moving quickly between us, but I don't care. I've never been the kind of person who worries about doing things too quickly or too late when it comes to dating and relationships. If something feels right, I go with it. And being with Becca and calling her my girlfriend feels right.

Her eyes light up as she slinks her arms around my neck. "I love the sound of that."

She leads me in a kiss that leaves me dizzy. When she pulls away and kisses down my bare chest, I have to grip both hands on the edge of the counter to keep upright. My skin is on fire as she works her mouth lower and lower.

"That means you're my boyfriend," she growls softly as she tugs at the waistband of my boxers.

A second later they're at my ankles. She licks me from base to tip, and my knees buckle at the surge of pleasure that rockets through me.

She looks up at me, her eyes bright and teasing. I watch through half-lidded eyes as my girlfriend takes me in her mouth, working me over until I'm shuddering and on the brink of collapsing. I thread my fingers through her hair, in awe of how this living angel can be so filthy with her mouth. With her hand on the base of my dick, she pumps faster and faster, swirling her tongue over the head of my cock until I'm seeing stars.

I spill into her mouth with a roar. As I pant, I catch a glimpse of her smiling up at me. She licks her lips, stands back up, and traces her finger along my jaw. "So what's the plan for the rest of the day?"

I laugh at her teasing tone. And then I lean down and chuck her over my shoulder. She squeals and slaps my ass as I march us back to my bedroom.

I palm her ass cheek and squeeze. "Let me show you what I have in mind."

Chapter 20

Becca

"I can't believe I'm meeting your family at a strip club." I grip Gage's hand tightly as we walk through downtown Denver.

He aims a teasing frown at me. "Hey, now. It's called a male revue."

"Right. That's what I meant."

He squeezes my hand. "Don't be nervous. It'll just be my brother and my cousins tonight. They're the fun ones in the family."

He leads me as we weave through a crowded patch of sidewalk. We turn right at the end of the block and stop at a two-story shiny black building. At the top is a fluorescent sign with the words "Club Onyx."

"I've never heard of this place," I say.

"It's new—and the only nightclub that was open to hosting a baby shower when I was researching places for Millie."

I turn to face Gage. "This is such a sweet thing you did, planning something so special for your cousin, especially when the rest of your family is upset about it."

He shrugs like it's no big deal. "I love my family, but our older relatives can be pretty old-fashioned at times. My cousin has compromised enough for them."

He tells me how she and her husband wanted to elope but agreed to have a big traditional wedding to appease their families.

"She deserves to do exactly what she wants today."

I go gooey at how supportive Gage is. At first glance, he comes off like a broody bad boy with his naughty TikTok videos and sexy scowls. But that's just his social media image. He's really an absolute sweetheart.

"Let me text my brother to see how far away they are." He pulls out his phone.

Just then a guy I recognize from the framed photo in his apartment rounds the corner toward us. He smirks when he sees Gage staring down at his phone, then runs up and jumps on him.

"What the—"

"Surprise noogie!" his older brother shouts as he ruffles Gage's hair.

Gage groans and shoves him off. His brother bursts out laughing.

"You're thirty-two years old," Gage says with a frown. "You realize that, right?"

"Aww come on. Are you ever gonna lighten up?"

"Never."

His brother laughs and smacks him on the back. A slight smile pulls at Gage's lips. He shakes his head before looking at me. "This is my brother, Tyler."

Tyler leans forward and flashes a dazzling smile at me while sticking out his hand.

"I'm Becca. It's so nice to meet you."

"She's my girlfriend," Gage says. My stomach flips. That word sounds so weird and wonderful.

Tyler pulls me into a hug. "My siblings' significant others always get hugs."

I laugh as I hug him back.

"Where's everyone else?" Gage asks.

"They hit traffic on the way." Tyler looks down the block. "Here they come."

A dark-haired guy and a red-headed guy who look like they're in their late twenties wave at us. There's a petite woman with dark hair and an adorably large baby bump walking behind them in a hot pink dress. Beside her is a tall woman with long, wavy black hair wearing a flowy floral romper.

"Holy shit," Tyler mutters.

"No way," Gage says.

It's not till the tall woman walks closer that I recognize her. It's Gage and Tyler's little sister Maya.

She runs up to hug them both. I step aside to let the three siblings have a moment together.

"What the hell? I didn't know you were coming." Tyler beams as he hugs his sister tight.

"Yeah, you said you were busy with work in LA." Gage lifts Maya off the ground with his hug.

"I wanted to surprise you guys." She beams and glances back at Millie.

Millie shakes her head. "I had no idea she was coming either. When I answered the door this afternoon and saw her, I burst into tears."

Maya steps over to her cousin and pulls her in a side hug. Millie reaches both hands around her cousin. "I'm just so happy you're here." She looks at me and beams. "And you too! You must be Becca."

Gage steps over and introduces me to everyone as his girlfriend. Everyone hugs me, and for a minute afterward, we stand together and chat pleasantries. Millie mentions a couple of her friends are joining and are in the middle of finding parking.

Gage looks over at Millie and pulls a hot pink square of shiny fabric from his back pocket. He shakes it out, revealing a sash that says, "Hot Mama-To-Be." Millie squeals and grabs it from him. Maya and Austin help her put it on.

"Millie, I think I speak for all of us when I say that this is the weirdest baby shower ever," Gage says. Everyone laughs. "But that's why we love you. You're an amazing person and are going to be an incredible mom. You deserve all the joy and happiness in the world. And we can't wait until that little baby is here so we can spoil the hell out of them."

Millie flashes a shaky smile. Her bright brown eyes are teary, and she fans her face with both hands.

She blinks quickly. "I love you, Gage. You're the greatest. You all are." She spins around to everyone. "Thank you for being such good sports and celebrating my unborn baby in such a ridiculous way."

We all laugh. Gage leads us inside. It's a typical dimly lit nightclub space with dance music booming from the speaker system. The walls and floors are dark with metallic touches. At the far end of the open space is a stage.

He points us to an elevated seating area off to the side of the stage. The words "Hot Mama" are spelled in gold balloons along the seats.

Millie squeals and takes a photo with her phone.

I look over at Gage, who's smiling as he watches his cousin. There's that warm feeling in my chest again. I'm completely in awe of this guy. Not only is he ridiculously sexy, but he's an absolute sweetheart. Seeing him plan such a thoughtful party for his cousin makes me weak in the knees. A hot, sweet, kind, and thoughtful man who's incredible in bed. I've hit the jackpot.

A tall shirtless guy with the most ripped torso I've ever seen waltzes up to Millie and introduces himself as the server. He sets down a tray of champagne flutes at the table.

"Congratulations to the beautiful mom-to-be." He grabs Millie's hand and kisses it. She blushes. "I'll be your server tonight. Please enjoy some sparkling grape juice to kick things off."

Gage hands the guy cash and thanks him. Then he pulls out two fat stacks of singles from both pockets and hands out cash to everyone. "I'm sure you all brought cash to tip, but just in case, here's extra."

We all sit down and sip our drinks. Gage, Tyler, Austin, and Declan want something harder to drink, so they head to the bar. Millie and Maya chat with me while they're gone.

"I'm so happy you came," Millie says as she grabs my hand. "You must think we're such a weird family, having a baby shower at a strip club."

"The Grant-Calzado clan are a pack of stone-cold weirdos," Maya says. "We should have warned you."

I chuckle and shake my head. "Not at all. I think it's so cool how you're all so open and supportive of each other. Not a lot of families are like that. You guys are really lucky."

A warm look passes between Millie and Maya. "You're right about that," Millie says. "We're cousins, but we grew up next door to each other, so we're practically siblings. We always want to be there for each other, no matter what."

"Even if we're apart," Millie says, pulling her cousin in yet another hug. "I still can't believe you're here."

"I know. We thought you went off-grid completely," Tyler says as he and the others return with their drinks.

Gage settles next to me and slides his arm around my shoulders. I let out a quiet hum at how good it feels for him to be so openly affectionate.

Maya stiffens slightly, sitting up straighter. She sweeps her long, wavy hair over one shoulder. "I'm not off the grid. I'm just busy and don't like to be glued to my phone."

"Except to post on Instagram, right?" Tyler elbows her lightly.

She rolls her eyes. "So I like posting to Instagram. Sue me."

"But you'd think that if you're posting on Instagram all the time you could at least send a text to your big brothers."

As teasing as Tyler's tone is, I can tell this is a soft spot for him. He probably wishes his sister would keep in contact more often, just like Gage does.

"Why? So you can lecture me for the millionth time about how I travel too much and should focus more on finding a solid career?"

My eyes go wide at Maya's pointed tone. I glance between her and Tyler, wondering if they're about to have a full-on argument right now.

"Tyler, we all wish that Maya would call us more, but she's allowed to live her life how she wants. And there's nothing wrong with liking Instagram *and* taking a break from your phone," Austin says. He winks at Maya, who flashes him a grateful smile.

"You always take her side," Tyler mutters before sipping his drink.

"And I always will," Austin says. Maya blows him a kiss.

"Maya and Austin are best friends," Gage says to me in a low voice so only I can hear. "She was the first person he came out to when he was a teenager. Some of our relatives weren't very supportive of him when they found out he was gay, and Maya blasted them over it. All of us cousins have been supportive of Austin and defended him, of course, but Maya has always been the closest to him. They've always stood up for each other. It's kind of like them versus the world."

"That's great that they have each other," I say.

"It is. We all give each other shit, but we don't dare go against Maya and Austin together. We wouldn't stand a chance."

I laugh along with Gage. When I look around, I see the place is packed now. A trio of young women joins us, and they're introduced as Millie's friends. The lights above us and onstage dim.

"Who's ready to get wild?" a low, growly, teasing voice booms across the speaker system.

Everyone screams and cheers.

"That's what I like to hear! Let's give it up for the strapping young lads who will be your entertainment tonight!"

The noise in the club is deafening as six tall, muscled, and oiled-up men appear on stage wearing nothing but fitted jeans and work boots. They kick off with a choreographed dance routine before they start to wander into the audience.

Gage glances over at Millie, who's cheering. "Get ready."

"What do you mean?"

Before he can answer her, one of the ripped dancers waltzes up to our section. "Who's the lucky lady?"

Gage points to his cousin. "Right there."

Millie's eyes go as wide as her grin as the dancer holds out his hand to her. He helps her down the steps and onto the stage, where there are four empty chairs, and guides her to sit in the one near the middle.

I gasp and smack Gage on the arm. "A lap dance!"

He chuckles. "Yup."

A sexy soul jam blasts through the club. I catch Tyler giving Gage a look. "I'm glad Millie is having a good time, but I'm not really in the mood to watch my cousin get worked over by a half-naked dude."

"Me neither. Wanna grab a drink at the bar?"

"God, yes."

"I'm coming with you," Austin says.

Tyler claps Gage on the back. "We should shotgun a beer for old time's sake."

Gage rolls his eyes. "No way."

"Just one."

"I said no."

"You're too stubborn for your own good, little brother."

Gage doesn't even acknowledge Tyler and instead turns to check on me. "You're okay staying here?"

I nod. "Yeah, I'm having a great time."

He grins wide before giving me a quick kiss. "Need a drink?"

I shake my head. "I'll stick to the alcohol-free stuff. Solidarity with Millie and all."

He leaves me with a kiss on my forehead and a smile that makes me melt. I catch Maya glancing at me. She steps closer to me. "I've never seen my brother smile this much."

There's a tingle in my chest. "Really?"

She nods. "He's always been so serious and brooding. You make him so happy, Becca."

There's a warmth in her smile that sends a thrill through me. "He makes me happy too. Like, so, so happy."

Part of me feels weird talking about how much I like

Gage with someone I've just met, who also happens to be his sister, but the other part of me feels excited. His siblings and cousins have been so welcoming to me, treating me like I'm a member of the family when they've known me for less than an hour.

But I guess that's a testament to how kind they are. And it makes sense because Gage is the same way too—incredibly sweet and supportive of me from the get-go, even before we were a couple.

"I know we literally just met," she says, "and I know he'd kill me for saying this, but I have to. My brother hasn't been the kind of guy who brings the people he's dated around our family. He's only done it, like, twice ever. And that was years ago—one time in college and one time after that. And that was after all of us had badgered him to let us meet who he was dating. I've never seen him so relaxed and happy in a relationship before."

What feels like a million tiny fireworks explode in my chest. "Seriously?"

She flashes a warm smile. "Seriously. He's nuts about you."

"Oh damn," Declan says, staring ahead at the stage. We both look over and see one of the dancers kneeling between Millie's open legs and pressing a kiss to her knee before kissing her swollen belly. Her head falls back as she shrieks and laughs.

"Yes, Millie! Get it!" Maya screams. Declan and I yell, "woo!" The performance ends, and Millie returns to our area.

Her tan skin is flushed ruby red, and she's breathing a little harder than before. "Well. Holy hell."

Gage, Tyler, and Austin return with their drinks. Gage

takes in his cousin's dazed stare. "Did you have fun up there?"

"A blast."

As the next performance starts, Gage settles next to me. "How about you? Are lap dances your thing?"

The corner of his mouth quirks up into that sexy-as-hell smile I adore. "Honestly? Not sure. I've never had one before."

After the performance ends, the emcee announces that the dancers will be heading into the audience to do some on-the-spot lap dances.

Gage turns to me and quirks up his eyebrow. "Wanna pop your lap dance cherry?" There's amusement in his gaze. I bite my lip and nod.

"Who wants one, ladies?" the announcer booms.

Gage waves his arm. "Right here!" he shouts, pointing at me.

Nerves and excitement crash inside of me.

My boyfriend is going to watch me get a lap dance.

This is something I never, ever thought I'd do, but I'm actually into it. The thought of Gage watching me while another man dances sexily over me is strange and wild—but it's also kind of thrilling.

A burly dancer with wavy blond hair and golden scruff walks up to me. "You ready, darlin'?"

My heart pounds. Gage looks on from a few feet away, an amused smirk on his face.

"I think so." I hate how my squeaky voice gives away just how nervous I feel.

The dancer winks at me. "Don't worry. I'll take good care of you."

He jerks my chair forward, stands over me, and grooves along to the beat of the music. He moves his hips closer and closer to me before stopping, and then he crouches down so we're eye level. Then he grabs my hands and places them on his bare chest as he continues to gyrate to the song.

My jaw drops. Maya, Millie, and Millie's friends laugh and cheer and tuck cash into the dancer's belt. My face is on fire as I touch this guy's sweaty, hot skin. I laugh. This is so freaking awkward. I look past his shoulder to Gage, who is chuckling softly as he watches.

"Hot, right?" he mouths to me.

I roll my eyes and laugh. Just then the dancer hauls me up in my chair against his chest.

"Oh, holy crap!" I yelp as I grip his pecs. I can hear everyone around me laughing and cheering.

He sets me down, and the song ends. "How was that, darlin'?"

"Memorable," I squeak out before covering my face with both hands. "You're extremely talented. And, um, strong. Very, very strong."

I let out another nervous chuckle. He winks at me. When he turns around, Gage stuffs a wad of cash in his hand.

"Aww, Becca, you're such a good sport!" Millie comes over and hugs me. Maya, Declan, Austin, and Millie's friends offer similar praise.

"You handled that like a champ." Tyler shoots me a thumbs-up.

Gage sits next to me, looking like he's holding in a laugh. "So? How was it?"

I shove his shoulder, and he laughs. "So awkward. But also fun. I'm glad I tried it."

"Want another?" he teases.

"Oh my god, don't you dare."

He bursts out laughing again before pulling me in for a

kiss. I've never had this before, a feeling of total comfort with someone. No guy I've ever dated before would have been okay with me getting a lap dance from another man in front of them. Ben would have had a jealous meltdown, no question. But Gage was so cool and casual about it.

This is what it must be like to be with someone genuine and secure and confident.

As the final performance winds down, sparkly confetti rains down from the ceiling.

I scream in shock, which makes Gage howl in laughter.

"Oh my god, there's glitter everywhere!" My arms and legs are covered in it. I make a face at Gage. "I've got dancer sweat and glitter all over me. I'm gonna need a shower ASAP."

A fire lights his eyes. "You got it."

Chapter 21

Gage

The second we walk into my apartment, I take Becca by the hand and lead her to the bathroom.

She giggles. "Where are we going?"

"You said you needed a shower."

I flip on the light and turn on the water in my rainfall shower. I spin around to face her and unbutton my shirt. I can't believe how tonight went. It was fucking perfect. *She* was fucking perfect.

My cousins and siblings loved her. As we were leaving the club, Maya and Millie pulled me aside to tell me how much they adored her. Maybe it's weird that my family liking Becca intensifies my feelings for her. But it's true. I want to be with someone I'm nuts about *and* who my family loves.

My chest swells yet again. Becca is special. I knew that from the moment I met her. But now that we're a couple, and now that I've seen her with my family, I feel myself doing something I haven't done often in my past relationships: I'm starting to picture a future together.

I blink and see a split-second image of Becca in a flowy white dress—a wedding dress.

It disappears as quickly as it flashed in my head, but I can't ignore it. Yeah, we've only been together for a few weeks, but that doesn't matter. What matters is how we feel about each other. And being with Becca feels right.

She watches me start to undress. Those doe eyes ignite in a heated stare. She starts to undo the buttons with me.

"You're joining me?" she asks with a teasing smile.

"If that's okay with you?"

She leans forward, dusting a kiss on my lips. When she gives my bottom lip a gentle bite and licks the spot, my knees buckle.

"More than okay." She shoves my shirt off my shoulders and tugs my belt loose. My jeans fall to the floor, and I'm left standing in my boxers.

I pull off her tank top and unbutton her shorts. Seeing her in matching black lace panties and bra has me drooling.

"God, you're fucking incredible," I growl as I grip her hips and pull her against me. "So fucking cute and sexy at the same time," I say between kisses.

She runs her fingers through my hair. When she pulls, I groan at the sharp pain.

"Do it again. Harder," I command against her lips. I slip my hand between her legs. She's soaking wet, and that makes me hard as titanium.

"You like that?" she asks, her breath ragged. "When I get rough with you?"

"Fuck yeah, I like that. It's the hottest thing in the world to see you get rough, angel."

She wobbles, her eyes dazed. Her legs tremble, and she leans against me even more. I don't know if it's what I've said or the way I'm working her in my hand. Maybe it's both. All I know is that I love seeing her like this: aching with pleasure, barely able to stand up straight.

I peel away her panties and unhook her bra, then kick off my boxers. I stick my hand in the stream of water, happy to feel it's the perfect temperature.

I lead her into the shower. Once we're under the stream, I get to work cleaning her up. I shampoo her hair, taking my time while I massage her scalp. Her eyes roll to the back of her head.

"That feels amazing, Gage."

My chest squeezes at the sight of Becca so blissed out, so happy. And that's when I realize how much seeing her happy means to me. When she's happy, I'm happy.

I swallow back the surge of emotion rising within me and soap her body. I glide my hand between her legs once more. She grips my shoulders with both of her hands as she starts to pant.

"Gage..."

Her eyebrows crash together, the look in her eyes dazed. I move my fingers faster. She's close. I can feel it.

She lets out a whimper and my dick throbs. Fucking hell, that sound. Such a sweet and hot sound, like she can barely handle the pleasure I'm giving her.

"Gage, I'm gonna come." She sinks her teeth into my shoulder. The sharp pain makes my dick jolt again.

"Come for me, baby. I'm gonna make you come over and over tonight."

Becca convulses against me as her orgasm hits. Her scream ricochets against my bathroom walls. She's so loud that I'm certain my neighbors can hear, and I don't care. Her pleasure is the only thing I care about in this moment. She's the only thing that matters.

She's clawing and biting at me, and it feels so fucking good. So primal. So carnal. So opposite of the sweet and angelic woman she is, and that's what I love most about seeing her come for me. Yeah, it's an insanely hot feeling and seeing her beautiful body writhe as a result of my touch, but it's also the fact that someone so wholesome and good becomes so damn filthy with me.

She aims a pleasure-drunk smile at me. "How are you so good with your hands? And your mouth? And your..."

She palms my rock-hard dick in her hand. I hum at how heavenly her wet, warm, silky hands feel on me.

"I took a class."

She bursts out laughing and pats my chest. She starts to glide her hand up and down my shaft. "Now it's your turn."

Wrapping my hand gently around her wrist, I pull her hand away. I quickly shampoo my hair and wash myself. "Not quite. If you do that, I'll blow, and that's not in line with what I have planned for the rest of tonight."

She grins, tracing her finger through the suds dotting my chest and stomach. "What do you have planned?"

I shut off the water and grab a towel. "Let me show you."

We dry off and head to my bedroom.

"Lie on my bed and spread your legs," I tell her.

Her lips part as she looks at me. She looks intrigued and turned on all at once.

A giddy smile pulls at her lips as she lowers herself onto the bed. I walk to the end of the bed and stand in front of her, drinking her in with my gaze.

"You're so fucking gorgeous, Becca." I give my dick a rough stroke, then pull my hand away.

Her gaze focuses between my legs, and she licks her lips. "You sure I can't help you with that?"

"Not yet. Show me how you touch yourself."

Her mouth parts open again, wider this time, like she's surprised at what I've asked her.

"You want to watch me touch myself in front of you?"

I nod. "I've been fantasizing about it long enough. I'm dying to see those beautiful hands get yourself off."

Her face and chest flush bright red. My dick pulses.

"Okay," she says.

When she licks the tips of her fingers, my eyes go wide. It's a movement that's as sweet as it is naughty. That perfect pink tongue sliding over those delicate, soft fingers...

The surge of arousal inside of me is so strong that I fall forward. I brace my hands along the edge of the bed. "Fuck, Becca. You haven't even started, and you're already getting me so hot."

That pouty mouth curves upward. So sweet and so smug.

She touches the pads of her fingers to her clit, moving in slow circles. Her eyebrows crash together, and her chest heaves up and down. "I usually need to warm up more, but I'm already so turned on by you."

I lower my face closer to her pussy, mesmerized.

"Look at how fucking wet you are, baby," I growl. Her fingers swirl faster and faster as she nods.

"That's how much you turn me on." She pants. "I-I've never had anyone watch me do this before."

"That's a damn shame. They missed out on a hell of a show."

My hands tingle with the need to touch her. My lips ache with the need to taste her. But I force myself to stay in place. Not just yet.

The insides of her thighs start to twitch. Her eyes are

closed, like she's lost herself in the ecstasy of the moment. She bites her lip and moans.

"Tell me how you feel," I growl.

"I'm so turned on, it hurts. I'm soaking wet. I'm aching so, so bad. Pulsing. Throbbing. My fingers feel so good." She opens her eyes and pins me with her stare. "But yours feels better."

I throw my head back and let out a frustrated laugh that sounds more like a growl. I'm so hard, I'm aching. "Fuck." I focus back on Becca. "Wider, angel. Spread your legs wider."

"Say please."

I grin at her rasped command and how shy her smile is when she says it. "Please."

She stretches those gorgeous legs even wider. She moves those fingers so fast. When I see that she's so wet she's dripping onto my bedsheets, I know I won't be able to make it much longer. I stomp over to my bedside table, grab a condom, and rip it open with my teeth. I sheath myself, then kneel on the bed. I hook my hands under her legs, wrapping them around my waist, and then I slide inside of her.

I almost collapse. She's so hot and tight and wet. I take a second to breathe, then thrust hard and fast.

"I couldn't wait any longer," I rasp. "I need you now."

"Good." She gasps. "Because I'm about to come. Come with me, baby. Please?"

Her whimpered request nearly sends me over the edge. Her leg starts to shake, a telltale sign that she's about to have an orgasm. My entire body goes tense and hot. I thrust as fast as I can, grunting and growling as I blow.

Becca shouts as she comes, squeezing her trembling legs

around me. I bury my face in her neck, bracing myself up on my forearms so I don't crush her.

"That was..."

"Fucking incredible."

I laugh at how perfectly Becca put it.

I kiss her. "Damn. My sweetheart is starting to get a filthy mouth."

"You must be rubbing off on me."

I pull away and toss the condom in a nearby wastebasket. When I lie back down in my bed, she cuddles into my chest. I take a second to silently appreciate just how perfectly she fits next to me, how good her head feels resting on my chest, the way her long, wavy blonde hair tickles my skin.

My heart beats so hard, I can feel it from the top of my head to my toes. I wonder if she can feel it, if she can feel just how crazy I am about her.

"Gage," she whispers.

"Yeah?"

"I'm nervous about meeting the rest of your family at the baby shower next weekend."

I smile and kiss her hair. "Don't be. They're gonna love you."

Like I love you.

Those four words pop into my head without warning. Where the hell did that come from?

I focus on the moment and try not to think about the four-letter word that just flashed in my mind, but it's like ignoring a siren or a spotlight. It lingers in the background, like an echo.

There's probably a reason for that...probably because I could definitely see myself falling in love with Becca.

You're already on your way.

She leans up to look at me. "Promise they will?"

I gently grip her chin in my hand and kiss her until we're both out of breath. When we break apart, I look her straight in the eye, my heart pounding in my chest. "I promise."

Chapter 22

Becca

I glance around the inside of Sweet Cheeks. Gage's family are happily chatting while enjoying the ice cream bar I set up. I breathe a sigh of relief that the ten tables I set up ended up being enough seating.

Tori refills a few of the toppings before heading over to where I'm standing behind the counter.

"Thanks again for agreeing to help with this, especially on your day off," I tell her.

She smiles. "It's no problem. It's been fun meeting Gage's family and friends. They're all so nice."

She tells me that she and Maya exchanged Instagram handles and started following each other.

"She hates mint chocolate chip, just like me. How cool is that?"

I laugh.

"And Millie wants me to come to the next girls' night she's having," Tori says.

Tyler walks by. I notice Tori eyeing him.

"Not a great idea, Tori. I like Tyler, but Gage told me

he's a commitment-phobic ladies' man. You loathe guys like that."

"Right. Hate that. Absolutely hate that," she says, her eyes on Tyler the whole time. I elbow her, and she blinks. That dazed look melts from her face. "What? I'm just looking. There's nothing wrong with looking at the menu as long as I don't order from it, right?"

I roll my eyes. "That is a ridiculous metaphor."

One of Gage's aunts walks up to us. "I'm so sorry, girls. I accidentally spilled on one of the tables."

"Oh, no worries at all!" Tori beams. "I'll clean it up for you." She grabs a washcloth and follows Gage's aunt.

I walk over to Millie, who's sitting at a table with her mom and Maya.

"How is everything?" I ask.

Her big brown eyes light up. "Amazing!" She pulls me down for a hug, the third time she's hugged me since she arrived an hour ago. "The ice cream bar is my dream come true." She points to her empty dish.

Her mom nods and gives me a thumbs-up. "So very yummy."

I smile at her. "Thank you so much."

"And you didn't have to put up decorations," Millie says. She glances at the clusters of pink and blue balloons hanging in the store. "I feel like I've imposed enough just having my shower at your shop at the last minute."

I pat her hand. "It's not an imposition at all. It's my pleasure, truly. And I didn't even put up the decorations. That was all Gage."

I look over to where he's standing at the far end of the shop, talking with his brother and cousins. He catches my eyes and smiles.

I go warm and tingly all over. I can't look at Gage too

long. Otherwise I'm sure his relatives will notice all the filthy thoughts playing out across my face. So I turn my attention back to Millie.

"I'm so happy you're having a nice time," I say to her.

"The best time." She winces. "Must pee again."

Her mom helps her up, and they walk toward the back where the bathrooms are.

"Your shop is so gorgeous," Maya says while glancing around. "It looks so much bigger than in your TikTok videos."

"You watch my TikTok videos?" I ask, hoping I don't sound as panicked as I feel. Just the thought of Gage's family seeing the sexy things I've posted has my stomach churning. I'm not ashamed of how I've chosen to take a sexier turn with my business's social media platform, but I don't want my boyfriend's family to watch it. That's almost as bad as if my parents saw it.

Maya chuckles. "Don't worry, I only watched a few of your videos from before Gage started filming videos with you." She grimaces. "I don't even watch the videos on his TikTok account. I love my brother, but I'd vomit if I had to see him do sexy stuff."

I wince and chuckle. "Totally get it. And thank you a million times over for not watching our videos together."

We laugh. Gage walks over and slinks his arm around my waist, pulling me close.

He kisses my cheek. "Let me guess. My sister's telling embarrassing stories about me."

Maya sticks out her tongue at her brother. "Not yet. But I will soon." She looks at me. "Remind me to tell you about the time Gage pretended to be sick so he could stay home from school and watch *The Young and The Restless*."

I laugh. "Oh my gosh, is that true?" I ask Gage. His cheeks are fire engine red.

"It's absolutely true," Maya says with a laugh.

He rolls his eyes, a flustered smile tugging at his lips. "I don't remember that. I must have been really little."

Maya's head falls back as she laughs. "You were in middle school."

I hunch over and cover my mouth, I'm laughing so hard.

Gage gives his sister a light shove on the arm. One of their relatives calls Maya's name, and she walks over to them.

Gage hugs me against him. "See? Told you my family would love you. My sister likes you enough to tell you embarrassing stories about me. And my mom is impressed that you own such a successful business."

I'm warm from the inside out. Gage's family has been so kind and gracious since the moment they all arrived. They treated me like family the moment they met me, hugging me, telling me how beautiful my ice cream shop is, and asking to buy ice cream to take home with them. His mom even brought me a massive bouquet of flowers as a thank-you for hosting Millie's shower at the last minute.

As I glance around the room at everyone chatting and laughing and enjoying themselves, my chest swells. Gage's family is so full of joy and love. It would be amazing to be part of a family like this someday.

I look at Gage, my heart thudding. After a second, I have to look away. This surge of emotion inside of me feels so raw.

I know this feeling. I'm starting to fall in love with Gage.

I also know it's fast. I've never fallen this hard, this quickly for someone before. That's why I take a second to collect myself before looking at him again. He'd probably freak out if I told him how I felt about him.

"Can you believe that a couple of months ago we met because I slid into your DMs, asking you to help me film sexy TikToks? And now I'm meeting your family," I say. I'm relieved at how casual and light I manage to sound.

He chuckles and cups my face in his palm. "It's a wild turn of events for sure." He hugs me tighter against him. "I'm one lucky bastard to have met you."

He dusts a light kiss against my lips. All of my insides tingle and throb.

"Sorry to interrupt you two love birds," Tyler says as he walks up to us and turns to Gage. "Auntie Ida and Uncle Sonny are taking off. So is Auntie Berta, and she needs help taking the party favors to her car."

"People are leaving?" I ask.

"Yeah, I think we'll start winding down. Millie mentioned she's feeling tired too," Tyler says.

"No problem," Gage says. "I'll help load her gifts into her car."

Tyler pats my shoulder. "Thanks again for everything, Becca. You saved the day."

"It was nothing. I loved doing it."

"It was everything," Gage says before kissing my cheek.

It's a blur of thank you's and hugs as everyone filters out and heads home. Gage and his mom are the last to leave.

"Becca, thank you again. This was so beautiful. And my goodness, what delicious ice cream you make. Best I've ever had." His mom holds my hands in hers. "You have such a beautiful shop too. I adore it." She beams at me. Joy swells within me at hearing Gage's mom say such lovely things to me.

"You know, dear, I'd love it if you could come to my birthday party in a couple of weeks," she says excitedly.

"Really?" My voice squeaks, I'm so heartened that she'd want me there.

Gage walks over and smiles at me. "I'd love it too if you could come."

I smile at him and his mom. "I'd love to come."

His mom hugs me again. "Wonderful! I can't wait to see you again, Becca."

Gage helps her carry some bags to her car, then runs back into the shop and pulls me into his arms.

"I've gotta drive my mom to the airport super early in the morning, so I have to stay at her house tonight."

I make a mock-pouty face. "I'll miss you."

"Believe me, I wish I were staying at your place." He kisses me. "Maybe I can convince my mom to take an Uber."

"No way you're ditching your mom. You're going to be a good son and take her to the airport. Then you can come over to my place."

"And I can have breakfast?" His eyes dart between my legs. He licks his lips.

I give him a light slap on the shoulder and laugh. "Go take care of your mom."

He gives me one last kiss before he takes off. I tell Tori to go.

"You sure? I'm happy to stay and help clean up."

I shake my head. "You've done enough. Go home and relax."

She beams, hugs me, and grabs her purse. "I'll see you tomorrow!"

For the next hour, I clean up, then start prepping online orders in the back. When I step back out in the front, it's nighttime already. I was so busy, I didn't even realize it had gotten dark.

I empty the garbage and walk toward the dumpster, which is half a block behind Sweet Cheeks. I chuck the bag in, then spin around and walk back toward the Sweet Cheeks entrance. When I'm almost to the door, I see movement in the corner of my eye. When I look up, there's a man I don't recognize walking toward me dressed in what looks like a white chef's coat.

"Excuse me, miss? I'm so sorry to bother you." He stops several feet away from me. Under the nearby streetlight, I can see his face. He's in his early sixties, with a handsome face that's furrowed in a worried frown. The longer I look at him, the more familiar he seems.

He hesitates. "Are you Becca Briarwood?"

I tense. "Who are you?" I say, ignoring his question.

He closes his eyes and shakes his head. "I'm sorry," he repeats. "I know I shouldn't be here, bothering you. But I've tried everything, and I can't..." He pauses. "You know my son. Gage Grant."

Oh my gosh. This is Gage's dad.

"Yes, I do know him," I say. "You're his dad?"

He nods, a sad smile tugging at his lips for a split second before his expression goes back to pained. "I'm Andre." He hesitates for a second. "Are you his girlfriend?"

I frown at him. "Wh-why are you asking me that?"

He closes his eyes again and shakes his head, like he's silently scolding himself. It's so weird seeing him like this. The few times I've seen him on TV, he always comes off as confident, charming, and unflappable.

But right now he looks disheveled in his stained chef's jacket. There's a thick sheet of gray scruff along his cheeks, and his blue eyes look tired, like he hasn't been sleeping.

216

"This is going to sound outrageous. And desperate." He huffs out a sigh and runs a hand through his thick gray-blonde hair. "I'm not sure if Gage told you, but he and I had a falling out. It was my fault. I realize now what a mistake I made, and I've been trying to get in touch with him to tell him I'm sorry." His lips tremble. "I-I don't have a relationship with my son anymore, and it's killing me."

His eyes turn glassy with tears. There's a sting in my chest at watching this broken man in front of me. I don't even know him, other than what Gage has told me, and yet I feel for him.

"He's cut me out of his life. I don't blame him. I really hurt him." He stops when his voice starts to shake. He clears his throat. "I just want the chance to tell him I'm sorry and to ask if he'll consider letting me back in his life."

I'm quiet for a few seconds as I process everything he's said.

"Why did you come here?" I ask.

He hesitates. "I know he has a big social media presence. That's how I found out about you and your ice cream shop, when I saw he was doing TikTok videos with you."

"Oh. Um, yeah. He's been helping me with my social media." I pause to clear my throat. "He's so generous and creative and talented, you know. And an incredible chef," I say, my tone firm.

Andre's shoulders slump forward, and his gaze falls to the ground. He looks so guilty, so broken. "He is. I want to tell him how proud I am of him and how sorry I am. I just need him to hear me out. Could you, uh...could you maybe talk to him for me? Ask him if he'll meet with me so we can talk?"

My stomach churns at the thought. "I don't know if that's something I should do."

"Please? I'll do anything for you to help me." He glances at the Sweet Cheeks sign. "You own this ice cream shop, right? I'll buy your ice cream and start serving it in my restaurants here in Denver. Or anything else you want—you name it, and I'll do it for you. Anything you want, Becca. Can you please just tell my son to call me?"

My mouth falls open. Part of me is appalled that he's practically bribing me. But the other part of me feels raw pity for the guy. To feel so desperate that he'd make such an offer to me, a total stranger, is beyond anything I can relate to or understand.

"Are you trying to bribe me?" I ask, still in disbelief.

He stammers. "No. I'm sorry, that's not how I mean to come off. I'm just desperate to have my son back in my life."

His lips start to shake again. That churning inside my stomach turns into an ache. I know how much Gage loathes his dad, and he has every right to. But seeing Andre standing in front of me, completely gutted, so desperate to reach out to his son that he's begging a total stranger for help, I feel for the guy. Yeah, he was a jerk for how he rejected Gage, but it sounds like he's truly sorry and wants to apologize to his son and try to make things right with him.

"I'll talk to him," I say softly.

"You will?" He looks so hopeful in that moment, it's heartbreaking.

I nod. "I promise I will."

That sad smile reappears. "Thank you, Becca. I'm so sorry again for coming to you like this. I-I know this isn't fair of me to ask you this. But..."

I nod. "I get it. He's your son, and you love him."

He looks relieved at what I've said. "Exactly."

He turns around, walks back down the street, then hops into a sporty-looking black car and drives off. As I lock up

Sweet Cheeks and walk up to my apartment, my head is a mess. I have no doubt Gage will be pissed when I bring up his dad and the idea of reaching out to him. But I made a promise to Andre.

Dread pools in my stomach as I crawl into bed. I barely sleep the whole night, and when I wake up, I still have no idea what I'm going to say to Gage.

Chapter 23

Gage

When I knock on Becca's door, I'm grinning like a maniac. It hasn't even been one full day since we've seen each other, but I'm giddy as hell to see her.

Giddy. I can't remember the last time I used that word to describe how I feel about someone.

But that's exactly how I feel. I'm smiling like a goober, and it feels like there are butterflies in my stomach at the thought of seeing her. Damn, that's different. I've never used the word "butterflies" in that way before.

That's how much I like her.

Love her.

This time when that four-letter word pops into my head, it doesn't feel as jarring. This time, it feels right.

But before I can think too much about that, she opens the door.

"Hey. Come in," she says with a small smile.

I shut the door behind me and pull her in for a hug. Those stunning baby blues look tired and swollen, like she's been up all night.

I hold her face and look at her. "Are you okay?"

She closes her eyes and shakes her head. "Not really."

My stomach bottoms out at the worry in her stare, at how weak her voice sounds. The urge to comfort her, to protect her, to make whatever is upsetting her go away, overtakes me.

"What happened?"

She grips her hands around my wrists and takes a breath. "I need to tell you something. After you and your family left Sweet Cheeks yesterday, your dad showed up."

"What?" I'm sputtering.

"He, um, he came up to me as I was taking out the trash."

"He what? What the fuck?" A tidal wave of anger levels me. What the fuck was my dad thinking, sneaking up on Becca at night when she was alone? He probably scared the shit out of her. And how the fuck did he even know about her or where her shop is?

I pull my hands away from her and shake them at my sides.

"Gage, it's okay. He just wanted to talk."

"About what?" Fury drips from my hard tone. I force myself to take a breath. I'm beyond pissed right now, but none of this is Becca's fault. I don't want to sound angry when I'm talking to her.

"He wanted to talk about you. He said he's been trying to get ahold of you for a while now. He wants to apologize for how he hurt you. And he wants to make things right with you, but he hasn't been able to get ahold of you after you cut him out of your life."

She explains how my dad admitted to following my social media and that's how he found out about her and

Sweet Cheeks. The whole time, anger steamrolls my insides. The fucking nerve of him.

"He mentioned seeing you in the Sweet Cheeks TikTok videos," she says. "I guess he thought that since he couldn't get a hold of you, he'd try me."

A bitter laugh drops from my mouth. I tug at my hair, infuriated. "Typical. He's such a fucking opportunist. Doesn't care how he makes others feel. Only cares if things work out for him."

Becca lets go of my hand. She looks jolted at what I've said. I close my eyes for a second, then I grab her hand in mine and look at her. "I'm sorry," I say in a softer voice. "He was out of line to approach you and put all of this on you. He practically stalked us both on social media, then cornered you to get to me." Just thinking about the lengths he's gone to makes me want to rage. "He had no right to do any of that. I'm so sorry he put you in that position."

"Gage, it's okay."

"It's not okay." I pull my phone out of my pocket, fury surging through me. I give Becca's hand a gentle squeeze before letting her go and dialing his number. I walk down the hallway toward her bedroom, my heart thrashing against my chest as I count the rings.

"Hello?"

"Dad, it's me."

"Gage?" he stammers. "I-I can't believe you called."

I can tell he's smiling as he speaks, and it makes me even angrier.

"Son, it's so good to hear from you. I'm so happy you—"

"Stop," I boom. My voice bounces against the hallway walls. "Listen to me. You crossed a line last night. How dare you corner my girlfriend to get to me."

"Wh-what? No, that's not—"

"Don't you ever come near Becca again, do you hear me?"

"Gage, that's not—listen, I'm sorry if I made her uncomfortable, but—"

"Uncomfortable? Dad, you creeped her the fuck out, sneaking up on her at night. What the hell were you thinking?"

He stammers for a few seconds before letting out a sigh. "I'm sorry. I wasn't thinking. I was desperate. All I wanted was to figure out a way to get to you so I could apologize, so I could try and make things right between us. I never meant to make Becca uncomfortable. I guess I made a mistake."

I grit my teeth so hard, I'm certain my jaw is going to shatter. "You think that's all you have to do? Say sorry and we're all good? You think 'sorry' makes up for the way you rejected me, the way you treated me? The way you practically washed your hands of me? Your own son."

"Of course not," he says, his tone soft and appeasing. It's a mind-fuck hearing my dad sound like this, so meek when he speaks to me. I'm so used to hearing him sound confident and assertive. He rules his kitchens like a commander, barking orders and telling anyone off who challenges him. He sounds like a completely different person right now.

"Gage, I know I have a lot to answer for." This time he sounds like he's actually pleading. It's disorienting to hear. "Just please give me a chance to make things right."

"No." I say it without even thinking, like a reflex. It's the only word I have for him.

A long silence follows on his end of the line. He starts to speak, but I stop him.

"Stay the hell away from Becca and her shop. And stay the hell out of my life."

I hang up, turn around, and walk down the hallway

back to where Becca is standing in her kitchen. I freeze when I see the look on her face. Her mouth is agape, clearly shocked at what I've said.

I walk over to her and reach for her, but she holds up a hand. "Wait. Why did you go off on your dad like that? You were pretty rough on him."

I almost laugh. "Becca, he accosted you in the middle of the night."

Her gaze on me turns pointed. "Gage, that's not true. Don't twist the situation. Yeah, when he first approached me, I was nervous, but once he introduced himself and explained what he was doing there, I felt fine."

I frown, confused about what she's even talking about. "What are you saying?"

"Maybe you should give your dad a chance to explain himself."

"What?"

"I know what he did to you was so hurtful. But I honestly think he's sorry and regrets it. I think he's changed his mind about you and your TikTok following. He wants you in his life again, Gage."

For several seconds, all I can do is stammer. I can't believe Becca is defending him.

"Are you kidding me right now? Are you seriously saying that you're siding with my dad?"

She squeezes her eyes shut and shakes her head. When she looks at me, her gaze is pleading. "No, of course not, Gage. I'm just saying that your dad made a mistake—just like we all make mistakes."

"He's a self-righteous jerk who shamed me for posting videos on TikTok. He thinks that because I pose with my shirt off every once in a while, I'm nothing. He thinks his own son is trash. I thought you of all people understood how much that hurts me, how messed up that is."

Panic flashes in her eyes as she takes a step toward me. "Gage, of course I understand. There's no excuse for how he's treated you. But it's been over a year since you two fought and you cut him out of your life. Do you think that maybe you've punished him enough? At least meet with him and hear what he has to say. Maybe he's changed. Maybe he's more understanding. Maybe—"

A bitter laugh falls from my mouth. "Maybe *you* think that because you had one conversation with my dad, you know our relationship better than I do? You think you really know him? You think he's a good guy? You think you know this whole situation better than me, who's spent almost my entire life dealing with his bullshit?"

Becca's expression turns anguished as she looks at me. She shakes her head and grabs my hand, but I yank it away.

"You don't know a goddamn thing, Becca," I mutter.

She winces like she's in pain. "Gage, please don't say that. I don't think I know better than you, I swear. I know I'm an outsider in this whole situation. No one knows your relationship with your dad better than you. But sometimes it helps to get an outsider's point of view in such an emotionally charged situation."

I shake my head, the frustration inside of me boiling over.

"Gage, your dad looked so broken last night. He's desperate to have you in his life again."

I let out another bitter laugh. "You think you know all that from one conversation? Come on, Becca. I thought you were smarter than that."

She exhales sharply as she looks at me. "Gage, your dad

offered to start buying my ice cream and featuring it on his restaurants' dessert menus in exchange for asking you to reach out to him."

My jaw falls to the floor. "He what?"

"That's how desperate he is to have a relationship with you again. He was willing to offer me, a total stranger, anything for just a chance to reach out to you."

What feels like lava seeps up my chest. "I can't fucking believe this. Anything to get your ice cream into restaurants like you said, right? Anything to make money. First, you use me to boost your TikTok, then you move on to my dad for something more high-end. Is that your plan?"

She gasps at my muttered words. Pain flashes in her eyes as she looks at me. What I've said is utter bullshit. It's a cheap shot, and I know it. But I'm so angry, I can't even think straight. Yeah, things moved quickly between us, but I'd never felt this way about anyone before. I thought we had a connection. It felt like she truly understood me, especially when I opened up to her about my dad. But I was wrong.

She blinks quickly. When I see the tears brimming in her eyes, it feels like a punch to the gut.

"You know that's not true, Gage," she says, her voice steady and firm. "I care about you so much. I'd never, ever use you like that. You know I wouldn't."

My hands ache to reach for her, to take her in my arms and hug her tight and tell her that I didn't mean it, that I'm sorry.

"Becca, I—"

"You need to leave."

Before I can say or do anything, she walks off toward her bedroom and shuts the door. My head falls back. I tug both hands through my hair and close my eyes. Fuck. I screwed this up so bad.

I contemplate staying and waiting until she comes back out, but I know that's not the right thing to do. I need to do what she asked me to.

I walk out of her apartment and drive home.

Chapter 24

Becca

I glance around Sweet Cheeks, taking in how packed it is. All the tables and chairs are full with customers, and the line at the register snakes out the door and down the block.

I let out a heavy sigh. Business is the best it's ever been, but I don't feel happy or relieved or any positive emotion. When I smile at customers, all the muscles in my face feel strained. I feel like I'm existing in a stupor, just going through the motions instead of enjoying what's happening around me.

I rush over to Tori to help her dish up ice cream for the family of five that just ordered. I check on Ellie and Aiden, the part-timers I hired to help with the influx of business we've gotten over the past couple of months, ever since our TikTok blew up.

"We're out of unicorn swirl and rocky road," Aiden says.

I ask Tori to help me fetch more ice cream out of the freezer in the back. Together we grab the flavors and walk back to the front.

"Becca, wait." I spin around to Tori, who's gazing at me with concern in her eyes. "Are you okay?"

I sigh. "Why do you keep asking me that? My answer hasn't changed from the last time you asked me—or the time before that, or the time before that."

I know that Tori means well. Ever since Gage and I fought a week ago, I've been a mess. She knows what happened. I called her crying after he left, and she came over to my apartment to console me. But Sweet Cheeks is busier than ever, and I don't have time to sit around and mope. I'm busy from the moment I wake up till we close. I'd rather channel my energy into my work than sulk and cry. I told Tori this. I just wish she'd stop pestering me.

She frowns and shakes her head. We walk back out and restock the flavors. I'm about to help another customer when Tori takes me by the arm and leads me into the back again.

"Tori, what are you doing? We have a line out the door. Customers are waiting."

"So? They'd be waiting anyway. What's an extra few minutes?" She crosses her arms and pins me with her stare. "Why haven't you reached out to Gage yet?"

"What?"

"Why haven't you texted him or called him?"

I stare at her with my mouth open in disbelief. Is she serious?

"Tori, you know exactly why. You remember what he did, don't you? You remember what he accused me of, how angry he got at me when I was just trying to help."

She purses her lips, then takes a breath. She rests her hand on my shoulder. "Bec, I love you. You know that. But I'm tired of seeing you stumble around all heartbroken like this when there's something you could be doing about it."

"What in the world are you talking about?"

"Look, no question, Gage was an asshole for saying that you used him and his TikTok fame for your business. That quip about his dad was shitty too. But I honestly don't think he meant it. I've seen you together. I've seen how happy you two are. I've never seen you like this with anyone before, Bec. Ever." She gently squeezes my shoulder. "You even said that he started to apologize to you before you kicked him out. And don't get me wrong, you had every right to kick him out for saying that crap to you. But it sounded like he knew it was wrong the second he said it. I'm not excusing what he did. He owes you one hell of a grovel for that. But we've all said mean and hurtful things to the people we care about."

I start to speak but trail off. She's right.

"And look, I'm about to say something that's going to piss you off, but it needs to be said: you were wrong too, Bec."

I'm stunned. "What?"

"You shouldn't have pushed Gage to forgive his dad."

I scoff. "Tori, how could you say that? His dad looked heartbroken when he came to me begging for help. Gage was being so mean to him."

"I know, Bec. But what you've seen isn't the whole picture. Gage has every right to feel upset at his dad. When you pressed him to give him another chance, I can see how that hurt him. He probably just wanted support from you in that moment more than anything else."

I go quiet as I think about what my best friend has just said. It never occurred to me that all Gage needed was for me to listen to him and support him, not tell him what I think he should do, then get upset when he refused.

"I know you aren't in the mood to hear any of that," she

says. "But I'm your best friend. We've always told each other the truth, even when it's hard to hear."

I exhale. "No, you're right. I needed to hear all of that."

She pulls me into a hug. Aiden runs over to us, out of breath. "We just got a vanload of soccer kids. It's all-hands-on-deck."

I peer around him and see a sea of middle schoolers crowded in the lobby. I smile to myself as my adrenaline kicks up. This is what I've always dreamed of, having an ice cream shop that's always busy, always full of happy customers.

I pat Aiden on the shoulder. "It's gonna be okay."

We start to head for the front, but Tori pulls on my hand. "Are you gonna talk to Gage?"

I nod. "As soon as we close up tonight."

* * *

I lock up the now-empty store and grab my phone. I pull up Gage's name and text him.

Me: *Hey. Can we talk?*

My heart leaps when I see those three gray dots appear almost immediately. But they fade as soon after, then reappear, then fade. Two more times, that happens. I watch the screen of my phone, my stomach in knots. My brain is a mess as I wonder how he's feeling, what he's thinking, if he's open to giving me, giving *us* another chance. Finally, he answers.

Gage: *I just need some time.*

My heart sinks. I guess I have my answer.

Chapter 25

Gage

"*Anak*, where's Becca? I thought you said she was coming."

I plaster what I hope is a convincing smile on my face and hug my mom. "She couldn't make it. Sorry. But here." I point out the massive bouquet of pink roses that I set on the table in the foyer of her house when I walked in a few minutes ago. "Happy birthday, Mom. I love you."

"Oh! How beautiful!" She pats my cheek with her hand. "Thank you. Is this from both you and Becca?"

I hold back a flinch. "Well, um..."

I knew this would come up. My stomach is in knots at the thought of being here without Becca. I think back to how Mom invited Becca to come today when she met her at Millie's baby shower and how excited she was to see her. I didn't want to upset her on her birthday of all days by telling her that Becca and I broke up.

"Hey, those are pretty." I point at the tall glass vase of lilies on the end table next to us, desperate for a distraction.

"Oh yes. So pretty." I notice her cheeks flush when she

looks at them. I see a small white card next to it with a heart scrawled in red ink and the letter "A" below it.

"Mom, you want some champagne?" Tyler hollers from the kitchen, bottle in hand.

Her gaze flits to him. "Oh, my favorite!" She hurries over. He pours glasses for the two of them, then hands the bottle to Declan.

I breathe a sigh of relief, thankful for my brother's interruption. I glance around Mom's house, at the crowd of relatives mingling and eating and singing karaoke. My chest aches. Becca would love this. I picture her laughing and sharing champagne with my mom, singing along with my little cousins at the karaoke machine, chatting with my aunties and uncles.

I glance at my phone and pull up our most recent text conversation, when she asked if we could talk. I read over my response for the hundredth time.

Me: *I just need some time.*

When she texted me a few days ago, I was surprised. Shocked, actually. After the way she told me to leave her place last week when we argued, I didn't think she'd reach out to me anytime soon. But she did. And a part of me was so damn excited to hear from her.

But the other part of me is so upset about how she thinks I should just forgive my dad. I think back to the day we fought in her apartment, that look of pure confusion and disgust on her face when she overheard me telling off my dad.

I think about how even after I explained how I felt and how I reminded her of how he fired me and cut me out of my life, she thought I was being too harsh on him.

I'm just saying that your dad made a mistake—just like

we all make mistakes…Maybe he's changed. Maybe he's more understanding.

I close my eyes as the memory of what she said to me cuts me yet again. I feel a bump on my leg and glance down at my cousin Walter's five-year-old daughter, Alodia, looking up at me.

"Uncle Gage, can I have some chicken nuggets, pwease?"

I smile. My first genuine smile in days. "Of course, sweetie. Here."

I lean down, scoop her up, and walk her into the kitchen, where a massive spread of food sits on Mom's kitchen table. I set Alodia down and grab a paper plate and load up some chicken nuggets for her along with some fruit and veggies so her dad doesn't go off on me for only letting her eat junk food. I set her up at a nearby table, where a couple of my other cousins' kids are sitting and eating.

She shoves a nugget in her mouth and says a muffled, "thank you," her mouth full.

"You're welcome." I kiss the top of her head and check on the other kids to make sure they have enough to eat and drink. I refill their cups with juice right as Tyler comes up and slaps me on the back.

"Room for one more?" He kneels down, champagne bottle in one hand and *lumpia* in another. He takes a gigantic bite of *lumpia* and chews loudly, making the kids laugh.

"You're so funny, Uncle Tyler," Alodia says while chuckling.

"Aww, I am, aren't I?" He ruffles her hair before elbowing my leg. "Uncle Gage on the other hand is being Mr. Grumpy Pants today."

The kids laugh again. Tyler looks up at me, his gaze

focused, like he can tell something is up with me. I shouldn't be surprised. I've been pretty cagey with him ever since things between Becca and me went to hell. We've met up at the gym a couple of times to work out, and he's asked about her both times. Both times, I gave evasive non-answers about us being too busy to see each other lately.

"Becca's not here?" he asks when he stands up.

"Nope."

"That's too bad. Millie was hoping she'd bring some more ice cream."

"Of course she was," I mutter.

He turns back to the kids. "Did you guys know that Uncle Gage has a girlfriend?"

I shove his shoulder. "Dude, shut up. You think they wanna hear about that?"

Annoyed, I walk off. Someone hollers that they need more ice for the drink cooler in the backyard, so I head to the garage to grab another bag out of the deep freezer. Behind me, I hear footsteps. I spin around to see Tyler shutting the door.

He looks at me and crosses his arms. "What's up with you?"

I grit my teeth and shove open the deep freezer. "Nothing's up with me, other than being annoyed by you, but that's not new."

"Ha-ha. I'm serious, Gage. What's going on? Where's Becca?"

I yank a bag of ice from the freezer and slam it shut. "She's not here," I mutter.

"Would you knock it off with the evasive bullshit? I know something is up."

Bag of ice in hand, I try to walk past him, but he shoulder-checks me.

I drop the ice and stumble back. "What the fuck?" I shove him. He leans back slightly but rights himself instantly.

"Did you and Becca have a fight or something?"

I glare at him. "That's none of your fucking business."

"Yeah, probably not, but whatever went down between you two must have been bad because you're not acting like yourself."

I scoff. "Dude, I'm not in the mood, okay? Fucking drop it."

He shakes his head. "Not a chance. I know I annoy the hell out of you, but I'm also your big brother. I notice when you're happy and when you're sad and everything in between. You're sad, Gage. Why?"

I try to shove past him to get to the door, but he blocks me again.

"Get out of my fucking way, Tyler."

"Talk to me. Tell me what's wrong."

I tug a hand through my hair. It feels like someone shook up a can of soda and shoved it into my chest cavity. I feel restless. I feel like I'm about to blow.

I let out a bitter laugh. "We broke up. There. Happy?"

I shove him again. Just like before, he stumbles back but quickly recovers. "What happened between you two?"

"None. Of. Your. Fucking. Business," I repeat through gritted teeth.

Concern flashes in his frown. "It *is* my business, Gage. You're my brother, and ever since you and Becca got together, I've never seen you so happy. And now that you're not, you're being an asshole."

I stand there, glowering at him, as my chest heaves with each breath I take. It feels like my lungs and my heart are about to explode.

"What went wrong?" he asks.

"Nothing. We just decided to call it quits," I lie, not wanting to get into something so personal.

He blinks, his expression neutral. I can tell he's not buying it. "Really? Sounds pretty amicable then."

"Yup," I huff.

He finally steps aside, and I make it to the door.

"Since it was mutual, you wouldn't mind if I asked her out, would you?"

My hand freezes on the doorknob. "What?"

"Well, I mean, she's smokin' hot. And sweet. Just my type."

Fury flashes through me. It feels like lava is burning through my veins. Slowly, I spin around to face him. "What the fuck did you just say?"

"I said Becca is hot. And I want a shot with her since you've made it clear you're no longer interested."

I stomp over to him and shove him against the wall. He lets out a wheezing sound as he clutches a hand to his stomach. He's hunched over as he catches his breath.

"You stay the fuck away from her, understand me?" I growl.

After a few seconds of coughing and gasping, Tyler starts to laugh.

"You think this is funny?"

He leans up, smiling through a wince. "Yeah, kinda. You're a dickhead, you know that?"

I move to shove his shoulder, but he blocks my arm. "I'm not going to ask Becca out, you dipshit. I'm not interested in her."

Relief washes through me.

"I only said all that to prove a point."

"What point?" I bark.

"That there's more going on than you're letting on. You're not fine, Gage. You're in agony. I can see it. Will you, for once in your life, quit acting like a stubborn bastard and just talk to me? I'm your brother. I just want to help. I just want to be there for you."

He grips my shoulder. Something inside of me softens. I can't remember the last time he's ever outright asked about my emotions.

I plop down on the dingy garage floor and rest my elbows on my knees. Tyler lowers himself next to me and assumes the same position.

"We broke up just over a week ago," I finally say, staring straight ahead at my mom's bright red Honda.

"What happened?" Tyler asks for the millionth time.

A heavy sigh rattles my body. "It's a long story."

"I got nothing but time, little brother."

A few seconds pass. "It all started after Millie's baby shower. After we all left, while Becca was closing up her ice cream shop, Dad showed up and cornered her."

Tyler whips his head to me, his eyes wide. "He did what?"

I explain how Dad introduced himself to Becca, how he fed her a sob story about our falling out, then guilt-tripped her into telling me that I should reach out to him and give our relationship another chance.

"We fought about it." I close my eyes and lean my head back against the wall. "She thought I was being too harsh on him. She thought that I had punished him enough for the way he treated me when he found out about my TikTok. She thought I should consider forgiving him and work on our relationship."

"And then what happened?"

"I was pissed. I couldn't believe that she'd think I should

do that. She was so supportive of me when I first told her about my falling out with Dad, and then she pulls a complete one-eighty." I shake my head. "She texted me the other day to say she wants to talk things out. But I can't. Not if we can't see eye to eye on this."

Out of the corner of my eye, I see Tyler shaking his head. "Look, I know you think I'm just giving you shit when I give you a hard time about being stubborn all the time. But I'm not. That's one-hundred-percent you, Gage."

I twist my head to look at him. "What's your point?"

"You've always been stubborn. It's a good thing and a bad thing. When you're standing up for what's right or defending someone, your stubbornness is admirable. You don't back down, and that's fucking awesome. But when you're wrong, it's infuriating."

"When I'm wrong?" I repeat, irritated.

"Gage, you can't honestly tell me that you don't think you've never been wrong about anything," he says.

"Of course I know that I've been wrong. Lots of times. But do you honestly think I'm wrong for being angry at Dad for how he treated me?"

"Being angry? Of course not. You have every right to be mad at him. He was an asshole to you. But to cut him out of your life forever? Yeah, I think you're wrong to do that. I think you're making a mistake."

I roll my eyes. "No surprise there. You've always given him more credit than he deserves."

"Jesus, Gage. The reason I have a relationship with our dad is because family is important to me." There's a bite to his tone that I'm not sure I've heard before. My brother sounds so serious and impassioned right now, not like his usual joking self. "Look, I don't live in a fantasy land. I know our dad is flawed as fuck. He's a workaholic who cared more about running a fine dining empire than being a present father to us when we were little. That's messed up. I'll always be hurt by that, and I'll always hold that against him. Always. But he's changed. He knows he messed up with us big time when we were kids. And he knows that we're all adults now and can see him for the flawed person he is. What he said to Becca about regretting how he treated you and wanting a better relationship with you? He's said that to me too. And Maya."

I'm sputtering. I had no idea.

"When you cut him out of your life, it scared him shitless, Gage. Right after that happened, he apologized to me for being an absent father growing up. And Maya told me he did the same to her. He makes time for me now. We try to see each other a couple times a month. It's not perfect, but I can tell he's trying his hardest to be a better father. Maya said that he calls her every week to catch up too when she's traveling. She and I had lunch with him the other day too."

I'm stammering. "W-Why didn't you tell me this?"

"Because every time we bring him up to you, you get pissed. You shut down. You don't want to hear anything about him. We get tired of you snapping at us, so we just don't bother anymore."

I'm dazed as I take in everything my brother's said. My dad has been actively rebuilding his relationship with my siblings—and seems to be doing a decent job of it. I can't believe it.

"People can change, Gage. It's not easy, but it's possible. Dad seems to be putting in the work to be a better father to us. I'm not saying that it'll end up perfect. Maybe it won't. But I think this is a relationship worth trying to salvage."

Despite everything Tyler has said, anxiety and anger rocket through me at the thought of seeing our dad.

"I don't know," I mutter. "It's a lot to think about."

"Is it?" Tyler twists his head to look at me. "I threatened to make a move on your ex, and you forgave me. After you knocked the wind out of me, but still. You gave me a chance to explain myself. You gave me a chance to make things right between us."

"You're my brother. Of course I'd do that for you."

"And he's your dad. Doesn't he deserve a chance too?"

I go quiet at the ironclad point my brother just made.

"You were wrong to get angry at Becca," Tyler says after a long moment. "You know that now, right?"

The realization lands like a kick to my gut. "Yeah."

He claps a hand on my shoulder. "Then make it right, little brother."

He stands up, grabs the ice, then walks back into the house, shutting the door behind him.

I stay sitting alone in the garage for what feels like minutes, in a daze. There are so many things I have to do to make things right that I'm dizzy just thinking about it all. But after a moment, the answer is so clear, so obvious.

I pull my phone out of my pocket and call the one person I never thought I would.

Chapter 26

Gage

When I walk into Seb'on in the upscale Cherry Creek neighborhood, my heart is in my throat. It's empty since it's nine in the morning and they don't open until noon. I take in the rectangular dining space with the open kitchen in the middle, like an island of stainless steel in a sea of black marble flooring and fixtures with dark walnut furnishings.

It looks the same as the last night I was here over a year ago...when my dad fired me and I cut him out of my life.

"Gage?"

I spin around at the sound of my name. When I see my dad standing ten feet from me, his blue eyes tired and hopeful, I hold my breath. I have no idea what I'm supposed to do or say right now. I didn't think that far ahead.

The corners of his mouth quirk up in a small smile. His short-trimmed beard has more gray in it than the last time I saw him. That thought sends a jolt of pain through me.

It's been so long since we've seen each other.

"You're here," he says.

"I said I would be." I clear my throat when I realize how hard my tone sounds.

He stops walking and frowns slightly. He gestures to a nearby two-person table. "Would you like to sit for a sec?"

I nod and take a chair. "Thanks for letting me come by."

"Of course. I was so happy when you called." He lets out a flustered laugh that unnerves me. He sounds so nervous, like he's not sure what to do or say to me right now.

"How's your mom?" he blurts.

I'm caught off guard by his out-of-the-blue question. "She's fine. Busy with work, but she just got back from a cruise with her cousins."

"Alaskan cruise?"

"Yeah. How'd you know that?"

"She always asked me to take her on an Alaskan cruise, but I never did. Too busy with work."

"Oh."

"Did she have a good birthday?"

I'm sputtering. They've been divorced ever since I was ten. He still remembers her birthday?

"Uh, yeah. We threw a party at her house. All her family and friends came. She had a great time."

A sad smile tugs at his mouth. He glances off to the side. I have no idea what prompted those questions about Mom.

I take a second to refocus on why I'm here. He turns back to me. I look him straight in the eye, my heart in my throat as I work up the nerve to say what I'm about to say.

"I owe you an apology." The words tumble from my lips like rocks tumbling down a mountainside. Fast, abrupt, hurried.

His eyebrows jump to his hairline before he frowns and shakes his head. "No, wait. I'm the one who should be apologizing. For so many things." He sighs. "Son, I need you to know how sorry I am for firing you, for saying those awful things to you about your social media account. I was wrong. So, so wrong."

He presses his eyes shut and shakes his head, like he's taking a second to collect himself. "I was a narrow-minded jerk. Ever since that day we fought, I've been thinking about a lot of things. I realize now that I've spent so much of my life focusing on the wrong things—on business and prestige and so much other stuff that doesn't matter. I gave up the most precious time in my life—raising you and your siblings —for material crap."

A hard swallow moves down his throat, and his eyes go misty. He blinks quickly. "I'll regret that forever. Just like I regret losing contact with you this past year. But I'm the one to blame for all of it."

For a moment I just look at him. As comforting as it is to hear him apologize and explain what he did wrong, I'm unnerved. I need a second to get used to seeing my unflap-pable, unfeeling dad like this: pained and regretful.

"I'm not used to hearing you like this," I say. It's prob-ably the wrong thing to say in this moment when he's being so vulnerable and open, but it's the truth. And it's the only thing I can think to say.

He surprises me by letting out a soft, sad laugh. "That's understandable. I've made a living as a rigid, uptight perfec-tionist."

"What made you change?"

"Losing you." He says it without missing a beat while looking me straight in the eye. "You and your brother and sister are the only things that matter to me, Gage. If I don't have you, I don't have anything." His voice starts to shake. "It's sad that it took me so long, that it took me being cut off by my own son, to realize that."

I'm speechless as I take in this moment with my dad. He's not the unrelenting and unfeeling robot I remember. He's human. He's emotional. He's imperfect. But I still love him. I always have. And I want him in my life again.

"I'm sorry too, Dad," I say after a quiet moment. "For cutting you out. That wasn't the right way to deal with things. I was just hurt by the things you said to me and how you fired me. And icing you out was the only way I could think to deal."

"I understand why you did it." He glances around his empty restaurant. "I'm sorry too for going up to Becca like that. That wasn't the right way to reach out. I was just desperate to have you in my life again. But I know that's not an excuse for the abrupt way I approached her."

I shake my head. "Becca really felt for you. I wouldn't be here sitting with you if it wasn't for her."

His eyes brighten. "She seems like a wonderful young woman."

My throat squeezes. "She is. I think I, uh, messed it up though."

His gaze on me turns concerned. "What happened?"

I pause for a second, letting the rawness of this moment wash over me. We've never had this sort of relationship before, where I've talked to him about personal things, like my relationships.

His expression turns sheepish as the silence stretches between us. "You don't have to tell me. Sorry, I didn't mean to pry. I know we don't normally talk about these sorts of things. But if you ever want to, I'm always here to listen."

I pull my lips into my mouth and nod. This feels so weird, sitting across from my dad, opening myself up like this. But the longer I think about it, the more I realize that's exactly what I want. I want to feel comfortable opening up to him. I want to feel comfortable talking to him about my life. And if that's what I truly want, I need to start now.

So I tell him about how after I called him to tell him off, Becca and I argued.

"She thought I was being too harsh on you and that I should reach out to you," I say quietly. "I was pissed. I couldn't believe my girlfriend would go against me. I was so hurt over it, and we haven't spoken since."

He looks pained. "I'm sorry I was the reason for your argument."

I shrug. "It's not your fault. I was a stubborn and angry jerk. I was being unreasonable."

"What made you change your mind and call me?"

"Tyler. He talked some sense into me and told me about how you've been reaching out to him and Maya and spending more time together."

The look on his face turns tender. "I see. Thank you for giving me a chance." He hesitates for a second. "I want you to know, I'm so proud of you, son, for the business you've built on your own. For how you've paved your own way. You're talented and hardworking. I'm so lucky you're my kid."

My chest swells. I've wanted to hear him say that for so long.

"Thanks, Dad."

He hesitates for a second. "How would you feel if I asked you to come back and work as my sous chef again?"

My mouth cracks open. I wasn't expecting that. "Honestly? I'm, uh, I'm not sure."

He nods, his expression resigned.

"It's not that I don't want to. I just..." I take a breath, careful with how I word this next part. "This is a lot to take in. We're getting to know each other again. I don't want to put too much pressure on things by working in the same kitchen again."

"Of course." His gaze is a mix of sad yet hopeful. "I just want you to do what makes you happy, Gage. That's all that matters to me."

In the quiet moment that passes between us, I picture what it would be like to work with my dad the way he is now: supportive, understanding, and open-minded. I think I'd like that.

He checks the time. "I have to take a work call in a few minutes. Sorry."

"It's no problem."

"I'd like to see you again. If that's okay."

I take in the hesitation in his tone and expression. My chest aches. "I'd like that too."

"Maybe Monday? I have the day off. We could, uh, get a drink or grab a bite."

"That sounds great, Dad."

When we stand up, he pulls me into a hug. It catches me off guard at first, but a second later, I squeeze him back. When he lets go, his eyes are misty, but he's smiling.

He starts to walk off but turns around. "I know I haven't earned the right to do this, but can I give some fatherly advice to you?"

I smile slightly. "Sure."

"Do whatever it takes to make things right with Becca. She sounds like a lovely person who makes you happy. You'll regret it forever if you lose her."

There's a look in my dad's eyes that I don't recognize, like he knows what it's like to lose the person he loves over something he could have made right if he hadn't been so focused on other things.

I think back to how he asked about my mom and her

birthday. I think back to that vase of lilies at her house, to the small white card with a red heart and the initial "A."

Andre.

My dad sent those flowers to her.

Determination surges inside of me. I tell him thanks before running out of the restaurant and to my car.

Chapter 27

Becca

"Tori, I'm really not in the mood to go out to dinner." I gaze out the window of the passenger seat of Tori's car as she drives us to Cherry Hill.

"I know that. But you need to get out, Bec. You've been working so hard. You deserve a nice dinner out."

I take in the smile on Tori's face as she looks ahead at the road. She's been in a great mood the whole day—the past few days, actually.

I think back to this morning at work when she surprised me with the news that she'd be taking me out for a late dinner to cheer me up after I'd spent the last week-plus working and sulking. I cringe when I recall how I groaned. God, what a brat I was to do that. My best friend is kind enough to plan a special dinner to cheer me up after my breakup, and here I am, acting annoyed.

I sit up in my seat, determined not to ruin the night. Sure, I'd rather be at home in my pajamas, eating a pint of ice cream, than wearing this little black dress and these heels, but that doesn't matter. I've done enough wallowing.

I need to make this a fun night for my amazing and thoughtful best friend.

She parks on the street, and we walk a few blocks to a white-brick restaurant front.

I frown up at the sign. "I'm not even going to try to pronounce that."

Tori laughs and loops her arm in mine. "It's French. I think."

Her long braid smacks my shoulder. "You look really pretty," I tell her. The gold mini-dress she's wearing makes her auburn hair look like fire. So gorgeous. "I'm sorry you're stuck with a sad sack for a date tonight."

"Hey. None of that talk." She gives my arm a gentle squeeze before letting go and opening the door to the restaurant. While she talks to the maître d', I take in the bustling space. Almost every table is occupied with happy-looking, well-dressed patrons chatting and eating. In the middle is an open kitchen. A dozen people in white chef's jackets move about in the space, prepping, slicing, plating, and cooking.

"Right this way, ladies."

We follow the maître d' to the far side of the restaurant, then toward the back.

I take in all the marble architecture and metallic accents. I touch Tori's hand. "This place is fancy."

We're shown to a small private dining room at the back. It's the size of an office with a dark wooden table that seats six.

"Tori, you planned all this for me?"

I catch the maître d' smiling as he sets a drink menu and two dinner menus on the table between us. "Your server will be right with you."

A knowing smile plays across Tori's lips as she looks at me. "Sure did. Let's decide what we're having."

I crack open the menu and skim the dishes.

"I think we should have something bubbly, like prosecco."

"Sounds great."

"How about we do the tasting menu?" she says, pointing at the menu.

My eyes bulge out of my head when I look at the price. Even though business is booming for Sweet Cheeks, and I've replenished my savings, I don't want to be careless. I still need to be careful with how I spend my month.

Tori reaches over and touches my hand. "My treat," she says.

"No way, that's too much."

She shakes her head. "Trust me, it's really not."

Before I can ask her what she means, the server comes in and takes our drink order. Tori tells him we'll each have the five-course tasting menu. He pours prosecco into our flutes and leaves us. Tori raises a glass. "To you, Bec. Not only are you the best ice cream maker on the planet, but you're an amazing friend and a truly wonderful person. You deserve all the good things in the world."

Tears prick at my eyes. It feels good to cry happy tears after all the crying I've done over Gage.

I sniffle. "Thank you, Tori. I don't even have the words to say just how much this all means." I sip my glass of prosecco, savoring the crisp flavor and the way the bubbles pop on my tongue. "God, that's good."

She beams at me. "See? Doesn't it feel good to get all dressed up and treat yourself?"

I nod and admit that it does. Soon our first course arrives: a slice of raw yellowtail with delicate shavings of jalapeno on top. The fish sits in a miso lime juice reduction and is dusted in dried seaweed.

"Mmm, oh my god," I say as I finish it in two bites.

I chuckle as Tori picks up her shallow plate and slurps the reduction. I copy her.

Next course is a white bean and endive salad dressed in a citrus vinaigrette, then a seared scallop in a pool of piping hot cauliflower and gouda soup.

"Oh my god, I wanna bathe in this soup." Tori moans as she licks her lips.

My eyes roll to the back of my head as I take a bite of the perfectly cooked scallop. I hum at the rich flavor and the crispy sear.

When the server drops off the fourth course, I cover my mouth and hold in a gasp. On the plate sits two lamb chops on a bed of roasted potatoes with herb gravy. A perfect sprig of mint tops the dish. This looks exactly like the dinner Gage cooked me the first time we had dinner together.

"Are you okay?" Tori asks.

I nod without even looking at her. "Yes. All good."

When I take my first bite, I'm transported back to that night. It's the same burst of flavors as the meal Gage cooked me.

I make sure to take my time as I finish the dish. I chew slowly, savoring the perfect blend of salt, fat, and herbs.

The server returns with dessert menus. "Ladies, the last course is your choice."

When he walks off, I look at the menu. As I skim the list of offerings, I halt at the very last one. My eyes go wide as I read the text.

This evening's featured dessert: chocolate torte with espresso ice cream from local shop Sweet Cheeks Creamery.

"What in the..." I look up at Tori. "H-How is my ice cream on the menu?"

She sips her water glass before taking a deep breath. "I have a confession."

"Okay..."

"I didn't plan this dinner. Someone else did. My job was to get you here."

"What?"

I hear footsteps behind me. When I look up, I see Gage standing in front of us.

I almost choke. For a second all I can do is look at him. My heart lodges in my throat as I take in the sight of Gage. He's wearing dark dress pants and a black dress shirt, no tie. The top two buttons are undone. Wow. That...that's super hot. Why have I never noticed just how hot unbuttoned men's dress shirts are?

I shake my head, annoyed with myself at how I'm focused on how sexy he looks.

"Wh-what are you doing here?"

His smile is slight, like he's hopeful but hesitant at the same time. "I wanted to talk to you."

Just then Tori stands up. "I'll give you two a sec."

She slips out of the room. Gage's chest heaves as he takes a breath. "Can I sit?"

I nod, still in a shocked daze at seeing him. "Gage, what is going on?"

"I, uh, planned this. This dinner. I asked Tori to bring you here so I could surprise you. And talk to you."

I go quiet. My mind is a cluster of shock and confusion. As happy as I am to see him, I'm also annoyed. He asked my best friend to bring me to some random restaurant so he could ambush me when we're not even on speaking terms.

"If you wanted to talk, you could have just called me," I finally say.

"You deserved better than an apology over the phone."

He clears his throat and pins me with his gaze. "This is my dad's restaurant. I worked with him here when he fired me, right before I cut him out of my life."

"Oh." I'm shocked. I wasn't expecting him to say that.

"We reconciled. We're working on our relationship. He asked me to start working here again as his sous chef, and I said yes. I'm working here a few nights a week."

I smile, heartened at the news. "Gage, that's wonderful."

"It's all because of you, Becca. You were right. I was wrong to cut him out of my life, I realize that now. He's changed a lot. He's so much more understanding and open now. He's supportive of me and my career. All he cares about is that I'm happy and doing what I love."

He pauses, and the look in his eyes turns pointed and raw.

"Becca, I'm so sorry. I had no right to lash out at you when you defended my dad after he came to see you. I was being a stubborn jackass. It took losing you and my brother talking some sense in me to realize how wrong I was about everything." Gage blinks, and the look in his eyes turns pained.

"I'm sorry too, Gage. I shouldn't have pushed you to reconcile with your dad. I should have just listened to you and supported you. I should have just trusted that you'd reach out to him when you were ready. And you did."

He shakes his head. "I was being so defensive. I'm so sorry for the hurtful things I said. I didn't mean them. That crap I said about you using me for TikTok and using my dad so your business could get ahead..." He grimaces like he's swallowing back bile, like the memory of his words makes him sick. "I'll understand if you never forgive me for that. I just need you to know that I regret ever saying it. I didn't even mean it. If I could take it back, I would."

I can feel the tension melting from my body as I observe Gage pour his heart out to me.

"I know, right now, this dinner seems like a ridiculous stunt. But I swear it's not. I did this because you deserve more than an apology from me. You deserve one hell of a grovel in a five-star restaurant. You deserve the moon and stars, you deserve the sun, the universe, everything. You are *that* incredible, Becca. I'm lucky you ever gave me the time of day. I'm lucky you ever cared about me."

When his voice starts to tremble, he stops and swallows. "I love you, Becca. I know that's probably nuts for you to hear since we've only known each other for a few months. But it's true. I've never felt this way about anyone before."

I'm breathless as I listen to him. My heart is pounding so hard, I can feel it in my ears.

"I don't expect you to say it back. I don't even expect you to accept my apology—"

"I love you too, Gage."

His eyes go wide. He blinks and shakes his head, like he can't quite believe what I've said.

He lets out a breath through a shaky smile. "You love me?"

I nod. "So, so much." I stand up and move to stand between his legs and cup his face in my hands. I lean down and kiss him.

His hands grip my waist. "God, I missed you."

"I missed you too." Closing my eyes, I lean my forehead against his. "That was a five-star grovel, Gage Grant."

He chuckles before kissing me breathless. "Was it?"

"I've never had anyone print up a fake dessert menu with my ice cream on it as a way to say sorry."

He leans back to look at me. "It's not fake, Becca. My dad wants to serve your ice cream on the dessert menu at all of his restaurants."

My jaw drops. "Are you serious?"

"Dead serious. He ordered your ice cream and thinks Sweet Cheeks is the most delicious ice cream he's ever tasted."

I fall into Gage's lap, stunned at the news. "I can't believe it." I stammer for a solid three seconds before hugging him. "My ice cream is going to be in restaurants! I've been dreaming about this!"

"It's happening. You made it happen."

"*You* did. None of this would be happening if you hadn't answered my drunk DM on a whim."

"Best decision of my life." Gage grins and laces his fingers in mine. "You deserve all the credit, Becca. Your amazing ice cream speaks for itself."

I shake my head. "It's a mix of everything, of both of us. Delicious ice cream desserts, flirty TikTok videos, and hard work. Over and over and over."

"Hmm." He quirks an eyebrow, his expression teasing. "Dessert, flirt, repeat. Sounds like a winning formula."

I kiss him. "It really is."

Epilogue

6 months later
BECCA

"What do you think about this? Too sexy?" Gage asks, his eyebrow quirked.

He shimmies his hips, and a dollop of whipped cream floats from his crotch to the floor. I burst out laughing.

I step over to him and press a kiss to his lips, careful not to get whipped cream on my clothes. "You are the perfect amount of sexy. Always."

He flashes that devastatingly gorgeous smile that's my kryptonite. Then he steps back, holds his arms up at his sides, and spins around. "You sure about that?"

"Positive. Despite the ridiculousness of your whipped cream bikini, you're still hot as hell."

His burnt sienna eyes go fiery, and the corner of his mouth lifts in a sexy half-smile. "I love it when you swear, angel."

That familiar heat flashes all over my body at my boyfriend's pet name for me. He leans forward and dusts a kiss on my lips. "If you keep looking at me like that, I'm going to have my way with you right now on the floor of your ice cream shop, and we'll never get around to filming this TikTok video."

My clit pulses at just the thought. We totally could. It's evening, Sweet Cheeks is closed, all the doors are locked, and the street we're on is completely empty.

Against every urge in my body to ravage Gage, I step back. "Let's get this filmed first. I promised Sweet Cheeks' followers something big, and I need to deliver."

"Big, huh?" Gage smirks down between his legs. I give him a playful shove on the shoulder.

The past several months have been a whirlwind. Almost nine months ago, my life was a disaster. I was fresh off a breakup and on the verge of losing my business. But one drunken DM changed all that. I have a hot and supportive boyfriend who is about to move in with me. Sweet Cheeks is thriving. Business has been booming, thanks to all the sexy videos Gage and I have been filming and posting on Sweet Cheeks' TikTok. Every day I sell out of all the ice cream flavors in the display case. Even now with winter in full swing, customers still line up out the door every day to buy my ice cream. I've had to hire a couple more employees to take care of all the online orders. And my ice cream is a staple on the dessert menus at Gage's dad's restaurants Avec and Seb'on.

Gage smiles at me, and it feels like fireworks exploding in my chest. I never thought life could be this good, that I could be this happy.

"Ready?" he asks.

I nod, then hit record on his phone, which is set up on his tripod.

"You sure this isn't going to scare off Sweet Cheeks' loyal TikTok following?" he teases.

I shake my head. "No way. They're gonna love this."

Sweet Cheeks just hit eight hundred thousand TikTok followers yesterday, and I want to do something fun to celebrate. I pitched the idea of having Gage decked out in a whipped cream bikini, and because he's such a good sport—and because he loves me—he agreed.

I turn to the camera and grin before leaning my face down to his chest. His pecs are covered in small mounds of whipped cream. I lick off a tiny bit of the whipped cream covering his left pec, then peer down between his legs, where a generous mound of whipped cream rests. Gage's naughty bits are out of frame, but that doesn't stop me from looking back at the camera and winking. I stand up straight and smile at Gage, who's flashing his signature scowl. A beat later, he does something he's never done in any of his TikTok videos or Sweet Cheeks' videos. He smiles—at me.

We kiss, careful to keep it lips only to avoid violating any content guidelines. We know we're already pushing it with the implied nudity.

I step out of the shot and stop recording. While Gage cleans himself up, I upload the video to Sweet Cheeks' TikTok and type out the caption I've been planning all day.

TFW you're the only one he smiles for ;) #aww #best-feeling #truelove #lovebirds #sweetcheeks #badboy #goodgirl

I pick a sexy slow jam to play over the video and post it. When I turn to show the video to Gage, he's standing naked in front of me.

"Aren't you cold?" I ask as I press up against him.

He shakes his head. "Nope."

In one smooth motion, he hauls me onto the counter. I wrap my legs around his waist, slink my arms around his neck, and lightly bite his bottom lip before kissing him.

Just then I hear the sound of keys rattling. "Becca? Gage? Are you here?"

I freeze at the sound of Maya's voice. "Oh no..."

"What the f—"

Maya shrieks when she rounds the corner and sees us. "Oh my god! Are you guys doing it?"

She covers her eyes with both of her hands and stumbles backward, bumping into the wall. Gage rolls his eyes as he quickly gets dressed, while I hop off the counter and resist the urge to curl into a ball and melt into the floor.

Gage walks over to Maya. "What the hell are you doing here?"

"Are you clothed? Please tell me you're clothed."

Gage exhales sharply. "Yes. Now do you wanna tell me why you barged into my girlfriend's shop after hours?"

Maya's hands fall to her sides, a sheepish expression on her face. "I'm sorry."

"How did you even get the keys to come in?"

She stammers. "Tori. I told her I needed to talk to you guys."

Maya and Tori have become good friends ever since they met at Millie's baby shower. Maya often crashes at Tori's place when we have girls' nights out.

I walk over to her. "Is everything okay?"

"Yeah, I just...um..."

I notice her expression turns nervous as she looks at her brother. "I, uh, have some news. I got a new job."

Gage rests his hands on his hips, his expression incredulous as he looks at his little sister. "*That's* what you barged in here to tell us?"

She winces. "Yes, because...well, I need to ask you a favor."

Gage nods once, lips pursed. "There it is."

I grab his hand and give him a silent look that says, "Be nice." Yeah, Maya can be a flake with how much she moves and changes jobs, but she's a sweetheart at her core. She's welcomed me with open arms since the moment she met me, and I want to show her that same kindness and support.

"This new job is in San Diego," Maya says. "I'm going to be the personal assistant for my friend Ingrid for the next three months. It'll be a temporary move, so there's no point in bringing all of my stuff with me."

"Three months?" Gage says.

Maya nods. "Her full-time personal assistant is on maternity leave."

She mentions something about how her friend Ingrid works for her family business, some massive global hospitality chain.

"I have to leave kind of soon," she says. "Like, right after New Year's. And I was wondering if you guys could take care of my plants while I'm gone? And, um, Mr. Pudding too?"

Gage rolls his eyes at the mention of the betta fish Maya bought at a pet store a couple of months ago.

I squeeze his hand. "Of course we can," I say. "It's no problem, right?" I look up at Gage, who, I can tell by the tight set of his jaw muscle, is holding back a "hell no."

He manages a slight smile that doesn't completely look like a grimace. "Sure thing, sis."

Maya beams and hugs me, then Gage. "Thanks, you guys. You're the best. I love you both so much."

"We love you too," I say.

Gage nods and mutters his affirmation. Maya says she'll

be by my place tomorrow to drop everything off. She starts to leave but spins around. "Oh, I almost forgot! Millie wants to know if you'll be making any more batches of unicorn swirl. She told me that nursing baby Evelyn is making her ravenous and your ice cream is her top craving."

I chuckle. "Of course. We'll drop some off this weekend."

Maya thanks us and leaves. Gage turns to me and lets out an exasperated laugh. "Well, that was a hell of a way to get cockblocked. My little sister, plants, and a betta fish."

I laugh and slide my arms around his waist.

"You sure you're okay with all this?" he asks.

"Of course. Maya is a sweetheart, and I'm happy to help her out."

Gage flashes a soft smile at me. "How did I get so lucky? You put up with my crazy family *and* you're beautiful *and* sweet *and* dynamite in bed."

He kisses me hard until I'm breathless. I claw at his shirt, desperate to feel his bare skin on me.

After a few seconds, he stops me with a hand on my wrist. "Let's take this upstairs. I don't want any more interruptions."

A second later he throws me over his shoulder. I squeal and laugh. Gage walks out of Sweet Cheeks and up the stairs toward the apartment.

"It's been a while since you've pulled out the 'sexy fireman carry' move," I say.

The low rumble of his chuckle echoes in the stairwell. "I knew it would get you hot."

When we reach the third floor, he sets me down and unlocks the door. As soon as he shuts it, I pounce. Our clothes are on the floor in seconds.

"Let's move this to your bed," he says against my mouth.

I lean back, breaking our kiss, and look up at him. "*Our* bed. You're moving in with me, remember?"

At that moment, as I gaze up at him, my heartbeat skids. I still can't believe this amazing man is mine.

Emotion flashes in Gage's eyes as he smiles at me. "I can't wait."

Want a spicy bonus scene with Gage and Becca?

Becca plans a sexy surprise for Gage their first night after moving in together...

Sign up for my newsletter to read it:

www.sarahsmithbooks.com

* * *

Thank you for reading *Dessert Flirt Repeat*! The Grant Siblings Series continues with *Snow, Ice, and Spice*! Maya's book! You're gonna love it because...it's a steamy, enemies-to-lovers (one sided) hockey romance! Get it in ebook and paperback. And keep reading for an excerpt.

Excerpt from Snow, Ice, and Spice

I take one last look at my reflection in the full-length mirror in my bedroom. My boobs are spilling out of this black lace top. If I lean over too quickly, they'll fall out for sure. Perfect.

I grab my purse, walk out of my bedroom, and head for the front door.

Yeah, this is petty. And immature. I don't care.

When I think about what Theo said to me yesterday, when he acted like a jealous psycho after I mentioned wanting to go out with Xander, anger surges through me like a flame.

Where the hell does he get off telling me who I can and can't date? Especially after that conversation I overheard between him and Xander at the arena the other day. I heard him say that he sees me as nothing more than a friend. Why the hell was he acting like the thought of me going out with Xander would send him over the edge? He had zero right. Even though I hate it when my older brothers pull that overprotective bullshit on me, at least it kind of makes sense. I'm their little sister. They just want me to be safe. But Theo? We're just friends.

I'm just trying to look out for you, Maya. Xander is a good guy overall, but no way in hell would I ever let any woman in my life within fifty feet of him.

Just thinking about the condescending way he spoke to me last night has me in a fury. He treated me like I was some helpless, defenseless damsel, like I can't navigate my own dating life without him intervening to save me.

I shake my head, annoyed. Whatever. I'm done being mad at Theo for his ridiculous and completely unreasonable jealousy. It's time to show him I don't need his advice.

When I walk into the main part of the house, Theo is standing at the kitchen island clad in sweats and a t-shirt, eating an apple and frowning at his phone. When he looks up, his eyes bulge out of his head. His jaw plummets to the floor, and a chunk of apple falls out of his mouth.

I mentally high-five myself. Just the reaction I was hoping for.

"Whoa…" he murmurs, his gaze fixed on my chest.

"I'm going out," I say without even looking at him as I head to the coat closet and fetch my coat. "With Xander."

Behind me, I hear a choking noise. I bite back a smile.

"Dressed like that?" His voice hitches up and I laugh. He's about to blow a gasket.

"Yeah. Do you have a problem with that?" I cross my arms, pushing my boobs up even more. Theo's peaches-and-cream complexion turns red as he glares at my tits.

"Nope. No problem," he mumbles as he glowers at his phone.

"You sure? Because you seem a little testy," I taunt.

His gaze cuts to my face. "I'm fine," he bites.

I purse my lips to keep from grinning. Yeah, it's a cheap

shot to wear the most revealing top I own on a date that Theo doesn't want me to go on. But I don't care. I want to make it clear as fucking day to him that he doesn't get to dictate what I do or who I date.

I step over to him. I'm so close that he stumbles back from me. "Do you think this top is too revealing?"

His jaw bulges, he's biting down so hard. He huffs out a breath. "Nope. You're actually pretty dressed up for a date with Xander. He prefers the women he goes out with to wear as little as possible. Naked is best, honestly."

Anger flashes through me. He wants to play dirty?

I grin at him. "Good. I like being naked."

A choking sound rips from his throat and his gaze is a crystal blue bonfire. Satisfied, I turn to walk away, but he catches me by the wrist and pulls me back to face him. In a flash, my ass is against the edge of the countertop and Theo is caging me in, his hands gripping the counter on either side of me. Our faces are barely two inches apart.

"What the hell are you trying to pull here, Maya?" he growls.

I bat my eyelashes and smile sweetly at him. "Whatever do you mean, Theo? I'm just standing here waiting for Xander to pick me up."

"Bullshit. You're doing this to fuck with me."

Like a brat, I tap the tip of his nose with my index finger. "Bingo!"

He blinks furiously for a second and shakes his head, like he's confused, but his stance over me remains.

"You're damn right I'm fucking with you, Theo. The next time you think you can comment on or control who I date, think again." I lean my face closer to him. "Think of me wearing this outfit while I'm on a date with whoever the hell I want. And know that it's none of your business."

His arms fall to his sides and he steps back. I start to walk off, but Theo grabs me by the waist and pulls me against him. Before I can think or say anything, we're nose to nose, his mouth hovering over mine.

"And when you're on your date, think of this," he rasps.

A split second later his mouth is on mine, and I'm in shock. Theo is kissing the absolute fuck out of me.

As much as I should push him away and curse him out, I don't. His mouth, his lips, his tongue...they all feel so fucking good.

If I thought our first kiss on New Year's Eve was good, this one blows it out of the water. This kiss is dynamite. This kiss is urgent, desperate. It's passion and fire and lust. His lips and tongue are firm and teasing, like he's savoring me. Like he's using his mouth to prove a point—that he can kiss the fuck out of me even in a moment when I can't stand him.

Because yeah, Theo pissed me off with that possessive act he pulled just now. But that's a distant memory in the wake of this earth-shattering kiss. I'd take a million knock-down, drag-out arguments with Theo Thompson if it meant that each one would end with a mind-bending kiss like this.

My knees wobble. My inner thigh muscles twitch.

When I feel that faint, tell-tale pulse between my legs, I moan into Theo's mouth.

"You like this, don't you?" he rasps.

"Yes," I whine. It falls from my mouth instantly, like a reflex.

I move my mouth in tandem with his, barely able to keep up, he's so rabid and desperate with his rhythm. God, Theo Thompson can fucking *kiss*. He's got the mouth and tongue of a demon. And as he laps his tongue against mine, I can't help but let my imagination run wild. Zero doubt that Theo's demon tongue would play my clit like a fiddle.

Almost like he can read my mind, I feel his hand start to slide from my waist to my hip. He gives me a gentle squeeze before tracing his finger along the waistband of my jeans.

I let out a desperate whimper against Theo's lips in anticipation of his fingers moving lower, right where I want them...

But then he leans back, breaking our kiss. He hovers his lips over mine, his hot, wet breath dusting over my mouth.

"Tell me how bad you want this, Maya. Tell me how much you want me to touch you."

He pins with me a cloudy, feral gaze.

That ache between my legs is a full-on pulse now. My thighs are twitching with the need to feel his fingers work my pussy.

"Please touch me...please..." I pant.

The corner of his mouth hooks up in a devilish smile that makes my knees buckle.

He unbuttons my jeans, yanks down the zipper, and slides his hand inside.

My eyes roll to the back of my head as I feel his palm, hot and firm and soft all at once. My clit jumps even though he's not even touching it yet.

I claw at his chest before snaking my hands through his thick, wavy, blond hair. When I tug my fingers through it, he growls into my mouth.

"Fuck, you're so wet. For me."

I nod and let out a whiny, "Yes," not caring one bit about how desperate and needy I sound. The only thing my body wants right now is for Theo to make me come.

He works the pads of his fingers gently over my clit. I

inhale sharply, and my legs start to shake as the pleasure in my core builds.

Theo leans back just enough to lock eyes with me. "You wanna ride my hand, Maya?"

I nod.

"Say it." His tone is low and guttural and demanding and god, do I like it.

"I wanna ride your hand."

"You wanna come?"

"Yes."

He swirls faster. The pleasure grows hotter within me.

"How bad?"

"So bad."

He traces his tongue along my bottom lip and I gasp. That's such an unexpected move. So erotic and teasing...

He shifts so he's palming my pussy. He gives a gentle squeeze that sends a jolt of pleasure rocketing through me. My eyes roll back.

"Ride my hand, Maya."

I grip a hand around his wrist while I do exactly what he says. It's not long, barely a minute before I feel that flash of heat and intensity.

My head falls against his shoulder, and I feel him shift and lean closer. His hot breath ghosts over the side of my neck. His lips land on my skin in a soft, gentle kiss.

"God, you're soaked," he murmurs.

He slides his hand farther down my panties and then I feel his fingers inside of me. I gasp when his thick fingers work my g-spot.

"Right there?" he grunts.

I nod quickly as I grind against his palm. My orgasm lingers right on the horizon. I start to shake as the pressure and heat build and build...

"Come hard, Maya. For me. Right now."

Theo's rasped command is the trigger for my climax. Soon I'm thrashing and shouting as I explode. He sinks his teeth into the side of my neck, which makes me come even harder. Wow. I didn't think I liked being bitten, but this is fucking hot.

I don't know how long it takes for me to start to come down, but by the time I do, I'm panting. My lungs are hollow and raw, like I've just sprinted a race.

I have to blink several times before those white bursts that filled my line of vision when I came start to dissipate.

He stumbles back and my hands drop from his body. He gazes at me, his eyes cloudy with arousal, chest heaving as he catches his breath.

He's the mirror image of me: panting, mouth hanging open, skin flushed, clothes rumpled.

My entire body is aching for more as I stare at him in disbelief. That really happened. I just rode Theo's hand until I came.

My gaze dips lower and I spot the bulge in his sweatpants. My mouth waters and the urge to fall to my knees and take him in my mouth throttles me.

But before I can, I notice his gaze shifts from pleasure-drunk to pointed in two seconds flat. He pins me with that razor-sharp stare as he slashes his tongue along his bottom lip.

"Have fun on your date, Maya."

Oh, right. I'm supposed to go on a date. With Xander.

Theo walks away to his bedroom and shuts the door behind him, leaving me a strange mix of confused, turned on, and pissed off.

Want the rest? Read it in Kindle Unlimited or paperback!

Also by Sarah Smith

Grant Siblings Series

Dessert Flirt Repeat

Snow, Ice, and Spice

Standalone Romances

Faker

Simmer Down

On Location

The Boy with the Bookstore

If You Never Come Back

I Heart SF Romance Series

The Close-Up

In Love with Lewis Prescott

Unlikely Pairings Series (written as Sarah Skye)

Sips & Strokes

Vibes & Feels

Whiskers & Sunshine

Acknowledgments

Thank you SO MUCH for reading Gage and Becca's love story! I hoped you liked it! If you did, please consider leaving a review on Amazon and Goodreads. Reviews make such a difference when it comes to a book reaching more readers and getting more visibility.

This book was an absolute blast to write and I have so many people to thank for that. Stefanie Simpson, Sandy Lim, and Rebecca Chase, thank you for your brilliant beta reader feedback. I don't know what I'd do without you all. Joanne Machin, thank you for your editing expertise. Elle Maxwell, thank you for designing yet another gorgeous cover. Thank you, Heather from @the_heather_effect_podcast, for naming Gage.

Thank you, Alex, for being the best husband in the world. Thank you, Maizie, for your neverending energy and cuteness.

And last but never, ever least, thank you to everyone who reads my books. You make it possible for me to write love stories for a living. For that, I adore you.

About the Author

Sarah Smith is a copywriter-turned-author who wants to make the world a lovelier place, one kissing story at a time. Her love of romance began when she was eight and she discovered her auntie's stash of romance novels. She's been hooked ever since. When she's not writing, you can find her hiking, eating chocolate, and perfecting her lumpia recipe.

instagram.com/authorsarahs
tiktok.com/@authorsarahs
bookbub.com/authors/sarah-echavarre-smith
facebook.com/groups/sarahsmithbooks

Printed in Great Britain
by Amazon